O9-AIC-196

New York Times and *USA Today* bestselling author
LAURA GRIFFIN

"DELIVERS THE GOODS." —*Publishers Weekly*

Praise for *FAR GONE*

"Perfectly gritty.... Griffin sprinkles on just enough jargon to give the reader the feel of being in the middle of an investigation, easily merging high-stakes action and spicy romance with rhythmic pacing and smartly economic prose."
—*Publishers Weekly* (starred review)

"Crisp storytelling, multifaceted characters, and excellent pacing.... A highly entertaining read."
—*RT Book Reviews* (4 stars)

"A first-rate addition to the Laura Griffin canon."
—*The Romance Dish* (5 stars)

"Be prepared for heart palpitations and a racing pulse as you read this fantastic novel. Fans of Lisa Gardner, Lisa Jackson, Nelson DeMille, and Michael Connelly will love [Griffin's] work."
—*The Reading Frenzy*

"*Far Gone* is riveting with never-ending action."—*Single Titles*

"A tense, exciting romantic thriller that's not to be missed."
—*New York Times* bestselling author Karen Robards

"Griffin has cooked up a delicious read that will thrill her devoted fans and earn her legions more."
—*New York Times* bestselling author Lisa Unger

Praise for the Tracers series

BEYOND LIMITS

"Another fast-action, high-octane read that grabs you from the first page to the last."   —*The Romance Reviews* (Top Pick)

"Daring escapades, honest emotions, and heart-stopping danger."   —*Single Titles*

EXPOSED

"Laura Griffin at her finest! If you are not a Tracer-a-holic yet . . . you will be after this."   —*A Tasty Read*

"Explosive chemistry."   —*Coffee Time Romance & More*

"Explodes with action. . . . Laura Griffin escalates the tension with each page, each scene, and intersperses the action with spine-tingling romance in a perfect blend."   —*The Romance Reviews*

SCORCHED

2013 RITA winner for Best Romantic Suspense

"A sizzling novel of suspense . . . the perfect addition to the Tracers series."   —*Joyfully Reviewed*

"Has it all: dynamite characters, a taut plot, and plenty of sizzle to balance the suspense without overwhelming it."
                —*RT Book Reviews* (4½ stars)

"Starts with a bang and never loses its momentum . . . intense and mesmerizing."   —*Night Owl Reviews* (Top Pick)

ALSO BY LAURA GRIFFIN

SHADOW FALL

LAURA GRIFFIN

Pocket Books

New York   London   Toronto   Sydney   New Delhi

Pocket Books
An Imprint of Simon & Schuster, Inc.
1230 Avenue of the Americas
New York, NY 10020

This book is a work of fiction. Any references to historical events, real people, or real places are used fictitiously. Other names, characters, places, and events are products of the author's imagination, and any resemblance to actual events or places or persons, living or dead, is entirely coincidental.

First Pocket Books paperback edition October 2015

POCKET and colophon are registered trademarks of Simon & Schuster, Inc.

For information about special discounts for bulk purchases, please contact Simon & Schuster Special Sales at 1-866-506-1949 or business@simonandschuster.com.

The Simon & Schuster Speakers Bureau can bring authors to your live event. For more information or to book an event, contact the Simon & Schuster Speakers Bureau at 1-866-248-3049 or visit our website at www.simonspeakers.com.

Manufactured in the United States of America

10   9   8   7   6   5   4   3   2   1

ISBN 978-1-4767-7925-6
ISBN 978-1-4767-7927-0 (ebook)

For Jessica

SHADOW FALL

PROLOGUE

The whole thing took four seconds, maybe less.

Exactly three minutes before it happened, Marine Captain Liam Wolfe was standing in the dusty court-yard feeling hot, hungry, and pissed off. The first two barely registered after four long tours in Afghanistan's summer fighting season. The last was pretty much standard since he'd started pulling personal security detail for a delegation of American politicians visiting the region.

It was an election year, and the base was thick with VIPs dropping in for photo ops. They wanted to mingle with the troops and eat in the mess hall and visit wounded children in hospitals staffed by inter-national aid workers. This afternoon's destination was a newly built school—a true nightmare from a tactical perspective. To add to the funfest, details of the mission hadn't been communicated until the last minute, giving Liam's CO almost no time to brief his team, which consisted of sixteen Marines squeezed into a three-Humvee convoy with a Virginia congressman.

Today, like all days, the team was locked and loaded and ready for anything. Bitter experience had taught them that no corner of the country was safe from bullets and IEDs, not even a school yard. Especially not a school yard.

Liam stood beside the compound's west gate, holding his M-4 loose but ready. The sun hammered down. His nerves jangled as children's high-pitched voices echoed around him. Just beyond the school's cinder-block walls, the sound of car horns and truck engines rose from the dirty street. Exhaust hung in the air as Liam scanned the surrounding rooftops for the hundredth time.

In some countries, PSD work was a cushy assignment. Not in Afghanistan. Here personal security detail was a tedious job requiring total concentration. It was a constant process of seeing and assessing—people, situations, and objects, no matter how inconsequential. Anyone from the kid on the moped to the ambling old man might be jocked up with explosives and ready to ruin your day. The mission was to spot something, anything, from a furtive look to a thread of wire in the road that signaled trouble.

The hours were long. No time for distractions. No time to think about getting food or getting a nap or getting laid. No time to do anything besides be in the moment and take all that it offered.

Liam squinted into the sun, his gaze skimming over the roofline. Sweat seeped into his eyes. He lingered on the two dark windows where Marine snipers had overwatch. He looked for any sign of foreign surveillance—not just by the Afghans but by the other countries that had been monitoring the American delegation since it first came to town.

He shifted his attention to street level. Trash tumbled along in an eddy of hot air. A bearded Afghan policeman was stationed across the road, and Liam gave him a long, hard look, paying close attention to his AK. Another policeman was positioned inside the school yard, manning the east gate. Liam had his eye on both of them.

He studied the street again as banged-up trucks held together by little more than duct tape whisked past. The people here were resourceful and could make a viable vehicle out of damn near anything with wheels. Liam watched the pedestrians coming and going. An elderly man carrying a basket approached the policeman, then glanced back at the school. Liam's fingers tensed. The old man shuffled away.

"Alpha, this is Bravo," came a voice over the radio.

"Alpha here."

"Yo, we're ready to roll out."

"Roger that."

Liam stepped through the gate and checked the convoy. The lead vehicle had a 50-cal mounted on top, manned by Tony Lopez, the team's best gunner. Liam caught his eye.

"Where's Burleson?"

Lopez nodded down the street, where two of Liam's men were milling on a corner. They were supposed to stay with the Humvees. As team leader, Liam had taken Burleson off point. He was probably still sulking.

Liam got him on the radio. "Get ready to move," he told him, then called up Bravo. "You guys coming?"

"Negative. Another photo op."

Liam scanned the street again. He scanned the courtyard. The policeman at the east gate shifted his weight. Eye contact.

And Liam knew.

In that fraction of a second, he read the deadly intent, and then everything happened at once.

The congressman stepped into the sunlight, surrounded by photographers.

"Gun!" Liam shouted, lifting his weapon, but there were kids and bystanders in the line of fire.

Liam launched himself across the courtyard. Gunfire erupted. Marines sprang into action. The congressman hit the ground—taken down by a bullet or a Marine, Liam didn't know.

Liam barreled into the shooter as bullets spewed from his Kalashnikov. They slammed into the dirt. White-hot fire tore through Liam's arm as he wrestled with the weapon.

A sharp *crack*.

Liam's vision blurred. The air around him was a mist of red.

CHAPTER ONE

EAST TEXAS PINEY WOODS
THREE YEARS LATER

Evenings were the hardest, the time when everything unraveled. Catie's mind overflowed, her chest felt empty, and the craving dug into her with razor-sharp claws.

Her shoulders tensed as she pulled into the park. All her life, she'd been addicted to work and approval and success. Now she was simply an addict.

Her high-performance tires glided over the ruts, absorbing the bumps as she eased along the drive. She turned into the gravel parking lot and swung into a space. *Forty-six days.*

Resting her head on the wheel, she squeezed her eyes shut. Her throat tightened, and she fought the burn of tears.

"One day at a time," she whispered.

She sat up and gazed through the windshield. She'd never thought she'd be one of those people who gave themselves pep talks. She'd never thought she'd be a lot of things. Yet here she was.

Catie shoved open the door and popped the trunk. She tossed her purse inside, then rummaged through her gym bag, looking for her iPod. On second thought, no music. She slammed the trunk closed, locked the car, and tucked the key fob into the zipper pocket of her tracksuit. She leaned against a trail marker and stretched her quads. A few deep lunges and she was ready to go.

She set off at a brisk pace, quickly passing the dog walkers and bird enthusiasts who frequented the trail. Her muscles warmed. Her breathing steadied. She passed the first quarter-mile marker and felt the tension start to loosen.

The routine had become her lifeline. She registered the familiar scent of loblolly pines, the spongy carpet of pine needles under her feet. She put her body through the paces, then her mind.

It was Wednesday. She was halfway through the week, another daunting chain of days that started with paralyzing mornings in which she had to drag herself out of bed and force herself to shower, dress, and stand in front of the mirror to conceal the evidence of a fitful night. Then she faced the endless cycle of conference calls and meetings and inane conversations as the secret yearning built and built, culminating in the dreaded hour when it was time to go. Time to pack it in and head home to her perfectly located, gorgeously decorated, soul-crushingly empty house.

But first, a run. Or a spin class. Or both. Anything to postpone the sight of that vacant driveway.

Almost anything.

Catie focused her attention on the narrow trail.

Thirst stung her throat, but she tried to clear her mind. Rounding a bend, she noted the half-mile marker. She was making good time. Another curve in the path, and she came upon a couple jogging in easy lockstep. Twenty-somethings. At the end of the trail, and still they had a bounce in their stride. The woman smiled as they passed, and Catie felt a sharp pang of jealousy that drew her up short.

She caught herself against a tree and bent over, gasping. Shame and regret formed a lump in her throat. She dug her nails into the bark and closed her eyes against the clammy onset of panic.

Don't think, Catie, Liam's voice echoed in her head. *Be in the moment.*

God, she missed him. Liam was way too smart and way too intense, and he didn't know how to turn it off. And she liked that about him. So different from David.

Liam never belittled her.

He knew evil lurked in the world, and he faced it head-on, refusing to look away, even relishing the fight.

Snick.

Catie's head jerked up. She swung her gaze toward the darkening woods as awareness prickled to life inside her.

The forest had gone quiet.

No people, no dogs. Even the bird chatter had ceased. She glanced behind her, and a chill swept over her skin.

Look, Catie. Feel what's around you.

She did feel it. Cold and predatory and watching her.

David would tell her she was paranoid. Delusional, even. But her senses were screaming.

She glanced around, trying to orient herself on the trail. She wasn't that far in yet. She could still go back. She turned around and walked briskly, keeping her chin high and her gaze alert. Strong. Confident. She tried to look powerful and think powerful thoughts, but fear squished around inside her stomach, and she could feel it—something sinister moving with her through the forest, watching her from deep within the woods. She'd felt it before, and now it was back again, making her pulse quicken along with her strides.

I am not crazy. I am not crazy. I am not crazy.

But . . . what if David was right? And if he was right about this, could he be right about everything else, too?

A sound, directly left. Catie halted. Her heart hammered. She peered into the gloom and sensed more than saw the shifting shadow.

Recognition flickered as the shape materialized. With a rush of relief, she stepped forward. "Hey, you—"

She noticed his hand.

Her stomach plummeted. All her self-doubt vanished, replaced by a single electrifying impulse.

Catie ran.

SPECIAL AGENT TARA Rushing drove with the windows down, hoping the cold night air would snap her out of her funk. She felt wrung out. Like a dishrag that had been used to sop up filth, then squeezed and tossed aside.

Usually, she loved the adrenaline rush. Kicking in a door, storming a room, taking down a bad guy—anyone who'd done it for real knew nothing compared. The high could last for hours, even through the paperwork, which was inevitably a lot.

Typically, after a successful raid everyone was wired. The single agents would head out for a beer or three, sometimes going home together to burn off the energy. But tonight wasn't typical.

After so many weeks of work and planning, she'd expected to feel euphoric. Or at the very least satisfied. Instead she felt . . . nothing, really. Her dominant thought as she sped toward home was that she needed a shower. Not just hot—volcanic. She'd stand under the spray and scrub her skin raw and maybe get rid of some of the sickness clinging to her.

Tara slowed her Explorer as the redbrick apartment building came into view. Her second-floor unit looked dark and lonely beside her neighbor's, where a TV glowed in the window and swags of Christmas lights still decorated the balcony.

She rolled to a stop at the entrance and tapped in the access code. As the gate slid open, her phone vibrated in the cup holder. Tara eyed the screen: US GOV. She'd forgotten to fill out some paperwork or turn in a piece of gear, or maybe they needed her to view another video.

She felt the urge to throw her phone out the window. Instead she answered it.

"Rushing."

If she put enough hostility into her voice, maybe they wouldn't have the balls to call her back in.

"It's Dean Jacobs."

She didn't respond. Because of shock and because she couldn't think of a single intelligent thing to say.

"You make it home yet?" he asked.

"Almost. Sir."

Jacobs was her SAC. She'd had maybe four conversations with him in the three years since she'd joined the Houston field office.

"They were just filling me in on the raid," he said. "Good work tonight."

"Thank you, sir."

The gate slid shut again as she stared through the windshield.

"I understand you live north," he said.

"That's right."

"There's a matter I could use your help on."

Something stirred inside her. Curiosity. Or maybe ambition. Whatever it was, she'd take it. Anything was better than feeling numb.

"I need you to drive up to Cypress County. They've got a ten-fifty off of Fifty-nine."

His words surprised her even more than the midnight phone call. Tara knew all the 10-codes from her cop days, but dispatch had switched to plain language, and nobody used them anymore. A 10-50 was a deceased person.

She cleared her throat. "Okay. Any particular reason—"

"Take Martinez with you. She's got the location and she's on her way to your house, ETA ten minutes."

Tara checked her sports watch.

"Stay off your phone," he added. "You understand? I need complete discretion on this."

"Yes, sir."

"And one more thing, Rushing."

She waited.

"Don't let the yokels jerk you around."

TARA DROVE NORTH on the highway hemmed in by towering trees. Barely an hour out of the city, she could already feel the change as they passed through the Pine Curtain. The night seemed thicker here, darker. She leaned forward, peering through the windshield at the moonless sky.

"Next exit," M.J. said, consulting the map on her phone. "We're looking for Dunn's Road."

Tara glanced at the agent beside her. M. J. Martinez was a rookie, not even a year on the job.

"You know, it's after one," M.J. said, looking at Tara. "I can't believe I'm even awake right now. I've had about three hours' sleep in the past three days."

Tara took the exit ramp. "At least you got a shower. I smell like gym socks."

M.J. didn't deny it. She'd been involved in the raid, too, but from a planning perspective. In her former life, Martinez had been a tax attorney. She was smart and organized but green when it came to fieldwork. Tara had her HPD experience plus SWAT training under her belt, so she tended to be more hands-on.

"This is it," M.J. said. "Dunn's Road. Hang a right."

Tara slowed, squinting at a sign marking a narrow road. Her headlights swept across tree trunks. The thicket gave way to jagged stumps, and Tara switched to brights. She thought the stumps looked ominous until the houses came into view, ramshackle wooden structures with sagging porches. Rusted septic tanks and dismantled cars littered the yards. Some of the homes were strangled by kudzu and had plywood covering the windows. None had seen a coat of paint in decades, unless you counted graffiti.

They passed the charred carcass of a house, and M.J. looked at her. "Meth lab?"

"Good bet."

The houses petered out, and so did the pavement. M.J. consulted her phone again because Tara's ancient Ford didn't have a GPS. The Blue Beast barely had a working heater. But the tires were new, and the four-wheel drive could handle anything. Tara changed the oil religiously so it wouldn't crap out on her.

"Looks like we're getting close," M.J. said, studying her screen. Instead of an address, Jacobs had provided her with GPS coordinates, along with the interesting factoid that FBI participation in this matter—whatever it was—had come at the request of the Honorable Wyatt H. Mooring, a federal judge.

"Veer left," M.J. instructed.

Tara buzzed down the windows, filling the SUV with cold, damp air that smelled faintly of rotten eggs. It was cloudy out but no rain in the forecast, although that was yet another aspect of tonight that might not turn out as planned.

"We should be veering left again," M.J. said, "after what looks like maybe a creek?"

They dipped down over a low-water bridge and heard the rush of water.

"Logging route," Tara said, noting the clear-cuts

on either side. They pitched and bumped over the rutted road, passing a rickety cistern and another rusted septic tank. They rattled over a cattle guard and passed through a gap in a barbed-wire fence. Tara glanced around but didn't see any livestock, or any other creature for that matter. Clear-cuts gave way to trees again, and a sense of foreboding settled in her stomach as they moved deeper into the woods. The road narrowed until the tree trunks felt like they were closing in.

She looked at M.J., wide-eyed and tense in the seat beside her.

"What the hell are we doing here?" M.J. asked, voicing the question in Tara's mind.

"I think Judge Mooring's from around here. Grew up in Dunn's Landing."

As if that explained why their boss had sent them scrambling into the forest in the dead of the night.

M.J. looked at her. "What's the difference between God and a federal judge?"

"I don't know."

"God doesn't think he's a federal judge."

Tara smiled, for what seemed like the first time in days.

A flicker of light caught her eye, a flash of white through the tree trunks. Her smile dropped.

"Whatever this is, I think we found it."

EMERGENCY VEHICLES LINED the side of the road—sheriff's units, an ambulance, a red pickup truck with the emblem of a local fire department on the door. A khaki-clad deputy in a ten-gallon hat waved them down.

Tara handed her ID through the window. "Special Agent Tara Rushing, FBI."

He examined her creds, then ducked his head down and peered into the window as M.J. held up her badge.

He hesitated and then passed Tara's ID back. "Pull around to the right there. Watch the barricades."

Tara pulled around as instructed and parked beside a white crime-scene van.

M.J. got out first, attracting immediate notice from the huddle of lawmen milling beside the red pickup. They looked her up and down, taking in her tailored gray slacks and crisp white button-down. Then again, maybe it was her curves they were noticing or the lush dark hair that cascaded down her back.

Tara pushed open her door. Tall and willowy, she attracted stares, too, but for a different reason. She was still geared up from the raid in tactical pants and Oakley assault boots, with handcuffs tucked into her waistband and her Glock snug against her hip. Her curly brown hair was pulled back in a no-nonsense ponytail. She grabbed her FBI windbreaker from the backseat, and the men eyed her coolly as she zipped into it.

Another deputy hustled over.

"Who's in charge of this crime scene?" Tara asked, flashing her creds.

He glanced at her ID, then her face. The man was short and stocky and smelled like vomit.

"That'd be Sheriff Ingram." He cast a glance behind him, where the light show continued deep in the woods.

"I'd like a word with him."

He looked at her.

"Please."

He darted a glance at M.J., then traipsed off down a narrow trail marked with yellow scene tape.

The men continued to stare, but Tara ignored them and surveyed her surroundings. Someone had hooked a camping lantern to a nail on a nearby tree, illuminating a round clearing with a crude fire pit at the center. Old tires and tree stumps surrounded the pit, along with beer cans and cigarette butts. Someone had cordoned off the area with yellow tape and placed evidence markers near the cans and butts.

Tara studied the ground outside the tape, where an alarming number of tire tracks crisscrossed the loamy soil.

Another khaki uniform approached her, no hat this time. "Who are you?" he demanded.

"Sheriff Ingram?"

A brisk nod.

"Special Agent Tara Rushing." She showed her ID again, but he didn't look. "And Special Agent Maria Jose Martinez."

If he was surprised the FBI had shown up at his crime scene, he didn't show it.

"We're here at the request of Judge Wyatt Mooring," M.J. added.

He glanced at her, then back at Tara.

With his brawny build and high-and-tight haircut, Sheriff Ingram looked like a Texas good old boy. But Tara didn't want to underestimate him. His eyes telegraphed intelligence, and he seemed to be carefully weighing his options. He stepped closer and rested his hands on his gun belt.

"I got a homicide." He nodded toward the woods. "Female victim. No ID, no clothes, no vehicle. Long story short, I don't have a lot."

His gaze settled on Tara, and her shoulders tensed. She could feel something coming.

"What I *do* have is an abandoned Lexus down at Silver Springs Park," he said. "Registered to Catalina Reyes."

"Catalina Reyes," Tara repeated.

"That's right. She was last seen there yesterday evening. Didn't show up for work today."

Tara glanced at M.J., communicating silently. *Holy crap.* She looked back at the sheriff. "How far's this park?" she asked.

"Twenty miles due southa here."

A deputy strode up to them. "Sheriff, you need to come see this."

Ingram trudged off, leaving Tara and M.J. staring at each other in the glare of the lantern.

Catalina Reyes was a north Houston business-woman who'd made a run for U.S. Congress in the last election. She'd been a lightning rod for controversy since the moment she announced her candidacy.

"She was getting death threats, wasn't she?" M.J. said.

"I think so."

Tara turned to look at the forest, where police had set up klieg lights around the inner crime scene. Workers in white Tyvek suits moved around, probably CSIs or ME's assistants. Tara saw the strobe of a camera flash. She noted more deputies with flashlights combing a path deep within the woods. They must have assumed that the killer accessed the site from the east, and Tara hoped to hell they were right, because whatever evidence might have been recovered from the route Tara had used had been obliterated by boots and tires.

The Cypress County Sheriff's Department didn't see many homicides and probably had little to no experience handling anything this big.

If, in fact, the victim was Catalina Reyes.

Tara bit the inside of her lip, a habit she caved into when she was nervous. Why had Jacobs sent them? Not just agents but specifically her and M.J.? As experience went, Tara came up short and Martinez was green as grass.

M.J. muttered something beside her.

"What?" Tara asked.

She started to answer, but Ingram approached. Tara looked at him, and she knew—she *knew*—that how she handled the next few moments would affect everything.

"Sheriff, the Bureau would like to help here," Tara said. "We can have an evidence response team on-site within an hour."

He folded his arms over his chest. "I think we got a handle on it."

Just what she'd thought he'd say. "I'd like to see the crime scene," she told him.

He gave her a hard look that said, *No you wouldn't, little lady.* But Tara stubbornly held his gaze. "Suit yourself," he said, setting off.

She followed him, with M.J. close behind. They moved through the trees along a path marked by

LED traffic flares. The air smelled of damp pine, but as they neared the bright hive of activity, the sickly smell of death overtook everything. Ingram stepped aside, and Tara nearly tripped over a forensic photographer crouched on the ground aiming her camera at the body sprawled in the dirt.

Pale face, slack jaw. She looked almost peaceful . . . except for the horrific violence below her neck.

Tara's throat burned.

M.J. lurched back, bumping into a tree. She turned and threw up.

Think, Tara ordered herself. She forced herself to step closer and study the scene.

A five-foot radius around the body had been marked off with metal stakes connected by orange twine. Only an ME's assistant in white coveralls operated within the inner perimeter. He knelt beside the victim, jotting notes on a clipboard.

Tara's heart pounded. Her mind whirled. She drew air into her lungs and forced herself to slow down. She felt Ingram's gaze on her and tried to block it out.

Think.

Rigor mortis had passed. Even with the cool weather, she'd been dead at least twelve hours. No obvious bruising on her arms or legs. Her feet were spread apart. Damp leaves clung to her calves. Toenail polish—dark pink. Tara looked at her arms. No visible abrasions, but the left hand was bent at a strange angle.

And her body . . . Tara forced herself to look without flinching. The woman had been sliced open from her sternum to her navel and eviscerated. Her organs glistened in the klieg lights.

Tara walked around, careful not to get in the photographer's way as she studied the victim's face again. The right side was partly covered by a curtain of dark hair.

"Who called it in?" She glanced at Ingram.

"Couple of teenagers." He nodded back toward the fire pit. "This whole area's a hangout. Kids come out to smoke pot, have sex, whatever they want. They're at the station house," he added, answering her next question. "I got one of my deputies interviewing them."

"He's finished up."

Tara glanced to her left, where the deputy she'd met earlier was slouched against a tree. He looked queasy, and she understood now why his breath smelled rancid.

"He got 'em on videotape," the deputy said. "Interviewed both of them side by side."

Tara looked at Ingram. "I'd like to talk to them."

"Who, the kids?"

"Yes."

"Tonight?"

"The sooner the better."

He gazed at her for a long moment, then stalked off.

Tara turned to M.J., who was standing off to the side looking shell-shocked. Tara arched her brows in a silent question, and M.J. answered with a nod.

The deputy turned and shot tobacco juice at the ground.

"Don't spit on the crime scene," Tara said, stepping around the photographer.

The deputy's face flushed, and his nostrils flared.

"We'll interview them separately," Tara told M.J. "Although it may be too late to get a straight story."

The photographer scrolled through her camera. "I have what I need here," she told the ME's people. "You guys are good to go."

The one holding the stretcher stepped carefully over the orange twine and crouched down beside the corpse. His partner unfurled a body bag.

Tara watched uneasily. They were taking away the body now, processing the scene, for better or for worse. Whatever chance Tara had had to involve the Bureau at this critical point in the investigation was gone. If that had been her boss's purpose in sending her here, then she'd already failed.

But she sensed there was more to it.

A knot of tension formed in her chest as she cast her gaze around the scene. The fire pit had been surrounded by evidence markers, but here near the body there were precious few.

Tara glanced at the deputy watching her sullenly from against the tree. She forced her attention back to the victim. An ME's assistant tucked the hands into paper bags, and Tara felt a twinge of relief watching his skilled movements.

Tara checked her watch. Almost two. She turned her gaze toward the dense thicket and shivered, suddenly cold to her bones.

How the hell had she ended up at this backwoods horror show? She felt unwelcome. Unsure of herself. She was even less sure of the politics in play, only that they involved a right-leaning judge and a left-leaning politician, plus a territorial sheriff backed by hostile troops.

She glanced at M.J. and wondered if she was having similar thoughts. This case was a disaster, and they'd barely started. The circumstances could hardly be worse.

A flash of light above the treetops, followed by a low rumble. Tara tipped her gaze up to the sky.

It started to rain.

CHAPTER TWO

Tara didn't dream of woods and gore but of a squalid apartment and a sunken-eyed child. She woke up with wet cheeks and stared, disoriented, at a crack in the wall.

The raid was over. The hollow feeling in her chest was her reminder that she'd been too late.

Now she was at the Big Pines Motel in Dunn's Landing.

Tara swung her legs out of bed, rubbing the crick in her neck as she glanced at the clock. She couldn't remember the last time she'd slept past 6:00, but it was 7:40. Her phone chimed across the room, and she lunged to answer it, cursing herself because she knew who it was even before she saw the screen, and she should have been prepared.

"Rushing," she said hoarsely.

"Jacobs here. Just read your e-mail. You're still up there?"

She cleared her throat. "The autopsy's at ten, sir. I thought—"

"Good idea. In the meantime, we're sending those reports you wanted. No confirmation yet?"

"Hopefully later this morning. The county coroner here is about eighty years old and decided to take a pass on this one. They're bringing a pathologist up from Houston."

"All right, keep me posted."

He hung up, and Tara blinked down at her phone. Her brain kicked into gear, and she texted M.J. on the other side of the motel.

They'd rolled in after four A.M. and roused the manager from his apartment behind the office. He'd been surly about it but less so when he learned they wanted two rooms for at least three nights. Better safe than sorry, Tara figured. The town had one motel, and depending on how the autopsy played out, they could have reporters converging by the afternoon.

Tara showered and rummaged through her hastily packed duffel. She was in Bureau casual today, a unisex outfit of navy golf shirt, desert-brown tactical pants, and boots. She holstered her weapon and sent another text to M.J. before walking across the street.

The Waffle Stop parking lot was crammed with pickups and SUVs. Long-haul rigs occupied the back third of the lot, making Tara optimistic about the coffee.

The aroma of bacon had her stomach growling as she stepped into the diner. The place was busy, but she found a corner booth, where she scrolled through e-mail as a scarlet-haired waitress filled her mug.

Tara was right about the coffee. As she sipped it, she scanned the customers, trying to get a feel for the town. Blue-collar, definitely. Mostly white. The breakfast crowd was a mix of locals who seemed to know one another, plus some loners at the counter—probably the truckers. The entire place was covered by two servers, Tara's and a peroxide blonde who looked at least sixty. In addition to handling the counter patrons, the blonde rang up checks at the register beside a case displaying the day's pies.

A cowbell clanged, and Tara glanced at the door as M.J. walked in. Her long hair was damp, and she attracted curious looks in her tailored gray suit.

"I feel like a city slicker," she said, scooting into the booth.

"You are."

The waitress stopped by to take her order. As she left, M.J. unzipped her computer bag.

"Just toast?" Tara asked.

"No appetite this morning." M.J. opened up her laptop and clicked into a file. "So, I downloaded those reports from Jacobs."

Tara scanned the screen, reaching over to tap the keyboard as she read through the documents.

"Four incidents within two months, all the summer before the election," M.J. summarized.

Each event was detailed in a 302, the standard Bureau interview form. In the first three instances, Catalina Reyes was listed as the interviewee. The fourth report was different.

"Liam Wolfe," Tara said, skimming the notes. "Security consultant?"

"That's her bodyguard, evidently. Some special

forces badass. I heard the deputies talking about him last night."

"Why were they talking about him?"

"His firm—Wolfe Security—it's headquartered around here. Although I couldn't find a listing, so right now it's not much of a lead."

Tara spent a few minutes reading the 302s. The first two incidents consisted of threatening letters. The third incident involved a Molotov cocktail thrown through the living-room window of Catalina's house, injuring no one but resulting in a call to the Silver Springs Fire Department.

"No one injured, no fire," M.J. said. "Evidently, the bomb was pretty amateurish."

"Still, it kicks up the threat. Looks like that's what prompted her to hire the bodyguard."

The fourth incident consisted of someone tagging Catalina's car with the words *wetback whore* while it was parked at a restaurant in Houston.

The waitress appeared with their food, and M.J. slid the computer over so Tara could continue reading. Tara stabbed at a sausage link as she skimmed the page. In the fourth incident, Liam Wolfe had personally confronted the vandal and escorted him to the police station.

"*Escorted.* Ha."

"Yeah, I noticed that, too." M.J. spread grape jelly on her toast.

Tara took out her phone and did a Google search of Wolfe Security. No listing. She tried a different search engine. Nothing. She tried the name Liam Wolfe and got a real estate agent in Naperville, Illinois. Definitely not the same Liam Wolfe.

"Where is this guy?" She looked at M.J.

"No idea. I couldn't find a trace of him."

Tara dug into her omelet, thinking. She did a search of images and got publicity shots of the real estate agent. They were all the same, except for a candid at a charity event in Chicago.

Tara ran across another candid photo, a man standing beside a limousine with a beautiful blonde in a black micro-dress. "Ashley Somers arrives at SXSW, accompanied by bodyguard Liam Wolfe," read the caption.

Tara zoomed in on the bodyguard. He was tall, broad-shouldered. The cut of his dark suit didn't quite conceal whatever serious weapon he had holstered at his hip.

"Damn, he's ripped," M.J. said. "Wonder what his face looks like."

Tara did, too. It was hard to tell with the mirrored aviators. He had a strong jaw and a military-short haircut. His mouth was set in a firm line.

"South by Southwest. That's the film festival in Austin," M.J. said.

"I thought she was a singer."

"Whatever." M.J. shut down her laptop and zipped it into her bag. "She's a celebrity, so he doesn't just protect politicians."

Tara made a dent in her breakfast and watched M.J. nibbling her toast.

"You nervous?" Tara asked.

"About what?"

"The autopsy."

She shrugged. "I'll be okay. Last night I was just, I don't know, caught off guard. What I'm really nervous about is this assignment. What was Jacobs thinking?" She pushed her plate away. "I mean, *you* I can understand. You used to be a cop. But I barely have a year on the job."

"You'll do fine."

Tara downed the rest of her coffee. The conversation made her antsy because she'd been thinking along the exact same lines.

"Y'all need a refill?"

Tara glanced up at the waitress. "Thanks. Great omelet, by the way."

She smiled as she poured. "I'll tell Donny you said so. He's a keeper."

"Hey, I have a question," M.J. piped up. "You wouldn't happen to know a Wolfe Security in town, would you?"

She lifted an eyebrow. "I've heard of them."

"You know where they're located?"

"Sure, up the highway. Second turnoff on the right, just past the old sawmill."

Tara checked her watch. They had more than an hour to burn before the autopsy.

"Think we have time?" M.J. asked.

"We'll keep it quick."

The waitress dug out their check from her apron and gave Tara a pointed look. "Good luck."

"Why?"

"I bet you don't get past the gate."

THE SECOND TURNOFF past the old sawmill was a gravel road that curved into the forest. After 2.8 monotonous miles, the road dead ended at a solid black gate.

No guardhouse. No keypad.

Tara surveyed the eight-foot game fence stretching in both directions.

No mailbox or nameplate or wrought-iron depiction of the family brand above the entrance. The sole indication of the property's owner was a sleek black security camera aimed straight at Tara's windshield.

Tara stared up at the all-seeing eye.

"Not really camouflaged, is it?" M.J. observed.

"Think that's the idea."

Tara took out her phone and tried another search, but she still couldn't find a listing, much less a phone number.

M.J. huffed out a breath. "It's like he doesn't exist online. He's invisible."

Tara made a three-point turn and headed back toward the highway, tamping down her annoyance. She'd just have to roll with it. No one was really invisible, and she'd find another way to access Liam Wolfe. In the meantime, they could be early to the autopsy and maybe get a moment alone with the pathologist.

The Cypress County morgue was in a sixties-era brick building that housed the county's administrative offices with the exception of the sheriff's department, which shared the courthouse across the street. Tara and M.J. picked up visitors' badges from the receptionist and followed her directions through a labyrinth of cinder-block hallways. After half a dozen turns, Tara started reading placards beside the doors, thinking they'd missed it. Then she rounded the corner and spotted a pair of khaki uniforms receding down the hallway.

"Sheriff."

Ingram turned around, hat in hand. Fury swelled in Tara's chest as she strode up to him. He smelled like menthol, and she noticed the ointment glistening over his upper lip.

"We're here for the autopsy," Tara said.

"Looks like you just missed it."

"You said ten o'clock."

He shook his head. "Doc showed up at seven, so we went ahead and got started."

Tara gritted her teeth. Behind Ingram, his deputy—Jason of the vomit breath—was already tucking a lump of chaw into his lip. He looked pretty pleased with himself.

The sheriff arranged his hat on his head. "I'll be sure to get you ladies a copy of the report," he drawled, "soon as I have it in hand."

Down the hallway, a door opened, and a man in blue surgical scrubs walked out.

Tara sidestepped Ingram and caught up to the doctor as he headed into a break room.

M.J. snagged Tara's arm. "You handle this. I'll see what I can get out of the staff here."

"Thanks."

Tara turned back to the pathologist, who was pouring coffee into a Styrofoam cup.

"Dr. Greenwood?"

He glanced up. "You must be one of the feds who was running late."

"Not late. Misinformed." And it was her own fault, because she should have seen it coming. "I'd like to ask you a few questions about the autopsy."

Greenwood was short, portly, and bald as a turkey vulture. He took a sip and made a face, then set the coffee aside and regarded Tara with bloodshot gray eyes.

"I'll finish my report by tomorrow," he said. "You can read about it."

"I will, but in the meantime, I'd like to at least get the basics."

He leaned back against the counter. "You want an ID, I presume."

"That's right."

"Were you at the crime scene?"

She nodded.

"Then you have an idea what we're dealing with." He folded his arms over his chest and looked up at her. "I compared the dental records of Catalina Reyes to films of the victim. Looks like a possible match."

"Possible?"

"Several teeth were knocked out. I'd like to get confirmation from a forensic odontologist before we go public with a name." He arched his eyebrows. "Given the circumstances."

"I understand," Tara said, even though it meant more delays. But she didn't blame him for being thorough. She could only imagine the fallout if he got the ID wrong in such a high-profile case.

"What about fingerprints?" she asked.

"So far, we've come up blank. In terms of the other findings, manner of death, obviously homicide. I'd say time of death was between six and ten on Wednesday night. Livor patterns indicate the victim was moved sometime after she was killed. Cause of death, asphyxiation—"

"Asphyxiation? She was gutted like a deer."

Greenwood frowned reproachfully.

"Sorry."

"Cause of death," he repeated, "asphyxiation due to manual strangulation, evidenced by minor petechial hemorrhaging. The mutilation to the body occurred postmortem. At least an hour, I'd say. The instrument was a large blade, six inches or more. You might also be interested to know I recovered a shard of glass embedded in her left hamstring."

Glass was good, in Tara's world. Glass might yield prints or DNA from the killer.

"What kind of glass?" she asked.

"I'm not sure. The Delphi Center crime lab might be able to help you on that count. I had it couriered over to them, along with the other trace evidence. Their forensic odontologist will be getting the films. And that"—he heaved a sigh—"is about all I can tell you until I pull my report together."

"Thank you." She tried not to sound disappointed.

"Also, I put in a phone call," he said. "Mia Voss in the Delphi Center's DNA lab is a top-notch analyst and a personal friend. I let her know the urgency surrounding this matter. I'm sure she'll do her best to be quick."

He started to leave, but Tara stepped forward. "Just one more question. Is there anything in your findings that might"—she struggled for how to phrase it—"shed light on the perpetrator?"

"Besides the obvious? That we're dealing with someone exceedingly violent?"

"That's right. I'm talking about anything forensic. Anything that might give us an idea about who we're looking for."

Greenwood bowed his head and looked at his feet.

"You know, I posted two traffic fatalities last night, both sixteen-year-old kids texting and driving. Now this." He gazed up at her, his look somber. "I can't shed light on this for you. I wish I could. I can document her injuries and X-ray her bones and weigh her organs. But ultimately, she is a stranger to me."

TARA EYED THE sheriff's units parked in front of the courthouse as she pulled out of the lot.

"Well, I picked up some gossip," M.J. said.

"I knew you would."

M.J. had something Tara lacked: the gift of gab. It was a skill that came in useful during investigations.

"One of the clerks said the pathologist was notified and put on the schedule last night," M.J. said. "By Sheriff Ingram himself."

"Figures."

"So, anything from the doctor?"

Tara filled her in, getting angrier by the minute as she recounted all the critical developments they'd missed by being shut out of the autopsy.

She drove through downtown Cypress, passing the town square with the white gazebo in the center, the library, the VFW hall. It seemed like such a quaint Southern town, but Tara knew better, and so had Jacobs when he'd sent her here. *Don't let the yokels jerk you around.*

Tara tried to calm her temper. She had a problem with certain types of men, a problem that manifested itself as a tight knot in her chest that refused to loosen. It was a constant struggle for her to let go of all the crappy things she couldn't control and focus on the things she could.

She took a deep breath and tried to shake it off. She'd underestimated the sheriff. It wouldn't happen again.

Tara passed the Dairy Queen, whipped into a gas station, and pulled her old Explorer up to a pump.

M.J. pushed open her door. "Think I'll grab some coffee now that I'm not worried about losing my breakfast. Want any?"

"No, thanks."

Tara popped open the gas tank and surveyed the town as she fueled up. GO VIPERS! read the Dairy Queen marquee. Across the street at the local hardware store, spirit signs decorated the windows.

Tara studied the traffic—a mix of pickups and SUVs and logging trucks. She spied a few gas rigs, too, and remembered last night's rotten-egg smell, which resulted from hydrogen sulfide being released during the production of oil and gas. Fossil fuels were more lucrative than timber, and Tara knew logging was becoming secondary to petrochemicals in this part of the state. And then, of course, there was the other cottage industry. Meth labs had been sprouting up like weeds, providing a steady source of income and misery throughout the region.

M.J. came back. "Brought you a snack," she said, holding up a pack of powdered-sugar doughnuts.

"How'd you know?" Tara slid behind the wheel. She opened the doughnuts and demolished the first in two bites. The sugar dissolving on her tongue seemed to dissolve some of her bitter mood.

"Okay, new plan," Tara announced, firing up the

Explorer. She started to pull out, then jabbed the brakes. "Son of a bitch."

"What?" M.J. glanced up.

"Hardware store. Black pickup."

Tara watched the man as he loaded lumber into the truck bed. Tall, lean, mirrored shades. She couldn't see his eyes, but she recognized the military-straight posture.

"It's him." She looked at M.J.

"Who?"

"Liam Wolfe."

M.J. leaned forward and squinted. "How can you tell from here? I can hardly see his face."

"Trust me."

Tara watched, riveted by the sight of him. His size, his moves—the man oozed confidence from every pore. He strode around to the driver's side and got behind the wheel.

Tara drove to the opposite end of the lot as the black pickup pulled into traffic.

"You're going to follow him?" M.J. sounded alarmed.

"Sure, why not?"

Tara pulled out but hung back, allowing a few cars between herself and the truck. She didn't need to get close because she knew where he was going. He got on the highway and headed south toward Dunn's Landing.

"But the ID isn't confirmed yet," M.J. said. "What if the victim isn't Catalina Reyes?"

"Either way, she's missing, which is why we're here. Liam Wolfe's her bodyguard."

"*Was.*"

"He might have some ideas for us."

Tara tailed the truck, which looked like so many others on the road. She would have expected more of a statement—something with souped-up hydraulics or maybe a Hummer. But it was your basic black pickup, one of countless in the Lone Star State.

Tara studied the truck, memorizing the taillights, the chrome toolbox, the tinted back windows. The Chevy Silverado was a few years old. Loaded with lumber, it rode low to the ground.

"You think he's spotted us?" M.J. asked.

"I sure hope so. He's a security consultant."

The miles ticked by as they moved south on U.S. 59. Tara closed the gap and tried to read the license plate, but it was impossible to see with the wood hanging off the back.

He shifted into the right lane and put on his turn indicator. Tara's gaze narrowed. She'd never met the man, but she got the distinct impression that he was being a smartass.

He exited the freeway and passed the old sawmill, then hooked a right. Tara stayed behind him, wending her way along the gravel road just like before. Only this time, when she reached the end, the black gates magically parted.

Tara followed him through.

CHAPTER THREE

The gates slid shut behind her. Tara kept about thirty feet off his tailgate, close enough to watch his reflection in the side mirror.

"Cameras," M.J. said.

"Where?"

"Up in the trees."

Tara wasn't looking at the trees. Her attention was fixed on that mirror, but once again sunglasses concealed his eyes.

The trees gave way to a grassy clearing, and he swung a left. A house came into view.

"Wow," M.J. said.

It wasn't a house, really, but a lodge made of rough-hewn logs. One story, weathered wooden shingles. A wide breezeway connected two separate sections, each with a limestone chimney at the end. He drove past the building and pulled up to a row of trucks and SUVs with mud-caked tires.

Tara went to the end of the row and parked beside a battered Suburban with a swamp-camo paint job.

M.J. looked at her. "I hope you have a plan."

"We'll improvise."

Tara slid from the Explorer and walked over to the man now getting out of the pickup. Black T-shirt, faded jeans. Not combat boots, as she would have expected, but shit kickers.

"Liam Wolfe?" She strode up to him. "I'm Special Agent—"

"I know who you are."

He watched her, his expression unreadable. Tara didn't usually look up at men, but this one was tall.

He glanced at M.J., then back to Tara.

"You're here about Catie," he said. "There's been an ID?"

"Nothing definite." Tara paused, gauging his reaction. His eyes were still hidden behind mirrored shades. "Probably by tomorrow."

Something shifted in his posture, a subtle bunching of muscles. Almost as soon as she noticed it, he looked relaxed again.

"Nice place you've got here," M.J. said, stepping up beside Tara. "Is this your company headquarters or—"

"That's right."

M.J. smiled. "Mind if I look around while you two talk?"

The sunglasses shifted to Tara.

"I just have a few questions," she explained. "It shouldn't take long."

"Look around all you want," he told M.J. "Jeremy can take you."

They turned to see a man standing behind them—six-three, two-thirty, brown hair, blue eyes. He wore Army green fatigues and heavy black boots that Tara had somehow failed to hear crunching on the gravel.

M.J. thrust her hand out and introduced herself with a smile.

"Jeremy Owen," he said briefly, shaking hands with both of them and then giving Liam a look that seemed loaded with secret communication.

Tara shot M.J. her own secret look. *Are you okay with this?* M.J. answered with a subtle nod before walking off with the big commando. He led her across the clearing to a corrugated metal building, where he held the door open as she stepped inside. A wooden sign above the doorway read SEMPER FI.

Tara returned her attention to Liam Wolfe. "Like I said, I just have a few questions."

"And I have things to do. Hop in."

He turned away, and she stared at his back, startled. After gritting her teeth for a moment, she trekked over to the passenger side of his truck. The instant she pulled the door shut, he was moving.

"So, Mr. Wolfe—"

"Liam."

He glanced over, and she noticed he'd finally ditched the shades. His eyes were deep green, the color of the woods around him.

"How did you hear about Catalina's disappearance?" she asked.

He steered his pickup over the gravel road. "David called me."

"David?"

"Her husband." He darted a look at her, probably

wondering why she didn't know this detail about the woman she was supposedly investigating.

"He called you Wednesday night or . . . ?"

"Yesterday morning. They notified him after her car turned up."

Her car. Interesting. Hadn't David Reyes already known his wife was missing when she didn't come home that night? Maybe he'd been away for some reason.

Tara looked around the truck. No fancy stereo or expensive gadgets. It was toasty warm inside and smelled of wet earth. She glanced in back and saw muddy work boots on the floor. Size thirteens, if she had to guess.

She looked outside. They were no longer on a road through the trees but simply *in* the trees, following a route he seemed to know well. Tara listened intently and then buzzed down her window.

"Is that—"

"Our firing range," he said. "Straight west of here."

It wasn't pistol fire she was hearing but rifles. "How long's the range?" she asked.

"A thousand yards."

She tried not to look impressed. "How many acres you have here?"

"Twelve hundred."

"And people?"

"Here, only a handful. I keep most of my guys in the field."

His guys. Again, she tried to mask her reaction. A twelve-hundred-acre facility, plus vehicles and employees. It was a large operation for a man who looked to be thirty-five, tops. Evidently, private security paid better than government work.

She turned to study him. Athletic body, peak condition. Ripped, as M.J. had said. His wide shoulders seemed to fill up the spacious cab.

He pulled over, and Tara's window buzzed up as he pushed open his door.

"Stay inside if you want," he said. "It's more comfortable."

Tara hadn't come here to be comfortable. She got out and zipped her jacket against the cold. They were deep in the woods, and it was dark as dusk. A layer of pine needles carpeted the forest floor. She walked around to the back of the pickup where he was unloading wood.

Tara grabbed a pair of two-by-fours and carried them to a growing pile at the base of a tall wooden frame. Someone was constructing a tower, it looked like. For rappelling? She stacked the wood and glanced around, noting the group of tires arranged on the hard-packed path. Farther down the trail she saw parallel bars and a wall made of logs. Nestled out here in the woods, the PT course reminded her of the one at Quantico.

"You train your people here?" she asked.

"Yep."

She returned to the truck. He scooped up an armload of two-by-fours like they were Styrofoam pool noodles. Tara grabbed two. "What are you building?" she asked.

"A cargo net."

She gazed up at the frame. "What is that, sixty feet?"

"Seventy." He looked at Tara, and the corner of his mouth lifted in a smile. "SEALs train on a sixty. Can't be outdone by a buncha frogboys."

A warm tingle filled her. Something about his eyes without the sunglasses, especially when he smiled. She looked at the frame again. "Impressive," she said.

There was no point in denying it. Liam Wolfe was impressive. His operation was impressive.

But she hadn't come here to be impressed.

He hauled the last of the wood as Tara stood there shivering. He seemed immune to the cold in his thin T-shirt. His muscles rippled as he stacked the lumber, and Tara watched him, suddenly struck by the certainty that he'd killed men before, probably with his bare hands.

"You used to be a Marine?" she asked.

"Retired." He looked at her. "There's no 'used to.'"

"Mr. Wolfe, what sort of threats was Catalina Reyes concerned about?"

"Liam." He slammed the tailgate on the now-empty truck bed. "And I don't know."

"Weren't you her bodyguard?"

"Security consultant."

She crossed her arms, annoyed by more semantics. "What's the difference?"

He leaned back against the truck. "In some cases, life and death."

"Okay, so you were her security consultant for how long?"

"We worked together about six months. She terminated the arrangement after she lost the election."

"You were her security consultant for six months, and you don't know what kind of threats she was worried about?"

"Lately? No."

She tipped her head to the side. "I find that hard to believe."

"That doesn't much bother me."

She watched him, trying for a read, but his body language didn't offer many clues.

He wasn't defensive. Or evasive. Or nervous. He seemed relaxed but alert. And she somehow knew he was keenly aware that he was being interviewed by a federal agent who might consider him a suspect in the disappearance—and probable murder—of a woman he knew.

Yet he seemed calm.

Tara looked over her shoulder at the path snaking through the trees. They'd been here ten minutes, and not a single trainee had come pounding down the course. They were alone, with only the chirping of birds and the distant pops of gunfire coming from the range.

Tara looked at him and caught him checking her out. His gaze lifted, and she felt a hot flush of sexual awareness.

"How'd you meet Catalina?" she asked.

"A referral from a client."

"Mind if I ask who?"

"Yes."

She arched her brows.

"My clients are confidential."

She looked at the trees again, struggling not to let her impatience show.

This was a casual conversation, and he was having it willingly. She was lucky to be here. He could have asked to have a lawyer present or made her get a warrant to set foot on his property, but instead he was being cooperative.

Mostly.

"When was the last time you talked to her?" she asked. "Do you know that much?"

He lifted an eyebrow at the edge in her voice. "Probably a few months ago. I'd have to check a calendar to know for sure."

His tone was cool and businesslike. But there was nothing businesslike about the way he was watching her now. The simmering look in his eyes put a warm flutter in her stomach, and she had to remind herself that he was a suspect.

"When she called, do you remember what you discussed?" Tara asked.

"She had some concerns about her security system. I talked her through it."

Just the sort of info Tara had been hoping for. "What, she didn't think her system was up to par?"

"It was," he said firmly. "We installed it. She needed someone to explain a few things, put her mind at ease."

"Was there a specific threat she mentioned?"

"No."

"Was she having marital problems that you know of?"

He cocked his head to the side. "Are you married?"

"No."

"Me neither." He paused, watching her closely with those green, green eyes. "Every married person I know has marital problems. Catie wasn't different."

Catie again.

"What was your relationship with her?" Tara asked.

"I told you, she was a client."

"What about after that?"

"She was a friend." Tara waited, but he didn't elaborate.

"This phone call about her security system," she said. "It would be useful if you could give me a ballpark of the timing. You can check your calendar later."

"Before Thanksgiving." He pulled a phone from the pocket of his jeans, then checked the screen and answered it. "Yeah."

She watched him as he stared at the ground, listening. She hadn't heard the phone, so he must have had it on vibrate.

"Tell him five minutes." He ended the call and walked to the driver's side. "Back to work."

Tara dusted her hands on her jacket and climbed into the warm cab. The ride back was faster, maybe because of his meeting or maybe because he was ready to get away from her pesky questions.

He didn't talk. Sitting close to him in the silence, she realized it wasn't his size that captured her attention so much as his confidence. It was in the way he moved, the way he spoke. It permeated everything he did, even something as basic as steering his truck over the rutted road.

They reached the clearing, and Tara noted the shiny black Suburban parked at the far end of the house. By its dark-tinted windows and specialized antennae, she guessed it was Someone Important, probably one of his confidential clients. M.J. was standing beside the Explorer talking to Jeremy.

Liam rolled to a stop beside them. He turned to Tara and nodded. "Special Agent." She was being dismissed.

"Thanks for your time," she said, shoving open the door and pulling a business card from her pocket. "Please call me if anything comes up. I'll be in touch after we have more information."

He gave her a wry look and took the card. "I'm sure you will."

THE HILLY OPENNESS was a relief after the dense woods. Tara neared the Delphi Center crime lab, going over the facts in her mind. She'd been on the case thirty-six hours now, and yesterday's legwork had uncovered more questions than answers.

She and M.J. had spent the afternoon at Silver Springs Park, interviewing potential witnesses, including a dog walker who remembered seeing a woman matching Catalina's description on the trail around 5:40 P.M. They'd found two other people who had been at the park that evening, both bird watchers in their late seventies. They remembered seeing the white Lexus but not Catalina.

None of the witnesses recalled suspicious vehicles or people around the trail. Silver Springs PD and M.J. were checking out everyone's background, but all of their stories raised the same troubling point.

If the witness accounts were accurate, then whoever grabbed Catalina from the trail hadn't parked at the trailhead. The most likely alternative was a back access road used primarily by park employees.

But why hadn't anyone heard a struggle or a call for help?

Maybe Catalina's assailant had disabled her. But then he would have had to carry or drag her to his vehicle, a good half mile from the trail through thick woods. On the other hand, he could have forced her at gunpoint.

But Tara didn't buy that scenario.

A smart, educated woman—particularly one who'd been trained in self-defense by the likes of Liam Wolfe—would know better than to go willingly with an assailant, even one wielding a gun. Her chances were much better if she ran.

So maybe she hadn't been forced. Maybe she hadn't been murdered at all but simply walked away from her Lexus and her life. She could have run away with a secret lover. She could be running from tax problems or a bad marriage or anything at all. Until the ID came back on the victim in the woods, all Tara knew for sure was that Catalina Reyes was missing, and there were plenty of ways to be missing, not all of them bad.

But Tara knew what her instincts told her.

It was the same thing Liam Wolfe seemed to know, too.

Tara fully expected the victim in the woods to be identified as Catalina Reyes. Tara had glimpsed the body—under adverse conditions, yes, but she'd seen it. Liam hadn't, presumably, so what made him so sure? The answer was simple. Either he'd killed Catalina or he knew details about her death.

Assuming for a minute that he *hadn't* killed her, that meant he was getting info somewhere, possibly from one of those sheriff's deputies who'd been talking about him the night the body was discovered.

So . . . a murder suspect who had an in with the sheriff's office, an in that could easily be exploited. The prospect didn't sit well with Tara, but there wasn't much she could do about it. She was the outsider in this investigation—a fact everyone she'd met had made abundantly clear.

Tara spied the turnoff for the Delphi Center crime lab. She pulled onto the private drive and stopped at the gatehouse. As she showed her ID to the guard, Tara's phone chimed from the console. It was M.J.

"I talked to the husband," M.J. informed her. "He doesn't think it's her."

"He talked to you?"

"He had a lawyer present, but he agreed to the interview. I think he was worried about how it would look if he stonewalled us."

The guard handed back Tara's ID and waved her through.

"And he doesn't think it's her?" Tara asked.

"Says he's sure it isn't. Fact, he doesn't even think it was Catalina who drove the Lexus to the park."

"Who, then?"

"I don't know. But this guy's adamant. Says she never left work before seven. And she wasn't a jogger. She didn't take care of her health, according to him. He said she rarely exercised, and if she did, it was in the comfort of the air-conditioned gym at their country club."

Tara thought of the eyewitness account about a woman on the trail. But eyewitness accounts were notoriously unreliable. People saw what they expected to see. Or what they wanted to see. Or what they believed they *should* see. More and more, lawyers were managing to debunk eyewitness testimony in court.

"Well, how does he explain her Lexus?" Tara asked, curving up the road.

"He doesn't. He just insists she didn't drive it there. At least not to go jogging—and those are his words, not mine."

"And what's *that* mean?"

"I don't know, but we're looking into it," M.J. said. "I'm wondering if she had a boyfriend, maybe someone she was meeting at the park. Because—get this— the husband admits they were separated."

"Okay, hubs just catapulted to the top of my suspect list," Tara said. Ahead of Liam Wolfe.

"David Reyes says he moved out six weeks ago, says they'd been in counseling for months, but it wasn't working out. And I know your next question. Yes, we got his alibi, and no, we have not yet confirmed it."

The Delphi Center came into view, an imposing white building at the top of a hill. Tara had seen pictures but never visited in person. With its tall white columns and wide marble steps, it looked like a Greek monument. She pulled into the parking lot and found a space near the front.

"You need to vet that alibi," she told M.J. "The soon-to-be-ex-husband is looking like our prime suspect."

"Hence the lawyer," M.J. said. "And I'm inclined to agree with you, except for the obvious."

"What's that?"

"The *body*, Tara."

The emotion in her voice gave Tara pause. And she

knew what M.J. meant. The crime was horrendously violent. Could a man really do that to his own wife?

The answer was yes. But M.J. was new to the job so not as jaded as Tara was.

"It might also explain the lack of noise," Tara said logically, "or signs of struggle at the park. Maybe she knew her killer."

"But why go public?" M.J. said. "That's risky. If her husband wanted to kill her, why not do it at home and set it up like an accident?"

"We're not even sure it's her yet," Tara pointed out. "And anyway, maybe he wanted it to look like a stranger killed her. A random act of violence. Or a hate crime. Or someone stalking her for political reasons, like one of the people who prompted her to hire bodyguards when she was running for Congress."

"Yes, but if he wanted it to look like that, why argue with investigators about her driving her car to the park?"

They both got quiet, thinking it through.

Tara slid from the SUV, and a cold January wind whipped against her face. "I'll call you later. I'm at the crime lab."

"Good luck," M.J. said. "I hope you get some answers."

CHAPTER FOUR

Tara was looking for Dr. Walter Crumbley, and she expected a balding man in a white lab coat.

Instead she got an auburn-haired woman in faded jeans.

"I'm Kelsey Quinn," she said, striding up to the reception desk. "I understand you're here for Walt?"

"That's right."

"He's out this week. Knee surgery. I'm covering his cases." She glanced at the receptionist, who was handing Tara a visitor's badge. "We set here?"

"All checked in, Dr. Quinn."

Tara followed the doctor through the spacious lobby and down a sloping corridor where she stopped at a door and swiped her ID against a keypad. The door slid open, and they stepped into a wall of cold air.

"I'm in the Bones Unit," she told Tara over her shoulder. "They call it the Crypt because it's so chilly."

Another swipe of her ID, and she stepped through a door.

The temperature wasn't the only reason they called it the Crypt. The room was filled with stainless-steel tables. On each was a set of bones.

"You're a forensic odontologist?" Tara glanced at the doctor.

"Forensic anthropologist," she said, slipping into a lab coat. "I deal with the whole skeleton, not only the teeth. Come on back here and we'll have a look. I've been working on her since this morning."

Tara darted a look at the tables as she passed by. On some were full skeletons, on others just a few small bones no bigger than twigs. Atop one of the tables was a lone skull. Counters and stainless-steel sinks lined the wall. The room smelled like formaldehyde, and Tara stifled a shudder.

"You'll have to excuse the mess. It's our high season. We've been inundated with cases since November."

Tara followed the woman into a darkened room, where she switched on a light. Tara had braced herself for a corpse, but on the table in the center of the room was a microscope.

"Why November?" Tara asked.

The doctor picked up a large manila envelope from the counter. "Deer season."

Tara must have looked blank.

"Hunters are a forensic anthropologist's best friend," she explained. "See, in cities, bodies tend to be found quickly, and they typically go to the medical examiner. In rural settings, not so much. I get the cases where more time has elapsed, remains that have been discovered weeks or months or even years later. Remains that have been buried or otherwise hidden by nature. Around here, skeletonized remains are often discovered by hunters in the autumn and winter. Nature helps, too. When leaves fall, that increases visibility in the brush. So November to February is our busy time, but right now we're especially slammed because Walt's on medical leave."

"In that case, thanks for getting to this so quickly."

"Of course." She smiled. "Mia, our DNA specialist, said it's top priority. I think Greenwood called her."

The doctor pulled an X-ray from the envelope and clipped it to a light panel, which she then switched on to illuminate the film. Tara relaxed a bit. She could look at X-rays all day long. Autopsies were tougher to stomach.

"These are the dental records," she said. Then she tapped a few keys on a notebook computer, and a digitized X-ray popped up on the screen. "And these are the films Greenwood sent me for comparison. As you can see, it's a match."

A match.

The mutilated body in the woods belonged to Catalina Reyes, forty-two, former candidate for the U.S. House of Representatives. She'd been a controversial figure from the start of her political career, and her FBI file included death threats made within the last eighteen months.

The Bureau was officially involved now, even if it didn't turn out to be a hate crime.

Tara studied the skull X-ray and then the dental X-rays, looking for telltale similarities. But to her untrained eye, it could have been anyone.

"Actually, I'm not seeing it," Tara said. "You're going to have to help me out here, Doctor."

"Call me Kelsey." She pointed at the computer screen with her pen. "See the maxillary second molar here? It tilts inward, just as you see on this dental X-ray. Also note the slight malocclusion. She'd had orthodontic treatment, but either they didn't correct it completely or maybe she didn't wear her retainer."

Tara stared at the dental X-ray, thinking of Catalina—Catie to her friends, probably—as a teenager in braces. She studied the X-ray Dr. Greenwood had taken of the skull.

"What's that in her throat?" Tara asked.

"A tooth."

Tara looked at her.

"Her right first molar was knocked out around the time of death. Same with her second premolar. See here?" She pointed at a gap where a tooth should have been. "The molar she swallowed. The premolar's still missing. It was the only tooth she had with a filling, which is a very distinguishing characteristic. So that might explain Dr. Greenwood's reluctance to make a positive ID using dental records alone."

Anger tightened Tara's shoulders as she gazed at the X-ray and imagined the extreme violence of the attack. "If she swallowed her tooth," Tara said, "that suggests she was alive at the time she was struck, right?"

"That's what it looks like to me. Which would indicate she resisted her attacker, at least at first." Kelsey tapped the keyboard and brought up another autopsy X-ray, this one showing a hand and arm. "Approximately half the bones in the human body are found in the hands and feet, and I always pay close attention to the hands. They tell a story. See her wrist here? Fractured scaphoid. Also, her fifth metacarpal is broken, an injury known as a boxer's fracture. Another indication of a struggle."

So she'd fought hard. Good for her. "You think maybe she bit him?" Tara asked.

"I hope." Kelsey's gaze met hers. "You're thinking of DNA?"

"Yes. Where's the tooth she swallowed?"

"At our DNA lab. I can tell you there was blood on it, but whether it belonged to the victim or her attacker, I couldn't say. Our DNA specialist will have those results soon."

"I'll have what soon?"

They both looked up to see a woman standing in the doorway. Petite build, lab coat, strawberry blonde hair pulled back in a ponytail.

"Mia. Speak of the devil." Kelsey made introductions as Tara looked the woman over. The name embroidered on her lab coat said DR. VOSS, but Tara thought she looked young to be a doctor. Maybe it was the freckles.

"Dr. Greenwood speaks highly of you," Tara said, trying to keep the skepticism out of her voice.

The DNA expert smiled. "He said this case is top priority. I'm working on it now, as a matter of fact. That shard of glass is interesting."

"Interesting how?"

"It's not your typical glass. Honestly, I don't know what it is. I didn't find any DNA on it—besides the victim's—but I've sent it to one of our trace evidence examiners, who should be able to tell us more." She turned to Kelsey. "I just stopped by to let you know I'm working on that tooth now. Any word from Brooke on the other one?"

Kelsey glanced at Tara. "We sent one of our crime-scene techs to Silver Springs Park hoping to recover that missing premolar. It had a filling in it, according to dental records, so she went out there with a metal detector." Kelsey looked at her colleague. "No luck, though. So for now, we just have the one tooth."

"Well, one is better than none." Mia looked at Tara. "If I get anything useful, you'll hear from me."

As she left, Tara gave her a business card.

"I know what you're thinking," Kelsey said when Mia was gone.

Tara lifted an eyebrow in question.

"She's young but very good. No stone unturned," Kelsey said. "And her husband's a homicide cop, so she thinks like an investigator."

Tara didn't say anything, but she felt encouraged as Kelsey turned her attention back to the X-ray on the screen.

"Okay, where were we?" Kelsey continued. "The victim's hands. We have the fractured scaphoid, the broken metacarpal." Another X-ray flashed onto the screen. "What I *don't* see are any parry wounds. Defensive wounds made by a knife to the hands or arms. By the time the knife was used, she was likely already dead."

Thank God. "Greenwood concluded strangulation," Tara said. "Can you tell if it was manual?"

"He found no sign of ligature marks. You'll notice the broken hyoid bone." She pointed to a tiny bone fragment near what looked like the windpipe. "In about a third of strangulation cases I see, the hyoid is broken."

Tara took a deep breath, blew it out. "Tell me about the knife injuries."

She tapped her keyboard again and pulled up two images side by side: the torso and the pelvis. "A deep-penetrating wound to the sternum. See where it cut the bone here?" Kelsey pointed near one of the upper ribs. "The knife came all the way down, nicking lumbar three at the base of the spine."

Tara clenched her teeth, visualizing the attack. "Any chance of figuring out what kind of knife was used?"

"A very good chance. Our tool-marks examiner, Travis Cullen, is one of the best in the world. He's working on it now. He said he'd compare his findings to the Jane Doe from November."

Tara looked at her. "November?"

"We have some un-ID'd remains here from Cypress County."

"Same MO?"

"Hard to say. By the time I got involved there wasn't a lot to work with."

"But she hasn't been identified?"

"Just the Big Four," Kelsey said. "Age, sex, race, and stature. I entered my findings into the missing-persons database, along with the DNA profile. No hits yet." She paused. "Would you like to see her?"

THE BONES WERE clean and neatly arranged in their natural order in a long, flat drawer at the back of the osteology lab.

"She came in on opening weekend. Deer season," the doctor clarified. "A hunter found her while he was looking for his dog. I was really glad to be called in."

"Why?" Tara gazed down at the bones, brownish gray against the white parchment paper lining the drawer.

"These small-county coroners, they have good intentions," Kelsey said, "but they really don't have the experience to interpret bones. Sometimes they can't even tell whether we're dealing with animal or human remains, especially if we only recover a femur or a tibia, something like that. Animal bones can easily be mistaken for human. Also, teeth marks made by scavenging predators can be mistaken for knife wounds. I'm always glad when they bring us in rather than waste time and resources investigating a presumed homicide that's not really a homicide at all."

"But in this case you're sure?"

"Absolutely." Kelsey opened the file she'd retrieved from her office. "First off, we're dealing with a female; you can tell by the pelvis. Likely mixed race or Hispanic. I removed one of her molars." She tipped the cranium back so Tara could see. "The cross section gives me an idea of dental maturation. That plus skeletal development—the stage of union of the epiphyses—gives me an age estimate of eighteen to twenty. She was around five feet three inches tall."

"Hispanic, you said?" Tara was thinking about everything she had in common with Catalina Reyes. So far, sex, race, and stature, three of the Big Four Kelsey had mentioned.

"It can be hard to tell definitively. More and more, our society's a melting pot. But her characteristics are consistent with Hispanic."

"What about time of death?"

"That's been tricky." Kelsey turned to a computer

terminal and tapped a few keys, pulling up a satellite map of East Texas. "She was found here, about thirty yards west of the Trinity River. Based on the debris in her hair, it was clear the body had been in water. They'd recently had a flood, which might account for that."

"Did you see the crime scene?"

Kelsey rolled her eyes. "No, unfortunately. Which is a shame. It's always better if I can view the remains in situ. But in this case, the sheriff had everything zipped into a body bag and delivered here. What we got was partially skeletonized, no clothing or personal items. We removed the remaining soft tissue and cleaned the bones so they'd be easier to read."

"And?"

"And that's where it gets interesting. At first I was thinking she might have drowned in the flood. But it quickly became clear we were dealing with a homicide."

Tara's stomach knotted. "Was she strangled?"

"Broken hyoid again, fractured mandible. And also this." She pointed to some scratches on the vertebrae. "Knife marks."

Tara leaned closer to look at the scratches. "You sure it's not a scavenger?"

"Absolutely. I examined these marks under a microscope, and it's obvious they were made by a blade. As to what type of blade, that I don't know."

"But your expert can tell me."

"That's the hope. What I do know is that she's a homicide. What I *don't* know is her name." Kelsey looked at her. "And that's really the most critical piece of the puzzle."

"Most murder victims are killed by someone they know," Tara said.

"True." Kelsey nodded. "And I know you're concerned about justice. About prosecution and building a case."

"Aren't you?"

"Yes, but it's also my job to think about the families. Someone's missing this young woman—her mother, if no one else." Kelsey rested her hand on the parchment and looked down at the bones. "I want to give her a name and send her home so her family can put her to rest."

WIND RATTLED AGAINST the motel room's thin windowpanes as Tara sat at the table and searched the crime-scene footage for anything she'd overlooked.

"I can't watch anymore." M.J. rested her head on her arms and sighed heavily. "How can you stand it?"

Tara didn't answer. Her gaze combed over the forest floor, the leaves and twigs and evidence markers, all illuminated by the glare of spotlights. She'd been over it and over it, looking for any clue that Ingram's deputies might have missed. She squeezed her eyes shut, then opened them again to watch the footage. As the cameraman tromped down the trail, the lens bounced, making Tara slightly dizzy.

"I'm tapped," M.J. said.

Three hours ago, she'd shown up at Tara's door with a veggie pizza and a six-pack, and they'd made a dent in both. But their energy was flagging.

"So call it a night," Tara said.

Instead M.J. picked up the remote off the dresser and switched on the television. Tara turned her attention back to the computer.

"Still nothing," M.J. said, flipping channels.

The news anchor's voice filled the room, and Tara recognized the script. It was a replay of an earlier broadcast.

"Think they don't have it yet, or they don't care?" M.J. asked.

Tara listened for a moment as a meteorologist advised Houstonians to cover their plants tonight because of an expected freeze. Weather was still the top story.

"They don't have it," Tara said. "But they will soon, believe me. Enjoy this while it lasts."

M.J. sank onto the bed and lay back.

"Why don't you turn in?" Tara tapped the keys, rewinding the footage so she could watch again.

"What does Jacobs think?" M.J. looked at her.

"Of what?"

"Us. Of the fact that we got duped out of the autopsy by Sheriff Redneck."

"He didn't say anything," Tara said, which was about as demoralizing as it would have been if he'd reamed her out. He'd said nothing. Only silence.

Tara had called him with the ID as soon as she'd left the Delphi Center. He hadn't sounded surprised, and she'd wondered again if he knew more about the investigation than he was telling her.

Of course he did. And he should—he was the special agent in charge of the Houston office.

But she got the feeling she was being kept in the dark about some other important facts.

"He said nothing?" M.J. sounded skeptical.

"It was basically a pep talk. He said he needs us to be his eyes up here."

Actually, he'd said he needed Tara to be his eyes. And he hadn't said it like a pep talk but more of a warning. *I need you on top of this, Rushing. You're my eyes up there.*

Because of the victim's identity, the Bureau was all over the case, but they hadn't yet wrestled it away from the Cypress County Sheriff's Department. Tara wasn't sure what they were waiting for, only that Jacobs had a plan. He always did. And at the moment, that plan included keeping Tara and M.J. in Dunn's Landing to essentially spy on local investigators. Maybe Jacobs wanted her to squeeze info out of them under the guise of cooperation before the feds took over. Tara planned to try.

"What did he make of Jane Doe?"

Tara glanced at M.J. on the bed, staring up at the ceiling. She looked beat. "Hard to tell," Tara said.

"But he thinks it's unrelated?"

"Seems that way."

"What do *you* think?"

Tara turned back to her computer screen, considering it. She watched again as one of Ingram's clumsy deputies swept the camera over the fire pit near the victim's body. She could hear the deputy's labored breathing as he trudged around the site. Whoever Ingram had had filming this was way out of shape.

"I want the forensics results," Tara hedged.

She had a nagging sense the murders were related. But hours of mulling it over had filled her with doubts.

Two women had been killed, yes, and both deaths involved a knife. But what else did they really have in common besides geography?

Catalina Reyes was wealthy and successful, a public figure. She'd been abducted from a jogging path and her body dumped twenty miles away. People had noticed her missing within hours of her disappearance.

Jane Doe had been murdered last fall, probably dumped in or near the Trinity River. Four months after her death, her bones remained unidentified, even though a profile had been entered into various missing-persons databases, leading Tara to believe she was a transient or someone else on the fringes of society.

"And what about Liam Wolfe?" M.J. asked.

Tara's nerves jumped at the sound of his name. "What about him?"

"Well, he knew Catalina. And this second victim was discovered not far from his home, too. Coincidence, you think?"

"Maybe."

Tara turned back to her computer, not sure why she resisted the idea of Liam Wolfe as a suspect in the Jane Doe killing. He was definitely a suspect in Catalina's death. And it wasn't clear at the moment whether Catalina's murder and Jane Doe's were linked.

She thought about him back at his ranch, heaving lumber around like it was nothing. Certainly, he was physically capable, but the more she thought about him, the more she had trouble with the whole idea.

"I don't know. I keep thinking about it—" She glanced at M.J., whose eyes were shut now. "M.J., go to *bed*. Seriously. It's almost midnight."

She sighed.

"I mean it."

M.J. groaned and pulled herself to her feet. "I'm going. Don't let me oversleep." She grabbed her key card off the table. "We're meeting with the Silver Springs police chief at eight."

"Want the leftover pizza?" Tara nodded at the box.

"You keep it."

After she left, Tara returned her attention to the screen. Her eyes felt gritty. She rewound the tape again, cursing herself for not being pushier. She should have stood up to Ingram that first night. She should have called a halt to what he was doing and insisted on waiting for an FBI evidence response team. Instead she'd tried to be diplomatic, and now the original crime scene had been trampled on, driven on, rained on, and otherwise screwed up beyond repair. And there was no turning back the clock.

Tara rubbed her eyes and tapped play. Again. By now, she'd memorized the entire eighteen-minute loop. Deputy Lardass circles the fire pit, zooming in on beer cans and cigarette butts and evidence markers. He pans to the trees and then jerks back again, yelling at one of the deputies to get his butt over here, he missed a can. He tromps down the trail leading to the body, obliterating footprints and other possible evidence with his big boots. He pauses at the edge of the clearing, muttering softly as the body comes into view. Sheriff Ingram is standing there, his face twisted with revulsion. He waves his deputy over and orders him to get a 360-degree view of the area.

Tara sighed and picked up a pizza crust. She nibbled on it, watching the wobbly footage.

More back-and-forth with Ingram. The camera jerks down as the deputy picks up a spotlight. More wobbling as he adjusts the camera. He pans it around the scene, and the next six minutes is a collage of leaves, twigs, tree stumps, and pine needles, with the occasional glimpse of the deputy's boots as he combs the woods surrounding the crime scene.

Tara sat upright. She hit pause, then backed up the footage.

She watched again—leaves, twigs, tree stumps. A gnarled root.

"There." She hit pause and used the touch pad on her computer to zoom in.

Something small and white amid the leaves. A cigarette butt.

"Son of a bitch." Tara's pulse was thrumming. It was right there. Physical evidence, possibly *DNA* evidence, just a stone's throw from the body. And it hadn't been marked or flagged.

She chewed her lip, thinking. She reached for her phone to call M.J., then changed her mind.

"Damn it."

Tara stood up and glanced around. Her motel room was a sea of files and clothes and empty fast-food cups. She grabbed her jacket and checked the battery on her phone. Twenty percent. She stuffed it into her pocket.

Then she strapped on her holster and reached for her keys.

CHAPTER FIVE

Tara dipped over the low-water bridge, her headlights illuminating the narrow road. She rattled over the cattle guard, then rounded a bend and rolled to a stop before a police barricade.

She cut the engine and stared at the barrier. What was the point of it? The remote outdoor crime scene was impossible to wall off, so the wooden barricade did little more than signal to the morbidly curious that they'd found the right place.

Tara grabbed the heavy Maglite from beneath her seat and went around to the cargo space. She unlatched her evidence kit, which she'd made from a tackle box. Not wanting to juggle both the kit and the flashlight, she cherry-picked the items she would need: gloves, tweezers, envelopes, a glass vial. She tucked everything inside the pocket of her windbreaker.

She glanced up at the sky. Dark, moonless. The temperature had dropped at least ten degrees since she'd let herself into her motel room thinking she was in for the night.

She closed the cargo door and switched on the flashlight. She swept the beam through the darkness. It didn't take her long to find the path.

Tara passed the fire pit where forty-eight hours ago a huddle of deputies had stood watching her with skeptical eyes. Slicing through the darkness with the Maglite, she retraced her steps through the forest, scouring the ground for any further evidence that might have been overlooked.

High above her, an owl called out. *Hoo, hoo-hoo, hoo, hoo.*

Tara stared up at the pines. She glanced around. It was darker and colder than it had been the other night. Lonelier, too, which was good. She could concentrate without having to navigate the political obstacle course laid out by Ingram and his deputies.

She trained her gaze on the path, sweeping the light back and forth as she neared the location. Her footsteps slowed as she approached.

Catalina's body had been cleared away, along with the leaves and debris surrounding it. Only a sad patch of dirt remained. Tara identified the spot by the equidistant marks in the soil where CSIs had staked out the inner crime scene with orange twine.

For a moment, Tara stared. Wind gusted between the trees, biting her through her jacket. The air was damp and tinged with sulfur. She switched off the flashlight and stood still, just listening, letting the place and the darkness settle around her.

Silver Springs Park, then here. Two separate crime scenes, both part of the geographical region known as the Piney Woods. Yesterday morning, Tara had combed the park, interviewing people and looking for clues. But this site had more to offer. Silver Springs Park was about Catalina. She'd chosen it, for whatever reason.

This place belonged to her killer.

He'd brought her here, posed her, and left her. *He'd* chosen this place. Why? Tara didn't know, but it revealed something about him as surely as any fingerprint.

Bile rose in Tara's throat as she pictured the mutilated corpse. The body said something. The setting said something. The killer had selected a wooded spot but not a secret one. He'd chosen a known hangout with enough traffic to ensure discovery, a guaranteed audience for his show.

Tara switched on the flashlight. She sidestepped the empty patch of dirt and found the path into the woods. Ingram believed the killer had used the path moving to and from his vehicle. The reports weren't in yet, but the CSIs Tara had interviewed said the tire tracks were consistent with an SUV or a pickup, which in Texas narrowed it down to just less than half of registered vehicles.

Tara swept her flashlight back and forth until she spotted the tree, a sycamore. She recognized it from the video, and her pulse quickened as she stepped closer to examine its knobby roots. She scanned the dirt, the leaves . . . nothing.

She crouched down. Using a stick, she gently raked away pine needles and leaves until the base of the tree was swept clean.

Disappointment welled in her chest. She slipped

the phone from her pocket. She'd taken a screen shot back at the motel, and now she compared the image from the crime-scene video with the tree in front of her. It was the same.

Except the cigarette butt was gone.

Tara stood and tucked her phone into her pocket. It had been a fluke, but she'd been hoping. Frustration burned her throat. Her limbs felt heavy. Three weeks' worth of endless workdays and sleepless nights seemed to catch up with her, and she was suddenly so tired she could hardly stand. She closed her eyes and rubbed her forehead.

A rustle in the trees.

Tara went still. She listened. Switching off the flashlight, she turned toward the sound and strained to hear.

Icy fear gripped her as she realized she wasn't alone. Her senses sharpened. She heard something slinking through the trees.

Slowly, silently, she unholstered her Glock. The familiar weight of the pistol in her hand steadied her as she scanned the woods, straining to penetrate the gloom.

More rustling. A scrape of footsteps. Then a flurry of movement, and something crashed through the thicket. Tara moved toward it, a dog after a scent. She beamed her light at the noise and caught a flash of black plunging into the brush.

"Stop! Police!" she shouted, darting into the trees.

A searing pain clamped around her ankle. She dropped to her knees. Teeth bit into her flesh, and panic shot through her as she fell back against the dirt, kicking, trying to loosen the jaws. The flashlight was gone. She aimed her gun at whatever had hold of her and groped in the darkness with her free hand—

Metal. A cage. What had she stepped in?

An engine roared. She was blinded by headlights as a grille zoomed toward her. Her heart skittered, and she lifted her gun as the truck skidded to a halt and the door popped open.

"Freeze!" she yelled.

"Whoa there."

The voice was deep and male, and she knew it instantly.

CHAPTER SIX

Her heart hammered. She recognized the voice but couldn't make out a face.

"Hands where I can see!" she yelled.

The shadow shifted. The door slammed, and he moved toward her, a giant silhouette in the headlight beams.

"You're hurt."

Liam dropped to a knee beside her, apparently unbothered by the gun pointed at him. He took the flashlight and aimed it at her foot, which was encased in a mesh cage all the way up past her boot.

"You stepped in a trap." He looked at her.

She set her weapon on the ground and leaned forward, still trying to digest what had happened. Her pulse was racing, and her skin felt clammy.

"Looks like a crab trap," she said, and immediately realized how absurd that sounded.

"Possum." He handed her the flashlight and went to work unsnagging her jeans from the wire.

His face was cast in shadows, and stubble covered his jaw. She studied his features, still shocked to see him here.

"Nasty cut," he said.

She reholstered her Glock. She examined the cut, registering pain again as the adrenaline subsided.

Liam pulled a knife from the pocket of his jeans. He snapped it open and cut through the wire to free her boot. Then he got to his feet and lifted her by the arm, and the warmth of his hand seeped through her jacket.

"Can you walk on it?"

"I'm fine." She stepped forward and winced. "Really, I'm good." She pulled away from him and limped toward the truck. Her ankle was on fire.

"I've got a blowout kit," he said, going to the driver's side. He pulled the keys from the ignition and stepped over to the toolbox.

Tara leaned against the bumper. She felt self-conscious now. The wind whipped against her sweat-soaked skin, and she started to shiver.

It had been a person, not an animal, crashing through the forest.

"What're you doing out here?" He slammed the toolbox shut and came back with a red zipper pouch and a bottle of water. "Besides trespassing?" He tossed the pouch onto the hood, then unscrewed the lid off the water and crouched at her feet.

She pointed the flashlight at him. "I should ask you the same thing." He tugged up the cuff of her jeans and doused the wound, and she bit her lip as water trickled into her boot.

"I'm not trespassing. I own it."

She looked at him. Or, rather, at the top of his head. There was something very personal about his touching her clothes, but she didn't pull away. To have something to do, she rested the flashlight on the hood and thumbed through the zipper pouch.

"*You* own this land," she said.

"Yep."

Another fact to be added to her growing list: *Things I Should Have Known Earlier*. And another connection between Liam Wolfe and the murder.

She pulled away from him and propped her ankle on her thigh. He stood up as she tore open an antiseptic wipe and dabbed at the cut.

He watched her. "When was your last tetanus shot?" he asked.

"I'm good."

"When was it?"

She glanced up at him. "All my shots are current. It's a prereq for SWAT. We never know what we might bump into."

He watched her steadily as she cleaned the gash. He was right—it *was* nasty. She'd have to keep an eye on it, maybe swing into a drugstore tomorrow for some ointment.

"You're on a SWAT team," he stated.

"That's right."

"How much is female?"

She looked up. "What?"

"What percent?"

"What do you mean? My percent."

"Just you?"

"Yeah."

He shook his head.

"What?" she asked.

"Nothing."

She tore open another wipe. "So if you own this property, I'm assuming that trap's yours?"

"Don't know whose it is. At a guess, I'd say Alligator Joe."

"Alligator Joe? You can't be serious."

He looked over his shoulder. "He's got a little cabin down by the hollow, lives off the land."

"You let him squat on your property?"

"He's been here forever. Doesn't really bother anyone."

Sure. Except clueless federal agents stumbling around in the dark. Maybe it had been Alligator Joe crashing through the forest, scaring the crap out of her.

She finished cleaning her cut, acutely aware of Liam's tall, muscular body right beside her, so close she could feel the heat emanating from him. His unexpected presence here rattled her. And when she got rattled, she tended to be a bitch.

She pulled her cuff down and stuffed the bloody wipes into her pocket. "I need to get back," she said.

"I'll take you."

"Don't bother. My SUV's down the trail."

He walked around the front of the truck. "I'll take you to your SUV, then. Get in."

She watched him as he slid behind the wheel. He had a way of bulldozing people. She understood it completely because she had it, too.

She tucked the Maglite into her pocket and slid into the truck. Warmth surrounded her, and she looked at him in the glow of the dashboard. He had a strong profile, straight posture, broad shoulders. Again she was struck by the raw masculinity of him and felt a hot rush of attraction.

She focused on the view outside her window as he turned the truck around in the narrow space.

"How long have you owned this land?" she asked.

"Almost a year now."

"Why'd you buy it?"

"Case I want to expand."

"And you just let some guy live on it rent-free?" she asked.

"He pays in other ways. Works as a handyman around the place sometimes. He can fix damn near anything with a motor. He drives a truck even older than yours—an eighty-seven Chevy, blue and white, with a hundred-eighty-five-horsepower V-8." He glanced at her. "What's your Ford, a ninety-one?"

"Ninety-two."

"That's a first-generation."

She slid a look at him. "You sound like a mechanic."

"My dad was a mechanic. I grew up around cars," he said. "And you never answered my question."

"Which one?"

"What are you doing out here?"

She sighed. "I was looking for clues we might have missed."

"Find any?"

"Not really."

He glanced at her. "You sure?"

"Yeah. Why?"

"You seem jumpy."

Irritation bubbled up, and she stared out the window. But okay. She'd drawn down on him. He had good reason to think she was paranoid.

The truck bumped along the road, and she looked at him. She was used to being around big men. SWAT was second only to the military as a destination for jacked-up alpha males. But this one was especially large, and just sitting next to him made her feel small by comparison, weaker. And she didn't like feeling that way.

She gazed out the window again and realized her pulse was still thrumming. He unnerved her. It wasn't just his size, it was his attitude. Maybe she was self-conscious because he'd caught her flat on her ass. She was definitely embarrassed that she'd pulled her weapon on him.

She adjusted the vent and got a waft of hot air. His attitude bothered her, but she liked his truck. It smelled like leather and earth and felt deliciously warm. She forced herself to ignore the little flurry of nerves generated by being alone in the dark with him. The nerves weren't from fear but something else. And she wondered which was worse, being afraid of a man she was investigating or being attracted to him?

"You shouldn't come out here alone."

She looked at him. "Why not?"

"We've got more than a few meth heads around here. You don't want to walk up on something, not without backup."

She watched his face in the dimness, uneasy with

the protective tone of his voice. "We confirmed the ID today," she said.

"I know."

That ticked her off.

"Won't be long till the media has it," he added.

"Where are you getting your information?"

He didn't answer.

"And the other day," she said, "how'd you know we were here, me and M.J.? Are you having us tailed?"

Even if he was, he'd probably never admit it. But she at least needed to ask and get his reaction. Shadowing investigators could definitely be considered suspicious behavior.

Although she had to be honest with herself. She didn't consider him a real suspect. Despite his links to the victim, she simply didn't feel it.

"I'm guessing you filmed us approaching your property and ran my plate," she said.

The corner of his mouth curved. "Nothing that cloak-and-dagger." He glanced at her. "I'm friends with Crystal."

"Who's Crystal?"

"She waited on you at the Waffle Stop. Bright red hair, eyebrow ring. Her dad's Leo Marshall."

She just stared at him.

"The manager at Big Pines. Try to keep up." He was grinning now, and she knew he was teasing her.

She turned to face the window. "Small-town grapevine. And here I've been all impressed with your spying abilities."

"You should be." He pulled up to her Explorer and parked. "We're the best there is."

She looked at him in the darkness, so confident it

bordered on arrogance. And the crazy thing was she believed him—he was that good.

His eyes locked on hers, and the air between them felt charged with electricity. His gaze dropped to her mouth, and her heart skittered. Was he going to kiss her? He eased closer, watching her, making her heart pound.

"I'm sorry about Catie," she blurted.

He pulled back, as she'd intended.

"You were fairly close, I take it?" When he didn't answer, she kept pushing. "You knew her routines?"

He just looked at her.

"We're trying to understand how she ended up at the park that day," she explained. "Silver Springs Park. A witness might have seen her jogging, but her husband doesn't think so, and we didn't recover any clothes, so . . ."

His brow furrowed, and he turned away. "She went there sometimes. She liked the solitude."

"How do you know?"

"I showed it to her." His gaze met hers again.

Yet another circumstance linking him to the murder. And still Tara wasn't one-hundred-percent sure of his relationship to the victim, just that he hadn't told her everything.

Was it a love triangle? Was he part of Catie's marital problems? Even if they weren't having an affair, there could have been undercurrents of jealousy.

She pushed open the door. "Thanks for the help." As she said it, she realized he still hadn't explained why he'd been out here.

He put his hand over hers, warm and possessive. "Be careful, Tara."

She pulled away. "I will."

• • •

SHE TOOK OFF without a backward glance and Liam watched her in the rearview mirror. What the hell was it with her?

He shoved his truck into gear and got moving. She considered him a suspect, and so he ranked right up there with every lowlife scumbag she'd ever put in jail.

He drove through the woods, thinking about her, as he had been for days. He was a good judge of people, and the more he thought about it, the more he believed the way she acted toward him was just that, an act.

Tara Rushing was smart. And despite the incriminating circumstances—because they sure as shit were—he doubted she really believed he was a cold-blooded killer. There was something forced about her frosty attitude.

He'd caught the look in her eyes when they'd first met. And he'd watched her reaction to him tonight. Liam knew when women were attracted to him, and this one was, no question. And yet she held back. He wasn't sure what her hang-up was—probably something to do with work—but she seemed determined to keep him at arm's length.

He was determined not to let her.

A SWAT team. Damn. Now it was going to be even harder to get her out of his head.

His phone vibrated in his pocket, and he dug it out. "Yeah."

"You done yet?" Jeremy asked him.

"Just the northwest. I'm headed for the southeast corner now."

Silence, probably as Jeremy wondered what the holdup was. Then he said, "Okay, we're good to go in the control room. Everything's live."

"I'll finish this installation and be there in a few," Liam told him. "How's it running?"

"Right as planned."

CHAPTER SEVEN

Liam was right about the press, and by seven A.M., the parking lot of the motel was crowded with media vans. Teams of reporters staked out the Waffle Stop, too, collecting quotes from locals for their morning broadcasts. Tara and M.J. got their coffee to go and navigated through traffic to pick up U.S. 59 down to Silver Springs.

Compared with Cypress County, the administrative offices for Silver Springs were brand spanking new, housed in a two-story building with a facade of Texas limestone. Silver Springs was in transition. What had once been a sleepy logging town was now an affluent bedroom community on the outskirts of Houston. As they pulled into the parking lot, Tara wondered if the people who ran the town were modern like their headquarters or still mired in the past.

"Nice," M.J. said, as Tara whipped into a space beside the slot reserved for the police chief. It looked like he was already in, and Tara checked her watch to make sure they weren't late.

"Who's here again?" Tara asked as they got out.

"Chief Milt Becker and I think one of his officers."

They entered the building and were immediately approached by a rail-thin police officer in a blue uniform. "Special Agent Rushing?"

He'd been expecting a man, Tara could tell. They shook hands, and Tara introduced him to M.J.

"I been hearing about that raid the other day," he said. "What'd they call it, Operation Froyo? There ought to be a special place in hell." He shook his head. "Anyway, your guys down there, they did a good job."

"I'll pass it along," Tara said drily.

"Y'all come on back." He motioned them down a corridor. "Everyone's in the conference room."

"Everyone?" M.J. asked.

"The sheriff wanted to sit in. Him and Chief Becker go way back, so . . ."

He let the thought trail off as he opened a glass door to a room where half a dozen men crowded around a table, including Sheriff Ingram and his deputy, Jason Moore. They went through introductions, and Tara took a seat beside Chief Becker, a heavyset man with a silver buzz cut.

"You ladies want some coffee?" The chief nodded at a carafe on the table beside a half-empty box of fruit kolaches.

"No, thanks." Tara pulled out a notebook. "I assume everyone's had a chance to read the ME's report," she said, trying to set the tone. Jacobs was still pushing cooperation with the locals, and she was determined to try. "Dr. Greenwood concluded manual strangulation, and the forensic anthropologist at the Delphi Center backs that up. Greenwood's report also includes the tox results. She's negative for drugs and alcohol."

Becker whistled. "That came back in a hurry."

She assumed he meant the toxicology labs, and he was right. Typically, they could take a few weeks.

"You been to Delphi?" Ingram was frowning at her now.

"Yesterday afternoon," Tara said. "While I was there, I had a chance to talk to the forensic anthropologist about the Jane Doe case from November."

He bristled. "What about it?"

"It's been classified as a homicide." Tara glanced at the blank faces around the table. "A woman's body was recovered in Cypress County near the Trinity River, back in the fall."

"Opening weekend." Becker nodded. "I remember that."

"The victim has some broken bones and knife injuries," Tara said. "The tool-marks expert at the Delphi Center is analyzing the case now to see if there's a link."

Ingram looked irritated.

"I'm surprised you didn't think to mention it," Tara said pointedly.

"What's to mention? It's a dumped-body case, three months old. We don't even have an ID on her."

Dumped-body cases were among the toughest to solve. No witnesses, no murder weapon. And whatever biological evidence there was had been exposed to the elements. Tara sympathized with the challenges, but the sheriff didn't sound challenged so much as lazy.

"Did Delphi get my package, do you know?"

Tara looked across the table. The question was from the Silver Springs fire chief, Alex Sears, whose presence at the meeting hadn't yet been explained.

"What package is that?" she asked.

"Their lab out there—I sent in the lock and chain off the gate from the fire break," he said. "They were supposed to run it for prints."

Becker waved a hand at him. "Hold on a minute. Let's catch these gals up." He looked at Tara. "Alex here found evidence our perpetrator used the fire break north of the park. It's an access road, but it's gated off."

"Tire tracks match the ones y'all found," the fire chief said, although Tara wasn't sure how he could know that. "Looks like he used bolt cutters on the lock, then threw it in the bushes."

Tara took a long look at the fire chief. He was younger than the other men in the room, probably mid-thirties, and he kept himself in much better shape. She liked that he'd not only found a clue but followed up on it.

The lock was a valuable lead but unsettling, too. For the killer to access the park from a nonpublic route suggested a good deal of premeditation. He'd been familiar enough with Catalina's routine to know when to expect her at the park and then to get there ahead of time to lie in wait.

Or maybe it suggested that Catalina wasn't specifically targeted. Maybe the killer accessed the park through a back route and waited for a victim of opportunity.

"I'll check with Delphi on it," Tara told Sears.

"How about local suspects?" M.J. said, addressing the sheriff and his deputy. "You were compiling a list based on known offenders in the area?"

"Besides drug and alcohol charges, I got three possibles so far," Jason said. "Ross McThune, Donny Price, and Liam Wolfe."

"Liam Wolfe has a rap sheet?" M.J. sounded surprised. She and Tara had checked Liam out and come up with zip.

"He owns the land," Jason said. "Knows the area, the victim. Makes him a suspect in my book."

Tara couldn't argue his logic. "What about the other two?" she asked.

"Donny Price served a two-year stretch for aggravated assault. McThune just finished a year for simple assault on a woman in Dallas. We haven't had a chance to check 'em out yet. I'll probably interview Price today."

Tara jotted down the info as Jason eyed her notepad with suspicion.

"You might want to check McThune's arrest report," she said.

"Why?"

"I'm surprised he did a year for a misdemeanor, unless it got pleaded down from something bigger. How old is he?"

"Twenty-six."

She nodded. "So maybe it was a first offense and they cut him a deal. The original police report should tell you more." Tara wrote down the names and then looked at Ingram. "What about the guy who lives near the crime scene—Alligator Joe?"

Smiles around the table. Jason snorted.

"You ever met him?" Ingram asked.

"No."

"This that Cajun that lives down in the hollow?" Sears asked.

"Joe Giroux," Ingram said. "And he's older than two trees. I don't see him hustling down here to kidnap a woman, then hauling her home to cut her up."

Tara made a note of the last name.

"I'm following up with the teenagers today," Jason said. "Their folks are coming in, and we'll see if we can't sort out their stories."

"What about them?" Tara asked.

"Timing's off. This couple said they went out there around eight to meet some friends that never showed. But we talked to the friends, and they said they stopped by there and didn't see them. Somebody's lying."

He was right, but Tara figured the lies had more to do with the fact that they'd been out there having sex. She doubted that summoning their parents to the police station would do anything besides further muddy the waters, but she didn't want to waste time arguing about it.

As the meeting dragged on, Tara started to lose hope for getting any real help from the sheriff's people. They seemed to have the same sloppy approach to developing local suspects as they'd had to processing the crime scene. And so far, every "lead" they'd come up with would have to be reexamined by Tara or someone from her office. Day three of the investigation, and Ingram had yet to nail anything down.

"How about the husband?" Jason asked. "You guys bring him in yet?"

"We'll be interviewing him again this afternoon," M.J. said.

The Silver Springs PD had been more than happy to let the FBI handle the delicate matter of interviewing the powerful Houston attorney. David Reyes had a reputation for being litigious.

Ingram looked at Tara. "I thought the husband had an alibi."

"He does. He was in a mediation followed by a business dinner the evening his wife disappeared. But we're still looking at him."

David Reyes might not have killed Catalina, but he could have *had* her killed, and the pending divorce was a red flag. They needed more information, including financials, to really get a picture.

"Okay, back to the forensics." Tara scanned her notes. "I plan to be in touch with the Delphi Center, so I'll ask about that lock and chain." She looked at Sears. "You sent it for fingerprints?"

"And DNA, if they can get any."

"I'll check. We're still waiting on DNA results from a shard of glass they recovered from the body." She glanced at Ingram. "And I'm going to need a list of the items sent in from the crime scene, the cigarette butts in particular."

Ingram shook his head. "We didn't send them."

"Why not?"

"No reason to."

Tara looked at him.

"Waste of money, at this point," he said. "Till we have a suspect in hand, we'd just be running blind tests on a bunch of beer cans at a couple hundred bucks a pop."

Tara tried to swallow her frustration. "You're worried about the budget?"

He folded his arms over his chest.

"My office can help with that," she said. "Go ahead and send the evidence."

He obviously didn't like taking orders from a woman, but she didn't care. They had work to do, and she wanted to wrap this meeting.

"That's it, then." She closed her notebook. "The one other thing we should talk about is the press. Sheriff, I've been asked to let you know our media relations coordinator will be happy to handle any questions and interview requests. We ask that you direct reporters to us, so we get a consistent message out to the public."

Ingram looked like he'd bitten into a lemon. He was up for reelection next year, no doubt running on a tough-on-crime platform. She doubted he'd be able to resist the spotlight.

"If you *do* talk to any reporters," Tara said, "be careful not to discuss details of the investigation. When we get a suspect in for interrogation, it's going to be critical that we haven't tipped our hand."

"All due respect, this ain't my first rodeo." He stood and grabbed his Stetson off the table behind him. "Milt, Alex. I'll be in touch."

Five minutes later, Tara and M.J. were back in the Explorer.

M.J. looked at her. "What'd you think?"

"We came out with more to-dos."

"That's what you wanted, isn't it?"

"Yeah. And the lead from the fire chief about the

gate is good," Tara said. "But we're definitely on the sheriff's shit list."

"I think we were on it from the minute we got here. What do you think about the suspect list they're working?"

Tara didn't think much of it, but she shrugged. "We'll see where it leads."

Liam was on that list, and she had to admit—to herself, at least—that the idea bothered her.

Tara was treading on thin ice with him. She thought about the warm rush she'd felt during their first encounter. She'd felt it again last night, too. But she couldn't be influenced by that. She had the self-discipline to do her job, professionally and thoroughly, without letting a little thing like sexual attraction distract her.

M.J. scrolled through her phone. "I missed a call while we were in there. Mike Brannon." She dialed him back. "Hey, it's Martinez. What'd you get?"

Tara eavesdropped as she pulled out of the parking lot.

"Are you sure?"

She shot Tara a look. By the tone of her voice, Tara knew something was wrong.

"Can you e-mail the file?" M.J. asked. "Okay, thanks." She hung up.

"What?"

"I thought you said Liam Wolfe hadn't talked to Catalina Reyes since before Thanksgiving."

"That's what he told me."

"Well, it sounds like he lied."

CHAPTER EIGHT

Tara had stopped by the office to pick up an unmarked Taurus, hoping to maintain a low profile. The car reeked of lemon air freshener, but it had a built-in GPS, so it was a step up from the Blue Beast. Now she hung back, keeping the Silverado in view.

Her phone chimed from the console, and she put it on speaker.

"Where are you?" M.J. asked.

"Still shadowing him."

"To the airport or—"

"Austin."

Silence.

Liam eased into the right-hand lane, but Tara stayed where she was.

"You tailed him all the way to Austin?" M.J. sounded shocked.

"Tell me what you found out."

"I finally reached Jeremy Owen, with Wolfe Security.

He says Liam's out of town on business until tomorrow night."

Overnight created complications, but Tara had expected as much when she realized Liam was headed out of town. She eased into the right-hand lane as he exited the freeway.

"I need his cell number," Tara said.

"We don't have it."

"What about Catalina's phone records?"

She took the exit ramp. Following Liam, she hung a right into a residential neighborhood with large old houses and even larger new construction.

"The number's a landline," M.J. informed her. "Registered to WSI—Wolfe Security, Incorporated. What business would he have in Austin?"

"I don't know."

Tara slowed, letting him get ahead of her as he made a left turn, going deeper into the neighborhood. Now was the tricky part. If she lost him now, her entire day was down the tubes. But she couldn't risk getting too close.

"I'm not even sure it *is* business," Tara said, glancing at the manicured lawns up and down the street. "A lot of people say that when they leave town, whether it is or not."

"So what do you want me to do?"

She pulled up to a stop sign and spied him several blocks north turning into a driveway. She noted the street name and kept going.

"Try to connect with Jeremy again," she said. "That's a good angle. See if you can get him to tell you what Liam's relationship is with the victim. He's hiding something, I can tell."

Tara circled the block so she'd end up north of the house where Liam had stopped. She spotted him getting out of his truck, and she pulled over under the shade of a tree. He walked up to the front door of a Georgian two-story with black shutters. A blond woman stepped out. Liam pulled her against him and kissed her.

"And what are you going to do?" M.J. asked.

Liam followed the woman inside. The door closed, and Tara realized her heart was racing.

"Tara?"

"When I get the chance, I'll corner him," she said. "See if I can get some answers."

LIAM WAS ON edge tonight, and it wasn't just the job.

It was the setting, the timing, the distractions. And the fact that the threat to his client had recently been elevated.

He forced himself to forget all of that as he scanned the faces. He needed to stay in the moment—observing, collecting impressions, making eye contact. His stare made people uncomfortable, and that was fine with him.

Liam skimmed the tables in the ballroom, starting with the two closest to the stage. He was looking for suspects. His definition: anyone who caught his attention for any reason at all. Anything from a nervous glance to a forgotten backpack could signal trouble, and years of working in terrorist hot spots had taught him to trust his instincts.

Applause from the audience as the tuxedo-clad MC

finished his introduction. The guy stepped back from the microphone, and Jim Willet, candidate for lieutenant governor of Texas, stepped up to the podium.

Liam ignored his client and watched the audience. Look, assess, progress. Look, assess, progress. The mantra flowed through his mind as his gaze moved over the faces. Tonight's crowd included campaign donors and business cronies, along with dozens of bored-looking spouses. It also included reporters and party loyalists and—possibly—the author of a recent letter to Jim Willet that promised to put a bullet between his eyes.

Liam finished his survey of the audience and turned his attention to the podium.

Liam hated podiums. He hated stages even more. They created too much space between him and the protectee. Tonight's compromise had been to move the podium to the side of the stage, ostensibly so the audience would have a better view of the slide show while they ate undercooked pasta and rubbery chicken marsala. The real reason was so that Liam could station a man in the wings, just eight feet away from the client.

He scanned the crowd again, zeroing in on the man he'd labeled the Fidgeter. Ever since the dinner plates disappeared, he'd been messing with something in the pocket of his suit jacket. Liam caught the gaze of one of his men across the room. Lopez nodded. He'd noticed the guy, too, and was in a position to respond if anything happened. Such as what, Liam didn't know. But Jim Willet had his sights set on the second-highest political office in the nation's second-largest state. Rumor had it he ultimately had his sights set on the White House. Whether he got there would be a matter of planks and platforms and the pendulum swings of a fickle electorate.

Liam didn't give a shit about planks or pendulums. His job was to keep the protectee alive long enough to let the voters decide.

He checked the faces again, looking for tells. The relevant stats were embedded in his mind. A political attack in the U.S. would most likely be the work of a lone actor. It would be at close range, less than thirty feet. The most likely weapon was a handgun, which was why Liam always pushed for metal detectors. But campaign managers and sometimes the candidates themselves usually balked. Metal detectors created an "atmosphere of suspicion" that wasn't conducive to people getting out their checkbooks. Usually, Liam had to settle for ID checks at the event entrances, which carried the risk of someone sneaking in a weapon.

It wasn't that difficult, and tonight's event was a case in point. Aside from the six men from Wolfe Security, Liam knew of at least one spectator who was packing heat.

He glanced at the door in the back of the room. Tara stood in the shadows, invisible to the hotel staffers streaming back and forth. But she wasn't invisible to Liam. He'd felt her presence like an electric shock from the moment she slipped into the ballroom. He couldn't see her face now, but he knew she was watching him. Still. Her gaze had been on him since she'd first come in here.

He watched her from the corner of his eye. She was pure fed today, in a tailored dark suit and low heels. Sexy, yes, but not nearly as hot as when she'd shown up at his house in combat boots looking ready to kick his ass. He liked the way she'd pelted him with questions. And he liked the way she'd gotten her feathers ruffled when he'd refused to answer.

The SWAT thing fascinated him. He'd never met a woman so overtly physical, and he liked it. A lot.

"Wolfe, it's Lopez."

He adjusted his earpiece. "Go ahead."

"I've got a request here for a change of exit route."

"Negative. Plan is we're out through the kitchen."

"I know, but she wants it changed."

"She" was definitely Willet's campaign manager. It was the same song-and-dance with every PR flak on the planet. They wanted their guy in the crowd, mingling with the masses and getting photos snapped by the paparazzi. Liam wanted him as far away from both groups as possible, but he didn't always get his way. His standard compromise was a public entrance, complete with all the red carpet and fanfare the PR team could muster, and a private exit via an undisclosed route. Event endings were more dangerous than beginnings, so the last part was nonnegotiable.

"Tell her it's not happening," Liam said.

"I did, but—"

"Tell her again."

"Copy that. You want me and Chapman to sweep the exit route?"

"Soon," he said. "Wait until after he does the fishing bit."

"Roger."

A rumble of laughter from the crowd as Willet delivered a punch line.

Liam scanned the faces. Look, assess, progress.

Look, assess, progress. He couldn't get distracted, not even by Tara Rushing and the pistol on her hip.

But he *was* distracted. That was the problem. Like that first day back at the ranch, it took no time at all for her to get under his skin. There was something about her, maybe her go-to-hell attitude or her sexy mouth. Since the moment he'd seen her, he hadn't been able to stop thinking about her. Even now, while he was working, he was all too aware of her shadow in the back of the room.

Liam gritted his teeth. His job required total concentration, and Tara was screwing with him.

Focus.

He went through the faces again, every last one. He looked at posture, hands, eyes, searching for tells. The odds were stacked against him. He couldn't move faster than a bullet, so it was all about seeing and reacting before the bullet ever left the gun.

Liam noticed the woman making a beeline across the ballroom.

"Yo, incoming," Lopez said over the radio.

"I got her."

Willet's campaign manager halted in front of him. "*Who* authorized this change of plan?"

"What change is that?" Liam scanned the tables again.

"The limo's supposed to pick him up in front. We've got the CBS affiliate here."

Laughter boomed as Willet delivered his best fishing joke. Liam nodded at Lopez. Time to sweep the exit route.

"Did you hear what I said? CBS is here!"

"That doesn't concern me."

"Well, it concerns *me*. They want film for ten o'clock."

The Fidgeter was at it again. Liam watched him. He couldn't decide whether he was jonesing for a cigarette or waiting for a phone call.

Thunderous applause as Willet stepped back from the podium. The candidate smiled and gave his double thumbs-up.

"Exit clear," Lopez said over the radio.

"Roger that."

"Uh, *hello*? Are we having a conversation here?"

He looked down at her. "You're distracting my team, Greta. Don't do it again."

Her cheeks flushed. "Do I need to remind you who signs your paychecks? I freaking hired you people!"

The audience got to their feet, still clapping, as Willet waved and walked offstage. Liam moved for the exit, watching faces and hands. He glanced at the shadowy corner of the ballroom.

Tara was gone.

M.J. FOUND HIM at the general store. That's what it was called—just GENERAL STORE painted on a wooden sign mounted above the door. Hand-painted words in the window gave slightly more information: BEER BAIT AMMO.

Jeremy stood in the ammo aisle, and M.J. circled around to approach him from behind. Just for fun, she tried to be stealthy about it, but he turned to face her as if he'd seen her coming.

"Hi." She smiled up at him, determined not to

be intimidated by his stony expression. Or the fact
that he towered over her by at least a foot. "We meet
again."

He nodded.

"Smells good. Is that fried chicken?" She cast a
glance over her shoulder at the deli counter where
people were lined up for takeout. "Wow—bait,
ammo, chicken, and hushpuppies. Is there anything
you can't get here?"

"Cash."

She turned to look at him. "Excuse me?"

"Only ATM in town is at First and Main."

She tipped her head to the side and smiled. "Good
to know. Thanks."

He stared down at her without a word. Instead
of fatigues, today he wore an olive-drab T-shirt with
jeans, along with a leather bomber jacket that didn't
quite conceal his gun.

"So." She turned to face the shelf he'd been looking at. It was stocked with bullets and shotgun shells.
"What are you up to this nice Sunday evening?"

He reached for a bottle of CLP oil. "Not much.
You?"

"Oh, you know. Just getting some snacks for my
motel room. The diner's been flooded with press people."

He gazed down at her, and for the second time
since she'd met him, she noticed he had pretty eyes.
They were pale blue, almost gray, and if he bothered
to smile once in a while, he could actually be a chick
magnet.

She glanced down at the gun oil in his hand. "Need
some ammo with that?"

The corner of his mouth twitched as if she'd said something funny. "I'm good."

They walked toward the cash register, and M.J. grabbed a pack of Skittles. "So, you mentioned Liam's out of town. What's up at the ranch?"

"Not much."

"What, no keg parties while the boss is gone?"

He shot her a puzzled look, and she felt her cheeks warm. Yes, she was grasping at straws here, but this was like talking to a statue.

"Thought I'd hit the range," he said, finally throwing her a lifeline.

"You mean Liam's range? You guys practice at night?"

They reached the counter, and he gestured for her to go first. She watched him, waiting for an answer, as the cashier rang up her candy.

"Pistol range," he said. "It's indoors." He paid for his gun oil, and M.J. waited at his elbow, hoping he'd get a clue, but either he was oblivious or he didn't want company.

He held the door open, and they stepped into the cold night air.

"Sounds fun," she said. "Think I missed it on the tour."

He stopped and stared down at her, his brow furrowed slightly.

The silence stretched out, and she clenched her teeth to keep them from chattering.

"You want to see it?"

"Sure, I'd love to!" She beamed up at him. "I have to qualify soon, and I haven't been in a while. You mind?"

"No."

"Great, then. I'll follow you."

She jumped into her car and breathed a sigh of relief. "Jee-zus," she muttered, cranking up the heater and rubbing her hands together. She'd met some non-talkative men in her life, but this one was practically mute.

He drove a Ford F-250 in gunmetal gray, and she followed it back to Liam's ranch, scarfing handfuls of Skittles as she wondered how the hell she was going to get anything useful out of a guy who barely spoke.

On the other hand, just visiting the ranch again was useful. Even if Jeremy told her nothing of value, she'd get another chance to check out the living quarters of one of their prime suspects. And, as Tara had said, another chance to investigate Liam's connection to the victim.

She followed Jeremy through the gate and up the curving road through the pines. Instead of hooking a left toward the main house, he turned right and led her to a corrugated-metal building painted forest green.

M.J. parked her car and got out, glancing around. The building was tucked into some trees, and she hadn't even noticed it on the previous trip. Rock music emanated from inside, and a floodlight switched on as Jeremy stepped toward the door. M.J. glanced up.

"Motion sensitive," he said, pulling open the door.

The inside was loud and bright and smelled of sweat. In the room's center was a boxing ring, where two tattooed, shirtless men in sparring helmets were viciously going at it. They paused what they were doing to watch as M.J. followed Jeremy to a back room.

"Those guys live on the ranch?" she asked.

"Temporarily."

"How many are here right now?"

"Four."

"Where's everyone else?"

"We've got teams in Austin, Dallas, and Aspen."

He reached another door and tapped a number into a keypad, then ushered her into a room.

"Whoa," she said, stopping short. All four walls were lined with glass-fronted gun cabinets. "There must be, like, a *hundred* rifles in here." She walked over to the nearest cabinet to check out a heavy-duty rifle that looked like an A-15. The guns in the neighboring case she definitely recognized—all were MP5s like she'd trained with at Quantico. She did a slow 360-degree turn. "Damn, it's like an armory in here."

He cracked a smile. "It is an armory."

"And all this is for you guys?"

He shrugged. "There's a lot of us. We run training camps in the fall and spring. Usually fifty people at a time."

He was starting to loosen up. Maybe being surrounded by his favorite toys put him at ease.

M.J. glanced around. "What is that—knives, too?" She walked over to a table where tactical knives were lined up by size. She reached out and traced her finger over a long black handle.

"That's a Ka-Bar knife, standard Marine issue."

She heard the pride in his voice. "You know how to use it?"

"Sure."

She glanced around at the cabinets. "What's your favorite handgun?"

He looked at his feet for a moment and rubbed his jaw. Then he crossed the room to a small access-controlled cabinet and took out a pistol.

"An H and K MK23. It's a favorite in the spec ops community."

"Nice," she said, knowing it was an understatement. She wasn't really a gun person, but anyone could see it was a beautiful weapon.

"It's an ultra-rugged gun, takes a lot of wear and tear. And you can't beat it for accuracy."

He flipped it over in his hand and passed it to her, grip out. She hesitated.

"Go ahead."

She took the sleek black weapon. It was heavier than her Glock, but for a large pistol, it felt pretty compact.

She glanced up as he walked into yet another room. She followed. It was the practice range, and it consisted of six stations, each equipped with a storage shelf and ear protectors. Paper targets were clipped at the far wall, all human silhouettes.

She looked around, sponging up details to share with Tara. Tara *was* a gun person, and she'd love this room. Everything was state-of-the-art, even the earmuffs.

"Looks like Liam spares no expense," she said.

"Tools of the trade." He was standing in front of a shelving unit packed with boxes of ammunition. Probably a slight step up from what they carried at the general store.

"You ever bring clients out here?" she asked.

"Sometimes."

"Catie Reyes?"

He glanced up from the ammo. He knew she was here to pump him for information, and so far he'd been cool about it. Maybe he had nothing to hide. Or maybe he was just bored playing war games out here in the woods without any women around.

He walked over and plunked a box of ammo onto the shelf beside her. "She came out a few times."

"Was she any good?"

"At shooting? No."

She gazed up at him, waiting for more. What *was* Catalina Reyes good at? M.J. wanted details to add to what she already had on Catalina's background—which was a lot like her own.

Like M.J., she'd grown up in the Rio Grande Valley and worked to put herself through school—in Catalina's case, the University of Houston. Her first job had been in the HR department of an oil company, where she'd worked her way to management. Eventually, she'd left to start a staffing company that provided temp workers to businesses around Houston.

As for personal details about the victim, M.J. didn't know many, although her home revealed a few. Catalina had lived in a perfectly landscaped two-story house painted neutral beige with taupe shutters.

M.J. liked neutral. She understood it. Neutral was classy, an informed choice. Neutral signaled to Catalina's neighbors that she'd cut her ties to the Valley, leaving behind pink adobe and yard art. It showed them that they could rest easy, because she wasn't really Mexican but one of them.

But there was a lot more to Catalina Reyes than what she showed the public. M.J. was sure Jeremy knew plenty about the woman's private life, and she was determined to get him to talk.

But . . . given his aversion to conversation, it might take a while. She glanced down at the box of bullets.

"I don't recognize this brand," she said.

"They're a specialty shop. We're in their R and D program."

"Meaning what?"

"Meaning we test ammo for them. Give feedback."

M.J. ejected the magazine and loaded it as Jeremy watched her movements. Then she turned to face the target about thirty feet out. She glanced at the ear protectors and decided to skip it. She was finally getting him talking, and she didn't want to miss a word.

"You guys get paid for this service?" She glanced at him, and he was watching her now with his arms folded over his chest.

"It's more of a quid pro quo."

"You mean they provide equipment, and in exchange you help them fine-tune things?"

He nodded, obviously more interested in watching her shoot than talking about ammo suppliers. She spread her feet apart, lifted her arms, and took a deep breath. She waited, trying to get her focus. The din of rock music in the next room was the only sound.

She squeezed the trigger, and the force reverberated through her body. Relief washed over her, and she dropped her arms.

She glanced over, but he didn't say anything.

"Again?"

He nodded.

She settled into her stance and fired again. And again. The gun had a surprisingly smooth trigger pull. She went through the entire magazine. She managed to keep her expression blank the whole time, but inside she felt a surge of pride. She hadn't made a fool of herself.

She handed it over to him. He reloaded and stepped over to the neighboring station, where there was a fresh target.

She eased closer to watch. Wide shoulders, straight posture. He raised his arm and went perfectly still. Only his trigger finger moved as he fired the weapon.

She watched him, transfixed, as he fired shot after shot after shot. When the magazine was spent, she released the breath she'd been holding.

"Not bad," she said. Another understatement. She would have thought he'd brought her here to show off, but this had been her idea. She watched his totally relaxed expression as he pressed a button to bring in the target. He unclipped it from the wire. The ten bullet holes formed a tight grouping smaller than a quarter.

"Pretty good," she said. "Especially with your right hand."

He didn't say anything, but she thought she spotted the hint of a smile at the corner of his mouth.

"You *are* left-handed, right?"

"A lot of us are."

"Us?"

He tossed the target onto the shelf like it was nothing. If it had been hers, she would have pinned it up in her cubicle at work.

"The PSD teams," he said. "It's a tactical advantage."

She stared up at him blankly.

"I'll show you." He turned to face her and took a big step back. "Pull your Glock."

"What are you—"

"Pull it."

She reached into her jacket. In an instant, he was on her, his bulk surrounding her, his hand clamping around her arm like a vise. She blinked up at him, shocked by his speed.

"See?" He released her and stepped back. "Most people are right-handed. They attack from their dominant side, so in a face-to-face assault we have the advantage if we're dominant on the left."

"I never thought about it."

"We train for everything. But Liam's a numbers guy, so he has a hiring bias toward lefties. Anything for an edge."

"Over your competitors, you mean?"

"Over anybody," he said. "We're the best out there—and that's not bragging, it's a fact. We get a lot of applicants, so we can afford to be selective."

"Sounds like you do some of the selecting. Does that make you—what? Liam's XO?"

"More or less."

She glanced around the room at all the high-tech equipment, some that wasn't even on the market yet. She'd never seen a setup that compared, not even at Quantico. Her gaze landed on the USMC flag on the wall.

"Why'd you quit the Marines?" she asked on impulse.

She glanced over, and by his tight expression she could tell she'd offended him.

"I mean, you're obviously good at what you do," she said. "I would think they'd try to keep guys like you."

"I could see the drawdown coming."

"Everybody could."

He gazed down at her, probably thinking she was pushy. "I wanted to get ahead of it," he said. "Liam was staffing things up here, and he's the best CO I ever had, so."

She waited for more, but he didn't elaborate.

Still, he'd opened up some. Way more than she'd expected when she finagled the invitation. If she played her cards right, she might get him talking about Catalina again.

"You want to shoot some more?" he asked.

"Why, you want to change the subject?"

"Yeah."

She smiled and felt the tension relax. "Well, as long as we're here, I should practice with my Glock. It's not quite an MK23, but—"

"But it's your service weapon, and it could save your life someday." He nodded at her hip. "Take it out, let's see what you've got."

IT WAS A step up from Big Pines, but not the Ritz, thank God. Tara preferred a stocked vending machine to an overpriced minibar any day of the week. She grabbed some snacks and traipsed back to her room, checking out the vehicles in the parking lot, including a black Silverado similar to Liam's, only this one had one of those ridiculous lift kits that meant you practically needed a stepladder to get inside. Tara shook her head.

Cold air whipped around her shoulders, and she had a flashback of riding beside Liam in his toasty-warm, perfectly proportioned pickup.

She forced away the thought. Liam was officially a suspect until evidence proved otherwise. She had no business admiring his truck, his body, or anything else about him right now—or ever, if she knew what was good for her.

Her phone chimed as she stepped into her motel room.

"So guess what I found out," M.J. said.

"What?"

"He was in Aspen."

Tara dumped her snacks on the dresser. "Who was?"

"Liam Wolfe. He was in Aspen, Colorado, the night of the murder, meeting with a client at his ski condo. Jeremy mentioned something about it, and I double-checked with the airline. Liam's clear."

Tara stood in front of the mirror, noticing her appearance for the first time tonight. Wilted suit. Messy hair. Her blue eyes looked tired and annoyed at the same time.

Her heart was racing again, and again she blamed Liam.

"Tara, what's wrong? I thought you'd be relieved."

She was intensely relieved, damn it.

"What's wrong is I'm pissed," she said. "Why didn't he just tell us this, save everyone a lot of trouble?"

"I don't know."

Was he playing games with her? Was that what this was?

"Did you ask him?" M.J. wanted to know.

"Ask him what?"

"If he was out of town at the time of the murder."

"Why would I ask that?" Tara popped open her Coke and took a cold, syrupy sip.

"I don't know, I just thought you would. I mean, we shouldn't even bother with him if he has an alibi, right?"

Tara sank down on the bed and tried to get her thoughts straight. She was going on four nights with very little sleep. She was beyond stressed, and now she felt manipulated, too.

We shouldn't even bother . . .

"No, we should bother," she said. "This is a base we need to cover, or some defense attorney's going to make an issue of it later. Liam Wolfe is linked to the victim. He's linked to the abduction site. He owns the land where the body was dumped. And now we know he lied about talking to Catalina."

"But again, alibi. His is airtight."

The phone on the nightstand rang. Tara looked at it with suspicion. It rang again, and she put M.J. on hold as she picked up.

"Hello?"

"Meet me in the Mustang Lounge."

It was Liam.

"How did you—"

"Straight across from your hotel, ten minutes."

"You can't just—"

"Ten minutes, Tara."

He hung up.

CHAPTER NINE

He watched from the corner, waiting for her to see him. It didn't take long. She strode up to his table, a woman on a mission, and Liam's heart gave a kick.

"You know, you're starting to piss me off," she said.

"Starting to?"

She yanked out the chair across from him and dropped into it. She glanced at his glass, and Liam signaled the waitress.

"How's the inn?" he asked.

"How'd you know where I was staying?"

"Your office wouldn't go for five-star. Even for surveillance of a prime suspect."

The waitress stepped up to the table and smiled at Tara. "Something to drink?"

"Jack and Coke."

"Sure thing." She nodded at Liam's ice cubes. "Another for you?"

"Thanks."

When she disappeared, Tara folded her arms over

her chest, wrinkling the nice white blouse she wore under her suit.

"You're no longer a suspect," she told him.

"Then why are you here? Why are you guys tailing me and hounding my employees?" *And distracting the hell out of me.* He kept the last part to himself because he didn't want her to know the effect she had on him. It was a point of pride.

"We have unanswered questions," she said.

"Let's hear 'em."

She just looked at him.

"Bring it on, Tara. Let's hash this out, stop wasting everyone's time." He leaned back in his chair. "I'll answer any question you want, but I get to ask some, too."

She watched him suspiciously, probably sensing a trap. "Okay, me first," she said. "Why did you lie about when you last talked to Catalina?"

"I didn't."

"She called you three times on the day before her murder."

"You asked me when I last talked to her. I didn't talk to her. She left messages with my answering service."

She rolled her eyes. "You're being evasive."

"No, accurate. There's a difference."

The server delivered their drinks, and Tara scowled at Liam's glass. "What is that?" she asked.

"Seltzer water. I'm working."

She sipped her drink as the waitress swished off. "So what did her messages say?"

"Nothing, just her name." He leaned forward on his elbows. "And that's three questions. It's my turn."

"Fine, ask away. But I can't share details of an ongoing investigation."

"Why SWAT?"

She looked surprised by the question, then guarded. "What do you mean?" she asked.

"Why'd you sign up?"

"I don't know. Why not?"

"Now you're being evasive."

He watched her, and he could tell he'd made her uncomfortable by asking something personal, but he had to know.

She looked down at her drink, stirring it. "I got into law enforcement to enforce the law." She glanced up at him. "I promised myself I'd stay as far away from admin work as I could get."

"You don't want to be pigeonholed because you're a woman."

She just looked at him, not saying anything.

It was a shrewd career strategy, assuming she liked the work. Liam had seen plenty of women in the military get pushed into support roles. SWAT was about as far away from a desk job as it was possible to get, although working for a bureaucracy like the FBI would still mean plenty of paperwork.

"My turn," she said. "Why'd you quit the Marines?"

The word *quit* rankled, but he let it go. "I've never been good with authority. Didn't want to take orders my whole life." He didn't mention the shooting that had nearly ended it. It wasn't something he talked about.

"But you take orders from your clients," she pointed out.

"That's different."

"How?"

"They pay well. And I can refuse the job if I want."

She tipped her head to the side. "What would make you refuse?"

"You're getting a lot more questions than I am here."

She waited.

"My clients and I have an understanding. I have a certain way of doing things, and it works, but some people don't like it."

She watched him but didn't comment.

"What?" he asked.

"I thought you were going to say politics."

"Nope. I'm apolitical. Red, blue, purple—I don't give a shit what you are. If your money's green, I take it."

She lifted an eyebrow. "Anything for a buck, huh?"

"Just about."

He could tell she didn't buy that. "Okay, why is your cell-phone number impossible to find?"

He smiled slightly. "It's not."

She arched her eyebrows, which told him she'd tried and failed.

"Cell phones are tracking devices," he said. "They can carry viruses, spyware, remotely activated cameras or listening devices. If people can track me, they can track the clients I'm guarding. So I switch my phone all the time, stay a step ahead of the game. My clients reach me through my answering service. Only a handful of people have my cell number."

And at the moment, that handful included her. He had no doubt she'd gotten the number from the front desk of her hotel as soon as he'd ended their call.

She sighed.

"What?"

"Sounds paranoid," she said bluntly.

"Maybe to you. But some of the people I work with are victims of relentless stalkers. They come to me because I don't tell them they're paranoid. Instead I listen."

She watched him a moment. "And how long have you been doing this? Personal security?"

"This is our third year."

"Do you like it?"

"Beats government work."

She held his gaze, obviously trying to read more into that. Her eyes were sharp now, and he felt another question coming, something she'd been burning to ask him. "I want your opinion on something." She leaned forward and looked him in the eye. "What do *you* think happened? Based on your experience?"

Liam got that familiar twist in his gut. "You mean Catie?"

"Yes, Catie. Why do you think she's dead?"

TARA COULD SEE she'd struck a nerve. She'd meant to.

He leaned back in his chair, watching her with that same cool and assessing gaze he'd had earlier, when he'd been in bodyguard mode.

"You want my professional opinion," he stated.

"No."

His eyebrows tipped up.

"I want your take as a professional *and* someone

who knew her personally. You're in a unique position to help the investigation, as you obviously know."

If he picked up on the underlying guilt trip, he didn't show it. "Okay," he said. "Here's my take. I've been doing this a long time, even before I went out on my own."

"You were a bodyguard in the Marines?"

"Personal security detail—protecting high-ranking officers, visiting diplomats, people like that. In some places it's a cakewalk, but not in Afghanistan. Basically, I trained in a powder keg."

She nodded.

"I've studied political killings and failed attempts, both here and overseas. I've seen a few up close. And that's not what this is."

"How can you tell?"

He turned his glass on the table. "Most times it's fast and impersonal."

"Didn't seem that way when ISIS beheaded those journalists."

"Right, but this is domestic. It's different. Overseas you see a lot of bombs. And then you sometimes get hostage situations that end with murder. Stateside we're usually looking at a lone gunman. Sometimes a sniper but maybe something close-up and execution-style." He shook his head. "If Catie had pulled into work and been shot, I could see it being political. That's not what happened." He met her gaze. "I think whoever killed her, it was personal."

Tara had been thinking along the same lines. If the killer had just wanted Catie dead, there was no need to move her body, let alone butcher her the way he had.

"Back to the phone calls," she said, because she couldn't let it go. "Three calls to you right before her murder. Do you think she may have sensed some new threat and that's why she reached out?"

The muscles in his jaw twitched, and she knew she'd nailed it. She should have felt a little buzz from the victory, but instead she felt guilty. He obviously cared about this woman, and Tara was pouring salt on a wound.

"You're probably right about that." He looked down at his drink. "I don't know why else she would call me."

"Unless she wasn't calling you in particular."

"What do you mean?"

"She called the landline. Wolfe Security. Maybe she was looking for someone who works there?"

She waited for his reaction, but his face showed nothing.

"How many people were on her security detail?" she asked.

"Now my guys are under suspicion?"

"I didn't say that. But maybe they know something. Maybe one of them knew her personally."

"You mean sexually."

"She'd been having marital problems . . ." Tara let the idea trail off to see where he'd take it.

There was a glint in his eyes now. "My guys couldn't do this."

"Why not?"

"Because. Look at the crime. It's goddamn sadistic."

"You never know what people can do."

"I know my people," he said firmly. "Some better than I know my own brother. They've been through background checks, psych evals. Every man working for me, I'd step in front of a bullet for him." He meant it for real, she could tell.

"The people who work for you—do you know which ones smoke?" she asked.

"None of them."

"*None*? How do you know?"

"Piss tests."

She blinked. "You actually—"

"Absolutely I do."

"Why?"

"Because it's important." He paused. "You really want to hear this?"

"If it's relevant to the case."

He leaned forward on his elbows, and she felt the full power of his gaze. The intensity of it put a flutter in her stomach. "When we're working a job, the most important thing—the life-and-death thing—is focus. We have to be *in* the moment, every moment." Those green eyes held hers, and she couldn't look away. "Most attacks will happen in under five seconds, start to finish. We have to see it coming, interrupt it, and get the protectee out of harm's way. The way we do that is focus. All the time. That means no distractions. I can't have someone watching a rope line or a doorway or a rooftop, but they're not really watching it because they're thinking about their next cigarette or anything else. No cravings."

"What about food or sex or coffee? You're saying they don't crave that?"

"We minimize it."

"So you just expect your guys to be superhuman."

"In some ways, yes." He leaned back in the chair

now. "And since you asked about it, I don't have sex with clients. That would be the mother of all distractions. If someone working for me does it, he's gone."

She didn't hide her skepticism.

"You don't believe me?"

"I believe you to a point," she said. "Maybe you can control *you*, but you can't control other people. A lot of people can't even control themselves."

The corner of his mouth curved up. "Honey, you're a cynic."

"I'm a realist."

He watched her eyes, and she felt a warm tingle. His attention dropped to her mouth, and again she wondered what kissing him would be like. She'd been wondering since she first met him, first *saw* him. His intensity appealed to her. Hell, everything about him appealed to her. Except that even with an alibi, he was on the wrong side of this investigation. One of his guys might have committed the murder.

"You know, you never answered my question the other night," she said. "What were you doing skulking around in the forest?"

"Setting up surveillance cams."

Her eyebrows tipped up with surprise. "In the woods? Why?"

"They're my woods. I told you before, I own the land."

"I know, but—"

"Perpetrators sometimes return to the scene of the crime."

"Are you saying you're investigating this case?"

He didn't answer.

"Liam, you are *not* an investigator."

"If I find something important, you'll be the first to know."

"And who are you to decide that? You shouldn't be collecting evidence of any kind. You could destroy chain of custody or create holes in the case that a defense attorney will exploit at trial."

His expression darkened, and he leaned closer. "Let me explain something, Tara. Catalina was my client and my friend. Someone hunted her down like an animal and slaughtered her, and probably got off on it, too." He paused, holding her gaze. "I intend to find the man who did that. And I don't want him tried—I want him dead."

The words chilled her. If she'd ever wondered what sort of Marine he was, now she knew. He was hard, merciless.

Lethal.

And she didn't want to be hearing any of this. He should know better than to say it to someone with a badge, but he didn't seem to care. Did he think she'd cover for him if it came to that? Having seen the victim, Tara understood his desire to get revenge. But her job wasn't about revenge. She'd taken an oath to uphold the law.

She looked away and tried to think of a new topic. "So, I understand you have a lot of job applicants. I'm guessing that includes a lot of Marines?"

"We get people from everywhere."

"Okay, but a lot of military?"

"Yeah."

"Why is that, exactly?"

"Supply and demand." He took a sip of water, and she waited for him to explain.

"Thousands of guys are coming out of the service right now with very specialized skills," he said. "Police, fire, paramedics—a lot of those training programs are full up, including mine. I get a hundred applicants for every one I hire."

"And you run criminal background checks on all your people?"

"Every last one."

She'd bet that wasn't the only sort of check he ran. He probably went deep, and why shouldn't he? His business was all about hiring the right people. And it sounded like he could afford to be picky.

"I told you," he said now. "It's not one of my men."

"I didn't say it was."

He looked at her, and for a while they were locked in a staring contest. Tara felt a surge of annoyance, with herself and with him. She shouldn't be here like this. They had competing agendas. And just being in his presence made her lose focus on hers.

He watched her, and it was as if he could look right into her mind and see all those conflicting emotions. How did he do that? How did he make her feel as though he knew her innermost thoughts, including the ones she shouldn't have?

She took a last sip of her drink and forced herself to slide back her chair. "I should go."

He nodded.

But she didn't move. She just looked at him, and with every passing second his gaze grew hotter. She needed to leave before she did something stupid.

She reached for her purse, but he caught her hand. "I got this."

She watched him, feeling the weight of his fingers

through her sleeve, and she didn't know what "this" was. Not really an interview. Definitely not a date or even a pickup.

She stood. He stood, too, pulling out his wallet. He left money for the drinks, along with a big tip, and then he rested his hand at the small of her back as they walked to the door. Tara's nerves flitted. A moment later, they were out on the sidewalk.

Traffic whisked past. A cold wind whipped her hair around her face, and she brushed it away.

"Well, good night." She glanced up and felt her stomach drop as she read his look.

He leaned down and kissed her.

Her mind emptied as he pulled her into him. The firmness of his lips and the hardness of his body made her too shocked to move. His hands slid around her waist and splayed across her back, and then she *was* moving, sliding her fingers around his neck and letting herself be lifted right up onto her toes. She was letting him in, tasting him, feeling his tongue and his hands and the wall of his chest pressed against her. He tasted so good, and he felt solid and *male*.

She had a fleeting image of her hotel room across the street but pushed away the thought. And then he changed the angle of the kiss, and she couldn't think at all as his tongue tangled with hers and the kiss went on and on. She liked the way he kissed—strong and confident and unyielding. Not taking no for an answer. She didn't want to tell him no. She could feel his desire for her, and anything he could dream up she wanted to say yes to. The world seemed to fall away, and she was holding on to him, struggling for balance as lust spread through her. She made a small, needy sound in her throat, and he pulled her in tighter.

She leaned away, flushing. His eyes were dark and simmering, and she knew what he was going to say. *Come back to my room.*

She stepped away. "I have to go."

He watched her intently. But he didn't argue, and she felt a tug of disappointment.

Traffic hummed around them, and a chill swept over her skin as she glanced around. She brushed her hair from her eyes and tried to make her voice sound normal. "So . . . you're going back to Dunn's Landing tomorrow?"

He nodded.

"I'll probably see you around town, then," she said.

"Count on it."

CHAPTER TEN

Tara stacked by the door, staring at Brannon's back, the M-4 cradled in her hands. Her heart pounded and her throat felt dry as she waited.

"Alpha, you're a go." The commander's voice came over the radio, followed by a deafening boom as the battering ram hit wood.

Then they were pouring in, storming the apartment in a thunder of boots and flash-bangs. People screaming, running, diving to the floor. The room smelled of pot and fear. She sidestepped the chaos and scanned for her objective, quickly finding it beyond the tangle of obscenity-spewing bodies being cuffed on the ground.

"North hallway," she told Brannon, making a dash for it. One door left, two right. And a lone gray door at the end that pulled her like a magnet.

"Dead bolts." She tossed a look over her shoulder.

"Want me to—"

"I got it," she said, blasting it with a kick. The door bowed but didn't break.

"Here, lemme—"

"No!" She backed up and flew at it again, stomping so hard the force rocketed up her leg as the door burst open and smacked against the wall—boom!

Tara rushed inside, Brannon behind her.

The room was dark, and the stench hit—sweat and urine and other foul odors. The floor was a sea of cushions and sleeping pallets.

"Rushing!" Brannon darted across the room and through a door that stood ajar. "Check this out."

Tara was still scanning the blankets for any sign of life, but the room was empty, and her stomach knotted with fear as she followed Brannon through the doorway.

She knew the room from the videos—every detail, down to the wrought-iron bed and faded black comforter. The bed was empty now, the entire room empty. Her gaze went to the scarred wooden dresser where a frozen yogurt cup had once been.

Now it was gone.

A glint on the floor caught her eye, something peeking from under the bed. She dropped to her knees and pulled out a sequined pink flip-flop, a child's.

"Son of a fucking bitch."

"Hey!" Brannon's gaze snapped to hers. "You hear that?"

She listened. Turned. Behind a floor-to-ceiling curtain over what she'd assumed was a window, there was actually a door.

"Cover me," Brannon said, pushing it open.

Thin white legs. Bare feet. A mop of brown hair. It was a girl, maybe four, huddled beneath the sink. Tara rushed over, making soft shushing noises she didn't recognize—a nonverbal soothing that seemed to spring from inside her.

"Chhh, chhh, chhh . . . it's all right." She slung her gun to her back and crouched beside the girl. Brannon switched on the light, and Tara saw the glimmer of metal dangling from the pipe beneath the sink. The handcuff was attached to a tiny wrist, rubbed raw.

"Find a key," she ordered, and Brannon disappeared, leaving her alone with the child.

Matted hair, dirty cheeks. Her wide, dark eyes made Tara's heart pinch.

"Chhh, chhh, chhh . . . it's okay now." Tara reached for the girl, but she cowered back. *"It's okay. You're safe. We're going to get you out now, okay?"*

More squirming and pulling. In her flak jacket and helmet, she must look terrifying. Tara pulled off her helmet and prayed the social worker would get her ass over here. Then she grabbed a towel off a hook on the wall and wrapped it around the quivering shoulders.

Tara glanced back at the empty bedroom. She'd memorized every detail down to the stains in the Sheetrock.

She looked at the cowering child. *"The others,"* she said softly. *"Do you know where they are?"*

"He said don't talk."

"It's okay now. You can talk to me. Do you know where the others went?"

She nodded slowly, and Tara's stomach filled with dread.

"Where are they? You can tell me. Where are all the girls?"

Tara jerked upright, heart pounding. She stared into the darkness. She glanced around at the clock, the TV, the stripe of gray seeping through the curtains.

Another hotel room, this one in Austin. She brushed her hair from her face. Her T-shirt was soaked with sweat. She peeled the sheets away and walked into the bathroom, still disoriented as she groped around for a light switch. She blinked at her reflection in the mirror.

Damn.

Her skin was pale, her eyes bloodshot. The fluorescent light didn't do her any favors. Ditto the lack of sleep and the endless workdays strung together, week after week, until it was all a blur.

The most important thing—the life-and-death thing—is focus.

Liam's words echoed through her head like an indictment. When was the last time she'd focused on anything?

She stared at the mirror, straining to think objectively.

Before the raid.

That had to be it. Days before the raid, her focus had been razor-sharp. It was that utter focus that had allowed her to spot the yogurt cup in the back of a sex video. A small paper cup that she'd traced to a yogurt shop had broken the case wide open.

But that was days ago, almost a week. And now she was running on fumes.

She thought of Liam's eyes last night, so dark and observant.

Why SWAT?

She'd told him but only part of it.

Yes, she'd joined because she was determined to avoid being pigeonholed. Law enforcement was a boys' club, and in that sense the Bureau was no different from thousands of station houses across the country. Change was coming but at a glacial pace. People had to retire and die, taking their crusty attitudes with them to the grave.

She hadn't told him the full story, the emotional part. She hadn't told him the team was her lifeline. She needed it. Beyond the harsh and sometimes brutal camaraderie, she needed the raw, physical release. She needed to storm through those doors and stare into those faces and slap bracelets on those people who'd *hurt* people. It was her outlet, her antidote for the feelings of impotence that could swallow her, for that creeping sense of being invisible to all but the most calculating eyes. It was her way of slapping back.

Usually. But last week's raid had slapped back at her.

She had no one to blame but herself. She should have seen it coming.

Tara glared at her reflection. *Get over it.*

She had a job to do, and it deserved her full attention. In that, at least, she knew Liam was right.

She reached into the shower and set the water to scalding. She stripped out of her tank and panties and stepped into the hot spray just as her phone chimed from across the room. Cursing, she snagged a towel and rushed to catch the call—M.J.

"It's six thirty-two," Tara snapped.

"Are you in Austin?"

"Yes."

"Where's Liam?"

"At the moment, no idea," she said. "But he was here last night. Why?"

"We need you back here ASAP, Tara."

"Don't tell me—"

"We've got another one."

• • •

THE FOREST WAS damp and cold, and Tara's breath frosted in front of her as she slid from the car. She scanned the crime scene, marked off with yellow tape. She saw sheriff's deputies but no sheriff, and Kelsey Quinn's fiery hair stood out against the dull gray tree trunks.

The forensic anthropologist knelt on the forest floor, scraping at something with a small tool. The area around her was surrounded by metal stakes and cordoned off with blue twine.

Kelsey glanced up and climbed to her feet. "You made it," she said, dusting her gloved hands on her jeans. Her knees were black with dirt. "Agent Martinez must have called you."

"She did," Tara said. "Is she around?"

"I think she's with the sheriff."

"I'm surprised he notified you."

"He didn't. The coroner called," Kelsey said. "Cypress County's second skeleton in six months. I definitely think he's feeling in over his head. Anyway, I'm glad he notified me this time. I like to see the remains in place."

Tara looked down at the excavation site, which had been neatly subdivided into a grid of one-by-one-foot squares. Gray sticklike objects protruded from the soil. They didn't even look like bones, really.

"Who reported this?" Tara asked.

"Anonymous."

Tara raised her eyebrows.

"If I had to guess, I'd say hunters."

"Why's that?"

Kelsey tucked a tool into her pocket. "Deer season ended a week ago. Could be they were torn between civic duty and wanting to avoid being hit with a fine by the game warden." She tugged her gloves off. "Let me show you what we have."

She walked away from the grid to a separate area on the other side of the clearing.

"This is private property?" Tara asked, looking around uneasily. They were only a few miles from Liam's ranch.

"Belongs to a timber company out of Louisiana, I'm told. Here, have a look." Kelsey gestured to a smaller site designated with orange twine. Leaves had been cleared, and Tara noted the scoop-shaped depression in the soil.

"A skull?" Tara asked.

"That's right."

Tara glanced over her shoulder. "Is it unusual to find it so . . . apart from everything else?"

"That happens a lot," Kelsey said, "mostly due to scavengers, particularly when remains are buried in a shallow grave or not buried at all. And to make matters worse, we had a flood here not long ago, as I told you back at the lab. So anything could have scattered the bones—scavengers, people, Mother Nature."

"Where is it now?"

"The skull? I've got it boxed already. Don't worry—it's been tagged and photographed. We're extremely thorough, I can assure you."

"Any obvious cause of death?"

"No bullet holes, slugs, or lead wipe."

"Lead wipe?"

"Metallic deposits left in bone when a bullet penetrates. Of course, I'm just getting started, so there's still time." Kelsey rubbed her forehead with the back of her sleeve. Despite the cold, she looked flushed. Hunching over a grave site was obviously hard work.

"And gender?" Tara asked.

"Undetermined. Although based on a ring discovered with the hand bones, I'd guess female. I'll have the Big Four by tomorrow, along with postmortem interval and possibly cause of death." Kelsey met Tara's gaze. "If it turns out this is related to Catalina Reyes and our Jane Doe, then that's three victims."

Tara understood the implication. That many connected murders indicated a serial killer.

Kelsey peered around Tara and muttered a curse. Tara turned to see Jason crouched inside the blue grid.

"Deputy, I need your boots *out* of the excavation site," Kelsey commanded. "Nobody's allowed in there besides me and my staff."

Jason stood up, scowling. He took his time glancing around and then wandered back to the CSI van, where law-enforcement types were milling around.

"Unbelievable." Kelsey shook her head.

"How long do you think the recovery will take?"

She glanced at her watch. "Hard to say. The canine unit's still finishing up. Assuming we don't find any secondary sites, I'd say five or six hours?"

Tara was shocked. "Even with our evidence response team? They should be here any minute."

"I know, but it's slow going. An excavation like this requires small wooden instruments and animal-hair brushes to avoid marking up the bones. That takes time. And every scoop of dirt has to be sifted for evidence. A wad of chewing gum or a fingernail or a scrap of duct tape could contain vital DNA evidence." She nodded at the tent, where several workers in Delphi Center jackets knelt beside a sifter. "We have to go through everything, a thimble at a time."

"What can I do to help?"

"You've called your ERT people, so that helps a lot. I assume they're trained in body recovery?"

"They are."

"Hey!" Kelsey strode past Tara. "Did you just *spit* near the grave site?" She stalked right up to Jason, who was hovering over the sifters now.

"Huh?"

"Step away from my sifters, sir. That's a restricted area."

His cheeks reddened. "I'm deputy sheriff in this county."

"I don't care who you are. If you contaminate my crime scene again, I'll have you permanently removed."

Jason stormed off just as Tara heard a whistle from the woods. She turned to see a stocky young man walking over with a German shepherd.

"Something you need to see, Doc." He glanced at Tara, and she introduced herself.

Kelsey walked over. "Peaches alert on something?"

"About a quarter mile in," he said. "Follow me."

He led them back across the clearing and into the woods. A layer of pine needles covered the loamy soil, making it impossible to see footprints. The deeper into the woods, the darker and danker the surrounding air. The dog handler held a branch back so it wouldn't snap Tara in the face.

"Watch your step here," he said. "It gets steep."

Peaches led the expedition, confidently picking her way down an incline into a hollow littered with fallen trees and branches. She stopped beside a rotten log and thumped her tail on the ground.

"Down here," the handler said, peeling away a tangle of vines with his gloved hands.

Kelsey crouched beside him and took a look, then rubbed the dog's head. "She's good, isn't she?"

"The best."

Tara looked over Kelsey's shoulder to see a slender gray bone peeking out from the leaves. "Is it human?"

"Looks like it to me. I'd say a radius." Kelsey looked at Tara. "An arm bone. I'll examine the osteon pattern back at the lab to confirm." She dug a magnifying glass from her pocket and studied the specimen. "Slight scratches. They look postmortem, so my guess is they were caused by scavengers, possibly a raccoon or a coyote. I need to photograph it like this before we do anything."

They stood up, and the solemn look on Kelsey's face gave Tara a sinking feeling.

"Looks like we're dealing with a serial killer," Kelsey said.

"But how do you know scavengers didn't drag this over from the other grave site?"

"Because"—Kelsey nodded at the clearing—"that victim's arms are intact. This bone belongs to someone else."

• • •

TARA RETURNED TO her room at Big Pines practically drunk with exhaustion. Her shoulders ached. Her knees burned. Even her arm hurt as she reached to switch on the lamp.

She dumped everything onto the bed—phone, food, jacket, plus the map she'd picked up at the convenience store. Feeling faint from hunger, she sank onto the mattress and tore into her Snickers bar but quickly discovered she barely had the energy to chew.

She was wasted, both physically and mentally. And she knew sleep would be fitful tonight. Again.

Last night she'd drifted off thinking of Liam. She'd thought about his mouth and his taste and the warm slide of his hands. The buzz of it all had given her a few solid hours. But sometime around sunrise the raid had come back, just in time to wring her out emotionally before the start of the day.

The dreams would be different tonight. After spending hours hunched over the sifting screen, she knew tonight's visions would be about scoops of earth and musty smells and pitiful shards of human bone.

The familiar anger was back again, filling up her chest. She thought of those women murdered and dumped in the woods. What had their final moments been like? Had they run or fought or begged for their lives?

Tara believed so. It was something she knew.

She closed her eyes as the anger expanded, making her chest tighten and her hands clench into fists.

Honey, one day you're gonna snap in two, her grand-mother used to say, and some days Tara felt like she would, like she could physically shatter from the emotions she kept locked inside.

She hated the powerlessness. The feeling of weakness always lurking beneath the surface, making her confidence seem phony, making her feel like a fraud. Other people in her profession went about the whir of life so nonchalantly, and their ease had always felt alien to her. It made her feel estranged from everyone else. How could people see what they saw—especially social workers and beat cops who saw everything— and not be consumed with anger all the time? How did they do it?

Tara took a deep breath. She tried to manage the stress, and mostly she did okay. She was no shrink, but she had a minor in psychology and she wasn't an idiot. She knew she needed outlets in order to keep on an even keel, which was important for SWAT. Double standards abounded in law enforcement, and whereas a man in her office could lose his temper and everyone would shrug it off, if a woman did, she was labeled a bitch. Or worse, a head case.

Typically, she blew off steam by jogging or working out or doing some target practice. Nothing released tension better than burning a few mags on the pistol range. The force recoiling through her arms was a sort of release, and at the end of a session she'd feel okay. Sparring worked, too, going a few rounds with one of her SWAT teammates, landing a few solid kicks. And there was always sex.

Well, not always. And certainly not lately, which was part of the problem. She hadn't had time for shooting or sparring or anything she did to relieve tension, and it was building inside of her as the marathon work weeks continued.

Tara twisted the top off her drink and looked at her phone on the bed. Maybe she should call Liam to get her mind off everything. Was he back in town yet, or had he stayed an extra night in Austin with the blonde?

Ashley Somers. Tara had looked up the address. Liam was a player, apparently. He'd told her he didn't sleep with clients, but ex-clients seemed to be fair game.

So had he slept with Catalina Reyes? If he had, did it matter? What mattered most to Tara was that she still didn't believe she'd gotten a straight answer about his relationship to a murder victim.

Tara felt the sugar kicking in, and her energy perked up. She took a long, fizzy swig of Coke, then turned her attention to the map, unfolding it on the bed. An idea had been forming during her drive home, like vapor gathering into a cloud.

Two bodies, both deposited on private land owned by a Louisiana timber company and leased to hunters. Land where Kelsey Quinn suspected poachers had stumbled upon a human skull and then phoned in an anonymous tip.

After examining the map for a few minutes, Tara called M.J.

"Where are you?" Tara asked, glancing at the clock. It was after ten.

"Still at the sheriff's office in Cypress."

"Anything there?"

M.J. sighed. "Not a lot. We've got the security tapes

from the timber company, but they only keep two weeks' worth of history."

Tara had figured that might be an issue when she saw the low-budget surveillance camera mounted on the trailer that the timber company used as an office.

"Anyway, traffic is light there these days, according to the property manager," M.J. reported. "That tract's fifteen hundred acres, but they did a big timber cut last year, so right now that land's just sitting and all their equipment's tied up in the neighboring county. According to the timber company, the only people in and out have been some foresters inspecting the trees."

"Plus the hunters," Tara added.

"Yeah, I asked about that," M.J. said. "They tell me the people with deer leases come and go through the north access road. They've got a code for the gate there."

"We need a list of those lease holders."

"I know, Tara. Ingram's working on it."

"Sorry." She pinched the bridge of her nose. "I'm just tired."

"That's because you sifted dirt all day. Get some rest, okay? I'll finish here and we'll catch up in the morning."

Tara hung up and studied the map again, paying special attention to the layout of the roads and forests and access routes. She thought of the fire chief down in Silver Springs. Timber was a big business, and local fire departments were in charge of protecting it. Tara examined the roads and rivers in relation to where the victims' bodies had been found. Four victims discovered in three short months. Tara gazed at the map as her idea crystallized.

"Screw it," she said, pitching her candy bar into the trash and grabbing her keys. She wouldn't sleep well anyway.

SHE TOOK THE highway leading east from town and then retraced her path through the twisty back roads. Towering pines rose on either side. The road leading to the timber company's land was narrow and poorly marked, and Tara almost missed the weathered wooden sign: CORRINE TIMBER, RIGHT 2 MILES.

Tara turned and followed the unfamiliar route along the north edge of the property. She drove and drove through the woods, checking the map in her lap frequently. She'd almost given up finding it when she dipped over a low-water crossing with a rain gauge tacked to a post. She veered left, and a turnoff came into view. She hooked a right and saw the sign for the firebreak. *Score.*

She tossed the map aside and pulled onto a wide shoulder, careful to avoid any fallen logs. She got out, leaving her headlights on to guide her.

For a moment she stood beside her door and simply looked around, taking in the scene. It was eerily quiet. No din of emergency vehicles and first responders. Not so much as a barn owl to break the silence, only a faint rustle of branches as wind whispered through the forest.

Tara took out her flashlight and swept it around. She was surrounded by trees, completely hemmed in except for the narrow road behind her and the wide swath of emptiness directly behind the gate. The firebreak. A sign hooked to the barrier said, CYPRESS COUNTY FIRE DISTRICT NO TRESPASSING.

The air was misty, and the light of her head-lights shimmered off tiny droplets of moisture as she approached the gate. She aimed her flashlight at the sturdy metal arm stretching across the gap in the fencing. A rusty brown chain dragged on the ground.

No lock.

Tara's breath caught.

The gate was closed but not secured. Someone had removed the padlock, just as she'd suspected. The fire chief had found a discarded padlock at the crime scene in Silver Springs. What about this crime scene?

She glanced around, pulse thrumming. She wished she'd thought to ask Alex Sears precisely where he'd found the padlock.

Tara neared the gate, moving her flashlight over the area. If she'd parked her car at a different angle, she'd be able to see better, but she was too excited now to go back and move it. She eased inside the gate and aimed her beam at the ground, illuminating pine nee-dles and other natural debris but no discarded padlock possibly bearing a killer's fingerprints or DNA. If she recovered the lock, at the very least they might be able to match the tool marks. And matching tool marks could link this crime scene to the one down in Silver Springs. It was a long shot, but she had to look.

Tara moved farther into the forest and combed her light over the ground. Tonight she was on the lookout for snakes and spiders and animal traps ready to bite, but she saw only dirt and leaves.

"Come on," she muttered. She was onto something. She could feel it. For a moment she turned off her flashlight and simply stood there listening. The darkness seemed alive now, a breathing creature. Tara's pulse sped up.

Focus. Think like the killer.

She closed her eyes for a few moments. Then she walked back to the gate and eased through the opening, careful not to touch the metal. She stood beside the chain and imagined cutting the padlock with a heavy pair of bolt cutters. She imagined removing the lock from the chain as a victim lay dead or dying in a nearby vehicle. She tried to imagine what he'd be thinking and feeling as, moment by moment, his carefully crafted fantasy became real.

He'd be amped up, sexually aroused. He'd be nervous, too, maybe even nervous enough to do something stupid, like nick his hand on something sharp or forget to wear gloves. He'd get the lock off, then glance anxiously over his shoulder. Then he'd either pocket the ruined padlock or fling it away so he could undo the chain . . .

Roughly eighty percent of people were right-handed, including Tara. She scanned the ground until she spotted a rock. She picked it up and made what felt like a natural throw into a clump of bushes. The rock *thumped* against the ground, and she followed it into the brush with her flashlight.

No padlock nearby.

She glanced around, poking through the foliage. She pushed through branches, snagging her weatherproof jacket on thorns as she moved around, searching for metal. She dropped into a crouch, sweeping her flashlight around and peering under fallen logs. Months had elapsed since the victims had been brought here. Even if the lock had been left behind, it could be hiding beneath leaves or even inches of dirt. It could have been swept away in a downpour or cautiously removed by the killer himself.

Tara stood, frustrated. She walked to the clearing, where a good fifty feet of forest had been removed to create a challenge for all but the most determined forest fires.

She moved her light along the ground again. She walked to the other side of the firebreak, where the land dropped down into a ravine and the pines gave way to a thicket of oaks, sycamores, and scrub brush.

At the base of a tree, a glint of silver.

She rushed over. She crouched down and gently picked a leaf away to reveal a rust-spotted padlock. Shiny new gouges marked the place where a heavy-duty tool had chomped through metal.

"No way," she murmured, hardly believing it.

But then her disbelief was crowded out by the joy of being right about something, of following a wild hunch that panned out.

Practically skipping with excitement, she rushed back to the Explorer and grabbed some items from her evidence kit. As she returned to the site, she pulled out her phone. For a second she hesitated.

Maybe she should wait for a CSI. But what if something happened in the meantime? What if between now and tomorrow morning the lock got moved somehow, either by a person or a force of nature, like the cigarette butt she'd seen in the crime-scene video?

She couldn't risk it.

She went to work documenting the scene with her

phone's camera, taking pictures of the lock and the tree from every angle. Then she crouched down and brushed all the leaves away and used a twig to dislodge the mangled lock from the soil.

Carefully, she deposited the lock in a paper evidence bag and stood up. She tucked the bag into her pocket and looked around. Now she needed photos of the chain on the gate. Should she remove that now, too, or come back tomorrow? Her field kit didn't include a bag large enough to hold it, and anyway, it was heavy. She could come back with a cardboard box and a better camera to document the entire scene.

Crack.

She dropped to the ground, hitting her chin with a tooth-rattling *smack*. Her ears rang as her brain identified the sound:

Gun.

CHAPTER ELEVEN

Tara sprawled there, stunned, her mouth filling with blood as the word reverberated. *Gun gun gun.* She felt the hot sting of adrenaline in her veins. She lifted her head slightly.

Crack.

Dirt stung her eyes. She launched herself toward tree cover, and branches lashed her cheeks as she fought through the foliage. She flattened herself on the ground, pulse pounding.

Someone was shooting at her.

At her. What the hell?

She swatted at the branches but only managed to get more tangled, snagging her hair on thorns. She wrestled herself free from the bush and commando-crawled along the ground on her elbows, desperate to stay low. *What the hell what the hell what the hell?* She groped in the dark and encountered what seemed to be a sturdy tree trunk. She pulled herself behind it and felt a flicker of relief—and then the world fell

out from under her as she pitched headfirst into nothing, which quickly became something as she smashed
against a rock. She bumped over it, flailing her arms
as she careened down a slope, banging knees and
hips and elbows before hitting something solid and
immovable.

The impact had knocked the wind out of her, and
for a moment she was on a playground, blinking up at
the bright blue sky after falling off the monkey bars.
But there was no blue now, only an inky void. A feeling of unreality washed over her as she stared at the
blackness, and for a brief, disconnected moment she
thought she'd imagined the gunshots. But her ears
were still ringing from the noise.

She lay there, gasping. She felt like she'd been
body-slammed against a brick wall. Slowly, she
reached her hand up to touch it. The rough texture of
the bark under her fingertips told her a large tree had
broken her fall.

She kept still, clenching her teeth against the pain
as she forced herself to breathe in. And out. And in.
And out. Warm, coppery blood filled her mouth.
She'd bitten her tongue. Her head swam, and she registered a sharp pain in her elbow, along with a thick
throbbing in her skull.

Something trickled down her cheek. She touched
it gingerly, and her fingers came away wet. She didn't
think a bullet had grazed her, but something had,
maybe bark from the tree she'd been standing near
when the shot landed.

Just inches from her head.

Fear spurted through her now, and she commanded herself to *think*. Someone was shooting at her.

And it wasn't an accident, some stray shot by a confused hunter. It was the middle of the night, for one thing. And no hunter would confuse a wild animal with a human holding a flashlight and standing near a vehicle.

She rolled onto her side. Her breath came fast now as she realized her situation. She unzipped her jacket and took out her Glock. Gripping it made her feel better, reassured. She checked the magazine. The familiar motion steadied her, and her brain clicked into gear.

Two shots so far and possibly more coming as the shooter closed in. She tried to place the shot, tried to remember how far away it had sounded. A hundred yards possibly, but it was hard to know when she felt so disoriented.

She lifted her head. At the top of the ravine she saw the glow of her headlights. Her car was up there, keys in the ignition. She had to get to it. She couldn't stay here in the dark with some gunman stalking her. She'd lost her flashlight, and she didn't know the terrain.

Carefully, she sat up, bracing herself against the earthen slope by pushing against a tree with her foot. She did a quick inventory. Her flashlight was gone. Same for her phone. It had been in her hand when the shots rang out, and she must have dropped it on the way down. The phone case was deep blue, so she didn't have a chance of finding it in the dark.

She rolled to her knees and ignored the pain radiating up her legs as she flattened herself against the steep incline. Clutching her gun in her right hand, she used her left to grab hold of limbs and saplings and thorny branches, anything to help pull her up.

Her knees and feet dug into the mud as she clawed her way up the hillside, closer and closer to the light. She missed a foothold and slid down, down, down, bumping her chin on something sharp. Frustration burned in her chest. She squeezed her eyes shut against the pain. Digging her toes into the mud again and grabbing for a branch, she took a deep breath and inched her way toward the light.

Don't lose it.

She wasn't sure whether she meant her gun or her sanity, but the words fueled her efforts as she dragged herself up the incline one lurch at a time. Finally, she reached the top and pulled herself over the ridge, where she collapsed against the ground, chest heaving.

A distant rustle in the woods. She scampered behind a tree, glancing around frantically as she searched for threats. She couldn't look at the headlights, as much as her gaze was drawn to them. The glare ruined her night vision, so she focused on the shadows, clutching her weapon and envisioning her car parked at an angle on the other side of the gate. Forty feet away, maybe fifty. She could make a run for it, but she'd be out in the open where some sick bastard with a night scope might see her.

Because that's what she was up against. She knew it in her gut. And although she was trained in all types of firearms and defensive tactics, at this moment she had no body armor and only a short-range weapon that didn't do much good when her visibility was crap.

Cold air bit through her jacket, and she realized she was soaked with sweat despite the temperature. Her pulse raced. She tried to picture the layout. When she'd arrived here, she'd pulled off to the right, close to the tree line. She could use the trees for cover.

A snap of twigs spurred Tara into action, and she sprinted for her vehicle, staying low, keeping her head down. She crashed into the gate and frantically scrambled over it, landing on her knees on the other side. She lunged for the Explorer, jerked open the passenger door, and dived inside, yanking the door shut and then crawling behind the wheel. Sliding low in the seat, she stashed her gun in the cup holder and fired up the engine.

The ear-piercing screech rattled her.

It was running already. She threw it in reverse and rocketed backward, praying she wouldn't smash into a tree as she executed a lightning-fast three-point turn. She thrust it into drive and hazarded a peek over the steering wheel before stomping on the gas. No people or cars or other predators in the road, and if there had been, she would have mowed them down. She gripped the wheel, shoulders hunched, expecting an explosion of glass any second as she raced down the road, skidding through the turns.

Almost there, almost there. She glanced at the odometer. Another turn. Tires skidded, the car fishtailed. *Almost there.*

She reached the highway and punched the gas.

LIAM STOPPED BY the bunkhouse on his way in and found several of his men in the rec room watching Ultimate Fighting. Kyle Chapman was standing in front of the TV lifting barbells, and Tony Lopez was at the table cleaning his Beretta.

Lopez glanced up. "Hey, Chief." His smile faded as he took in Liam's suit. "How'd the funeral go?"

"It sucked."

"You just get back?" Chapman asked.

"Yeah. Where's Jeremy?"

"No idea."

"In town," Lopez said. "Think he went to shoot pool."

Liam left them to their entertainment and walked to his house, shrugging out of his suit jacket as he trudged up the stairs. His upper arm hurt like a bitch, which meant the weather was changing. It was his little souvenir from his last tour. After the attack on the Virginia congressman, Liam had lost full use of his rotator cuff but gained the ability to predict the weather.

Inside his house, Liam flipped the lights on and tossed his coat over a chair. He needed a shower and some comfortable clothes, but first he needed food. He yanked open the fridge and grabbed a beer as a shrill beep came from the control room. He plunked the bottle on the counter, took his phone out, and pulled up the app to see who the hell was at his gate this late at night.

It was a blue Ford Explorer with Tara Rushing at the wheel.

CHAPTER TWELVE

He heard her clomping around on the porch and met her out there, frowning down at her as she bent over to untie her boots. The legs of her jeans were coated with mud, and leaves clung to her hair.

"What happened to you?"

She glanced up. Dirt and blood streaked her cheeks, and Liam's heart lurched.

"Hey." He reached for her arm and realized she was shaking. "What the hell happened?"

Instead of answering, she slumped against him.

He stood there, shocked, and her shoulders quivered as he wrapped his arms around her. "Talk to me." But she didn't, and with every passing second his dread increased. "Hey, it's okay."

But it definitely wasn't okay. Someone had hurt her, and anger took hold of him as he waited for her to speak.

Abruptly, she pulled away. She yanked off her boots and tossed them by the door.

"Can I use your sink?" She stepped past him into the house. "Back here?"

He followed her to the hall bathroom and flipped on the light.

"Who's here tonight?" she demanded.

"Me." He took her arm. "What's going on, Tara?"

She shook off his grip, and the wild look in her eyes made his gut clench.

"Who else?" she asked.

"Chapman and Lopez are in the bunkhouse." He stepped closer. "Tara—"

"Someone shot at me."

He stared at her. "Someone shot *at* you or—"

"*At* me. Yes. As in they nearly took my head off, twice."

"Where?"

"Up at Corrine Timber, just a few miles from here." She looked out at the hallway. "Are you sure you're alone?"

He tipped up her chin to examine her cut.

"I bit my tongue." She pulled away.

"Your neck's bleeding, too. Jesus, what happened to your hands?"

He turned the faucet on and pulled her hands under the water. After holding them under the stream for a few seconds, he crouched down and rummaged through the cabinet for some first-aid stuff. All he found was a roll of toilet paper.

"Don't move," he ordered, and went into the bedroom.

He had to get his temper under control. She was rattled, and yelling at her wasn't going to help. When he came back with the first-aid supplies, her jacket was on the floor of the hallway and she was standing at the sink with her sleeves pushed up.

"Tell me step by step," he said. "Don't leave anything out."

He dumped the supplies onto the counter and turned her palms up to look at them. They were shredded, but the bleeding had stopped. Seeing the tremor in her slender hands made him want to punch something, but instead he waited for her to speak.

She took a deep breath. "You heard about the bodies today."

She stated it as a fact, not a question. She'd finally resigned herself to the idea that he was getting intel somewhere.

"Corrine Timber," he said, grabbing some ointment. "Scene was cleared two hours ago."

He dabbed her palms dry with some tissue, then gently applied the ointment. She didn't look at him, just stared at her hands as she struggled to get the story out.

"I was up there combing for evidence, and I found a broken padlock near the gate to the firebreak. Then someone took a shot at me."

"Twice, you said."

She glanced up at him. Her eyes were calmer now, but still she looked hyped up on adrenaline. And fear. "That's right, two times."

"Pistol shot or rifle?"

"Rifle. Definitely."

Liam swallowed down his anger. She pulled her hands away, then leaned close to the mirror to examine the side of her neck. She grabbed some toilet paper and dabbed the blood away while Liam watched, trying to control his reaction.

"You're sure it was a rifle?" he asked.

She glared at him in the mirror.

"Did you call the sheriff?"

"Are you kidding? What the hell would he do?"

Good point. Ingram was already neck-deep in murder investigations he couldn't handle.

She reached for the box of bandages. "Could I have a minute?"

She looked up, and something twisted in his gut. God damn it, when was she going to trust him?

"Please?"

He stepped out. She closed the door behind him, and he stood in his hallway, gritting his teeth. The water went on in the bathroom again. He returned to the kitchen and took a bag of peas from the freezer. He glanced at the bathroom and tossed the ice pack onto the coffee table. He paced the living room for a minute, then built a fire in the fireplace. When he had it going, the water was still running. He walked down the hall and picked up her jacket with the yellow letters FBI stamped on the back. The windbreaker was damp and muddy. The fabric under the sleeve was ripped.

He shoved open the door, and she jumped. "He fucking *hit* you?"

"What? No."

"Your goddamn jacket has a bullet hole." He pulled up her T-shirt to see for himself as she swatted his hands away.

"Hey!"

"You're covered in bruises, Tara." He ignored her protests and yanked her shirt up to see her abdomen. The entire right side of her torso was a big red welt.

"It didn't break the skin." She pulled away from him and tugged her shirt down. "Now, do you mind?"

"Yes, I fucking do mind. Where else?" He turned her around and lifted the shirt to look at her back. The skin there was smooth and pale. "What about your legs?"

"I'm okay. Could you please just give me a minute?"

He left her alone then and sat on the edge of his couch, fuming and staring at the fire. Finally, she came out. She'd cleaned the dirt and blood off her face. She picked up her jacket to examine the tear, then folded it neatly and placed it on the arm of the sofa.

He handed her the ice pack.

"Thanks." She pressed it to her temple, where she already had a bump forming.

She glanced around, as though she still didn't believe that he was alone, and then sank onto the edge of a leather chair.

"I was at the firebreak on the north edge of the Corrine Timber property."

Liam got up and walked down the hall to the control room. Tara followed him.

"Holy crap, what's all this?" She stood in the middle of the room, gaping at all the computer monitors as he sat down at his system and tapped a few keys.

A few moments later, he had a satellite map of Cypress County pulled up.

"This is where you monitor your security?" She was still gawking at all the screens.

"Yes. You were here?" He pointed to the firebreak along the north edge of the Corrine Timber tract.

She leaned over his shoulder and tapped the screen. "Here."

Liam studied the image. He zoomed out to look at a larger area.

"It sounded like, I don't know, a hundred yards away? It was hard to tell, though," she said. "Could have been more."

He clenched his teeth, thinking of the tear in her jacket that had been made by a bullet. An inch closer and she'd be dead.

"Luck could account for the first shot," he said. "Maybe he aimed for your flashlight. Two close calls, I'd say he had a night scope."

"I know."

She stared at him, her gaze somber. She'd calmed down some, but she still looked shaken.

She'd come *here*, to him. Probably not because she wanted to talk about bullet trajectories.

He stood up and took her hand and led her back to the living room. He sat her down on the sofa beside the fire and went into the kitchen. A few moments later, he joined her on the couch with a bottle of bourbon and two glasses of ice.

She immediately picked up the bottle and poured two generous servings. She downed a sip and winced.

"Thought you liked bourbon."

"I do," she croaked. "I don't usually drink it straight."

He watched her over the rim of his glass, and her

second sip went down more easily. Then she turned to look at him, and she seemed to be actually seeing him for the first time.

"Where have *you* been?" she asked.

"Funeral."

By her startled expression, he could tell she'd forgotten. Catalina's service had been that morning in Corpus Christi, where her family lived.

Tara sipped again, and he noticed her hands still trembled. He took her glass and set it on the table, then slid an arm around her. She tensed.

"I'll get your good clothes dirty."

"I don't give a shit. Come here." He tucked her head against his chest and pulled her in tight to stop the tremors. She felt both cold and warm at the same time—a weird combination that pissed him off. She was in shock, and he forced himself to lock down his anger.

What had happened tonight? He couldn't tell if she was giving him the full story. And why had she been out there by herself? He'd warned her about poking around alone in the woods, but she hadn't listened because she was so damn headstrong.

Frustration churned inside him. Frustration with her and with himself. She'd been only a few miles away, and he'd done nothing to protect her.

The shakes subsided, but still she was a ball of tension, and he could tell she didn't like being held. Or maybe she didn't want to like it.

She pulled away. "So, this new crime scene," she said matter-of-factly. "We recovered two bodies."

"I thought it was bones."

"Skeletonized remains. The forensic anthropologist should have an estimate of the time of death by tomorrow. But we're looking at four victims, and certain factors point to a similar MO."

"Such as?"

She paused.

"Such as what, Tara? Spit it out."

"I can't discuss the details. But basically, all four victims were discovered within a few miles of here. One you knew personally."

Liam bristled. "Are you telling me I'm a suspect?"

SHE COULD SEE the anger simmering in his eyes. And it wasn't just about her anymore.

"You have an alibi for the night of Catalina's death," she stated.

"Then what are you telling me?"

"I'm telling you, look at these murders. Look at where they happened and the fact that you knew one of the victims intimately."

She watched his reaction to the *intimately* part. She was still certain there was more to his relationship with Catalina, and his defensiveness reinforced her theory.

"You're no longer a suspect," she said, "but you have to admit there's a common thread here."

His gaze narrowed, and she could see he'd figured out where she was going with this topic.

"You said every man working for you has been through a psych evaluation," Tara said. "I'd like to see them."

"Not happening."

"They're relevant to our investigation."

He leaned closer. "I'll say it again. No."

She stood up. "Why are you putting up road-blocks? Someone *murdered* a friend of yours. Along with three other unidentified women, just a stone's throw away from where you live. Doesn't that bother you?"

He stood, too. "Bothers me a lot, but it wasn't one of my men."

"How can you be sure? Those psych evals could shed light—"

"Forget it."

"I could get a warrant."

"I doubt it."

She folded her arms over her chest and glared up at him. How could he be so hardheaded? How could he really know what the men working for him were capable of? Many were ex-military. They'd been trained in lethal tactics. What if one of them had a screw loose and was now back home unleashing his rage? And here was Liam, stubbornly guarding his privacy.

Tara shook her head and picked up her jacket.

He clamped his hand over her wrist. "Where are you going?"

"Back to my motel."

"You're not going anywhere."

"Like hell." She jerked her arm away. "You can't tell me what to do."

He stared down at her, jaw twitching.

He seemed to be battling with himself, and she

knew she was the reason. Her showing up here had activated his protective streak, but then she'd promptly pissed him off.

"I'll go with you," he said calmly, with obvious effort.

"I don't need—"

"Don't argue with me, *God damn it*! Someone almost *killed* you tonight!"

The blast of anger made her step back.

"Shit." He closed his eyes and rubbed his forehead. "Sorry."

"I need to go." She moved for the door, and he caught her arm again.

"Wait. Would you please just let me drive you home?"

SHE LET HIM follow her.

He trained his gaze on the bumper of the old Ford, going over everything in his head and cursing himself for acting like an idiot.

She'd shown up at his house shaken and bleeding, and he'd fucking yelled at her. Granted, she'd picked a fight with him, but that was just a knee-jerk reaction to what had happened. She was like him. When attacked, she went on the offensive.

He thought of the look in her eyes when she'd come to his door. It was a combination of fear and outrage and, worst of all, helplessness. He'd seen the same look in the eyes of men in combat after their outpost had been shelled by some invisible enemy hiding in the mountains. Liam had been through way more of those firefights than he wanted to remember, fights that had taken the lives of some of his friends. So he understood the fear and the fury and the need to lash out.

The neon sign for Big Pines came into view. She turned into the lot, and Liam followed. He pulled into the space beside her and buzzed down the passenger window.

"Stay here a minute," he said.

He got out and did a scan of the area. It was after midnight, and the parking lot was cold and silent. Full, though. The murder of a well-known politician had brought the media out, and several reporters were in it for the long haul, from the looks of it.

Liam scanned the highway and the woods beyond. He surveyed the Waffle Stop across the street, searching for anything unusual, but the restaurant was closed up for the night.

Tara sat in her Explorer looking impatient.

"Okay, let's go." He slipped out his Sig and followed closely as she walked to her door. He held out his hand for the key card, and she passed it to him with an eye roll. He entered the room, then ushered her inside. "Wait here," he ordered.

She stood by the door as he did a quick sweep of the place, checking closets and curtains. The room didn't have a balcony, which was good, but he didn't like the crappy window locks. He checked the bathroom. Her toiletries were scattered across the counter. A pair of running shoes sat beside the shower, and a white sports bra dangled from the towel rack. Liam checked behind the shower curtain and examined the rusty lock on the little window. He wasn't happy with it, but the window itself was too small for anyone to squeeze through.

Basically, the place was a dump.

"We good now?" she called from the bedroom.

"More or less." He joined her beside the door. "Your room's not great. Far as safety, I'd give it a four."

She lifted an eyebrow. "This one comes equipped with an armed federal agent. Any bonus points for that?"

"Maybe." He stepped closer. She was still a mess, but her eyes had calmed down. "Depends if you know how to shoot."

"I kick ass."

He didn't doubt it.

Liam eased closer. "I can stay."

She gazed up at him with those pretty blue eyes, and he felt a sharp pang because he already knew the answer. "I'm good."

"You sure?"

She nodded.

He pulled her against him. She stiffened at first, but then her arms went around his waist.

"Thanks," she said.

"For what?"

"Earlier."

She smelled like his soap now, and he wished like hell she'd change her mind. And he cursed himself because if he hadn't been such a hothead earlier, they'd still be at his house right now, maybe even in his bed, where she'd be safe and warm and he could do what he'd wanted to do for days now, which was fuck her blind. But instead he'd blown it.

She pulled out of his arms and reached to open the door. Message received.

"Call me if anything happens," he said.

She opened it wider.

"I mean it, Tara."

"I know."

CHAPTER THIRTEEN

The Waffle Stop was packed with locals and reporters, and Tara had to wedge herself into a space at the counter.

"The usual?" Crystal asked, plunking a mug in front of her.

"Sounds good."

The waitress filled her cup, then tugged a check from her apron and slid it in front of the trucker beside Tara.

Tara sipped the coffee, which was hot and strong and exactly what she needed on a bitter January morning following a restless night. As the caffeine seeped into her bloodstream, she felt her senses perk up.

With all the press in town, the servers behind the counter were a whir of motion, spinning from customer to customer and clipping orders to a wire beside the kitchen window. Tara watched the cook there—Donald Price, a.k.a. Donny—who made a mean cowboy omelet and also happened to be on Ingram's short list of suspects. He stood at the griddle now, and Tara observed him through a veil of steam. He loaded a plate with eggs and frizzled ham, then slid it through the window and slapped the bell.

"Order up!"

Tara noticed the prison tats on his knuckles as he wielded his metal spatula. His face looked sullen, and she wondered whether that was his usual expression or if he was pissed off for some reason, such as being dragged into a murder investigation by Sheriff Redneck.

"What happened to you?" M.J. walked up to her seat.

"Hey, how's it going?"

"You look like you've been in a cat fight," M.J. said. The trucker squeeze past her, and she took the vacated stool. "You want to tell me what happened?"

"It's a long story," Tara said, and then proceeded to tell it, keeping her voice low. She told her all about the padlock she'd discovered, and M.J.'s eyes bugged out when she got to the gunshot part.

"Oh my God, Tara!"

Tara rushed through the rest of it, barely touching on the part about going to Liam's house.

"Well, that explains that," M.J. said.

"Explains what?"

She tore open a packet of sugar and dumped it into her coffee. "When I went jogging this morning, there was a grumpy-looking Marine staked out in our parking lot."

Tara blinked at her. "He stationed a guy there?"

"*He* was there. Liam." M.J. sipped her coffee,

watching Tara over the rim. "I figured, I don't know, maybe you two had a lovers' quarrel."

Tara scowled. "Yeah, right."

"Well, what was I supposed to think?"

The older waitress, Jeannie, stopped by with a plate of food, and Tara shook her head as she cut into a sausage link.

"What?" M.J. asked.

She shook her head again.

"Really, what are you mad about? Sounds like he's concerned about you. So what?"

"It's insulting. I'm an FBI agent, for Christ's sake. I don't need a babysitter."

"He's a bodyguard, Tara. That's what they do."

"Security consultant."

"Whatever. Anyway, I'd think you'd be glad to have him watching your back considering someone took a *shot* at you. Don't you think we should get a team up there or something? See if we can recover a bullet?"

"I'm going after breakfast." At her look of disapproval, Tara redirected the conversation. "And then I'm going to the Delphi Center, if you want to come."

"Can't do it today," M.J. said. "I'm meeting with Ingram at nine."

"He's running late."

They turned to see Liam standing behind them. He looked showered and clean-shaven, not at all like a man who'd spent the night in his pickup.

M.J. smiled brightly. "Good morning, Liam."

"Morning." He reached between them and placed a cell phone on the counter.

Tara's pulse skipped. "Where'd you find it?" she asked, snatching it up.

"In the ravine."

The screen was cracked and the blue outer case was missing, but the phone came to life when Tara pressed the button. Thank God for small favors. She'd expected to spend half the day getting the damn thing replaced.

Liam set his own phone on the counter and tapped open a photo.

Tara looked at him. "Is that what I think it is?"

"Picture of the slugs from last night. One was embedded in a tree trunk, the other was in the fence post."

She touched the screen to enlarge the photo of the tree trunk. "How'd you find everything so fast?"

"Ingram met me out there with a metal detector," he said. "He dislodged these from the wood and had them sent to the crime lab. Although chances are you won't get much in the way of rifling marks. The slugs looked pretty mangled."

Tara glanced up at him. His expression was calm and completely unapologetic.

Perfect. Now a private citizen, one who'd recently been a *suspect*, no less, was helping collect evidence in her investigation. And he'd involved the sheriff, which meant Ingram knew all about last night's incident. Tara felt both embarrassed and undermined.

Not to mention pissed.

M.J. seemed to read her mood. She slid off her stool and smiled at Liam. "Sorry to run, but I've got to swing back by the motel." She looked at Tara. "Give me a call after Delphi."

Liam claimed the empty seat. He rested his elbow on the counter and faced Tara. "What's at Delphi?" He reached for her coffee mug and took a sip.

"A tool-marks expert. They're finished with the bone analysis."

Liam gave her a questioning look.

"They were examining the marks on the bones recovered in November and comparing them with the ones on Catalina."

At the name, he looked away, and Tara felt a twinge of regret. She probably sounded callous to someone who'd just been to the woman's funeral.

"I've been thinking," he said, skimming his gaze over the restaurant patrons. He had a habit of constantly assessing his surroundings, and he never seemed to give it a rest.

"About what?" She reclaimed her coffee.

"What are the chances you could get a transfer off this case?" His gaze met hers.

"I'd say zero."

"Doesn't your boss like you?"

"He likes me fine, which is why I don't plan to ask him."

"I think you could use a change of scenery," he said evenly.

"You're kidding, right?"

"No."

"I think *you* could use a reality check." She leaned closer. "I'm not your client, Liam. I don't need a bodyguard, and I *don't* take orders from you."

"Not orders, advice."

"That either."

Liam watched her pick at her breakfast, his expression carefully blank. But she could read it anyway, because she was learning his moods. Right now was suppressed annoyance. He couldn't tell her what to do, and it was getting under his skin.

Tara checked her watch. "I should go," she told him, sliding off her stool.

She paid her check. Liam silently followed her through the breakfast crowd, and together they stepped out onto the sidewalk.

The morning was bright and cold. She turned to face him, and in the glare of the sunlight she could see signs of fatigue around his eyes. She felt guilty for a moment but then squashed the thought. It was his own damn fault if he was tired. He was the one who'd chosen to spend the night freezing his ass off in a parking lot for no reason.

"What time's your meeting at the crime lab?" he asked.

"One o'clock. Why?"

He checked his watch. "Plenty of time."

"Time for what?"

"We need to go for a drive."

CHAPTER FOURTEEN

He exited the highway, and he could tell by the look on her face that she already knew where they were going. He drove over a bridge and turned at the sign for Silver Springs Park. Instead of pulling into the parking lot beside the trailhead, Liam kept going.

"You've been here before," he said.

"We were down the other day for a meeting with SSPD." She glanced at him. "You know Chief Becker?"

"I worked with him some on the threats to Catalina."

"Before the FBI got involved," Tara said.

"They were never really involved much."

She tensed beside him. "Not until she died, you mean."

He didn't say anything. It wasn't a matter of blame but simply a fact. Threats against elected officials were a dime a dozen. The Bureau couldn't investigate everything. And Catalina hadn't even been elected yet. She was only a candidate, not even a particularly viable one given her controversial stance on immigration and the demographics of her district. Her opponent had won by a wide margin.

Liam swung onto a dirt road and pulled up beside a metal gate. He got out. Tara did, too. She glanced around, and he saw her home in on the shiny new chain and padlock.

She glanced at him across the hood as he slammed the door. "This must be where Alex Sears recovered the lock," she said.

"Right over behind that rotten log." Liam nodded at it.

"So you know him, too?"

"Just casually."

Tara tromped over to the new chain and examined the gate. It was a low metal arm, not much of a deterrent for people or wildlife, but it kept vehicles off the road reserved for firefighters.

"Come on." Liam stepped over the gate, and Tara followed him.

They settled into a brisk pace. Their breath turned to frost, and Tara rubbed her hands together. She was in a new FBI windbreaker, he'd noticed. Maybe she'd borrowed it from M.J., who seemed to prefer business suits. Tara was more at ease in tactical pants and assault boots, which he found pretty damn hot.

Liam walked beside her, and she matched her stride to his. "This forest was logged back in the twenties," he said. "All the marketable trees were removed. Any leftover vegetation was burned and then the land was replanted to pine. The owner left everything alone for a while, and about ten years ago the state bought up the land, made it into a park. Fourteen hundred acres."

They continued through the woods as Tara glanced around. "You seem to know the history of this place," she said. "Why?"

"I run a business near here. Only makes sense to recon the area."

They trekked for a few more minutes along the road, and then he veered onto a narrow path. Tara looked at him. "This is how he came?" she asked.

"Close as I can tell."

They walked without talking as the woods grew denser and darker. He glanced at Tara. She looked tired. With her wild curls scraped back in a ponytail, her cheekbones stood out even more than usual. She didn't wear much makeup, but he noticed the faint smudge of something she'd used to cover the bruise on her jaw.

He thought of her reaction to his suggestion that she request a transfer off the case. She'd gotten her back up over it, as he'd expected. She was stubborn, and she didn't like people telling her what to do. Actually, they were a lot alike—which was something that both intrigued him and drove him crazy.

They walked into a clearing, and she halted. "Whoa."

She stepped over to an area of lichen-covered stones set in neat rows. It was a man-made arrangement, but nature had reclaimed it over the years. She walked to a brick archway shrouded in vines.

She looked at him. "What is all this?"

"Used to be a sawmill here."

She glanced around at the shell of a concrete building that was being swallowed up by nature. Liam looked around at the woods. It was a quiet spot, a place where it was hard not to think about nature and the life cycle and the relentless passage of time, all topics that had been on his mind since he'd come home from Afghanistan.

Tara walked over to a fallen log. Sunlight filtered through the canopy, casting thick white beams between the trees. She tipped her head back to look at the sky, and Liam's heart gave a hard thump.

"It's beautiful." She looked at him. Her gaze held his for a moment, and then she crossed the clearing to a cluster of trees. She picked a leaf off and smelled it.

"This is sassafras," she said. "Those down there are tupelos. I love how they turn fiery in the fall."

He walked over. "You know your way around trees. You do a lot of camping growing up?"

"Ha. That would be no." She rolled her eyes. "My mom's not exactly the outdoors type."

"What about your dad?"

"No idea. He left when I was two." She stepped over an old log and looked around. A breeze kicked up, and she tugged a pair of red woolen gloves from her pocket.

Liam propped his boot on the log. "What type is she?"

She looked at him.

"Your mom?"

She turned around and pretended to be interested in the trees again.

Investigative procedures and forensics she could talk about all day long, but she resisted anything personal, which made him want to push.

"She's smart," Tara said in a reluctant tone.

"But?"

"Book smart." She turned around. "She teaches English lit at the college in Nacogdoches. Her big hobby is community theater. She directs plays."

"Not exactly following in her footsteps, are you?"

"Not exactly." She looked away. "She was horrified when I told her I wanted to be a cop. Said it was 'pure insanity.' I would've gotten a better reaction if I'd said I wanted to join the circus."

Liam smiled.

"I take after my granddad." She looked back at him over her shoulder. "We're cut from the same cloth, you could say. He and my grandmother live in Lufkin, not too far from here. They have a little wooden house with a screened-in porch and a vegetable garden. Pretty simple life."

"Simple is good."

"He was the one who first taught me to shoot back when I was ten. He never understood my mom's thing for books and theater. Said she grew up with her head in the clouds." Tara turned around to face him. "Why am I telling you all this?"

"I don't know." He stepped closer.

"Why'd you bring me out here?"

"You needed to see it."

"Why'd you bring Catalina?"

He tensed at the question. She stared up at him with that clear, unflinching gaze, and he could tell she sensed there was more to this particular client relationship than he'd told her.

"Catie was a troubled soul," he said.

"How troubled?"

"She was dealing with a lot of pressures—the campaign, the death threats. A husband who was screwing around on her."

Tara looked surprised. By the fact that David Reyes was screwing around on his wife? Or the fact that Liam had revealed something highly private about a client? It was a breach of his ethics, which he didn't take lightly. But the circumstances were unusual, and he wanted Catie's killer identified, whatever it took.

"Not that Catie was any saint," Liam said. "They had a lot of problems."

"Was she an alcoholic?"

"Where'd you get that?" Liam couldn't picture David volunteering that info to investigators.

"The ME's report notes extensive cirrhosis of her liver."

"She had a drinking problem, yeah. Last time I talked to her she told me she'd quit."

"This was your conversation back in November?"

"She'd started a twelve-step program. It seemed to be going okay. She'd had a few setbacks, but she was getting through it." He looked across the clearing. "At least that's what she told me. She was also doing yoga, jogging. Basically trying to clean herself up."

"Why'd she tell you all that?" There was an edge in her tone again.

"I think . . ." He stepped closer. "I think she wanted me to be proud of her, if that makes any sense. I worked for her for six months. I'd seen her in some bad moments."

Tara tipped her head to the side. "Maybe she wanted you to respect her."

"Maybe." He paused, gazing down into Tara's blue

eyes that looked way too tired. "You know, threat assessment can be an ugly process. You turn someone's life inside out, put every aspect under a microscope. Then you work closely together trying to address the threat. Catie was starting from ground zero, security-wise. I overhauled her house, her office, implemented basic security procedures. I taught her defensive tactics."

"And all this is while her husband's running around on her?"

He gritted his teeth and looked away. "The guy's an asshole."

"I know. We interviewed him."

He looked at her.

"Were you in love with her?"

He wasn't surprised by the question, not from Tara, who didn't shy away from anything. But he was surprised at himself for not answering right away.

"I admired the hell out of her," he said. "She came from nothing, pulled herself up. Made a business and a life for herself." He glanced around the woods. He'd walked with Catie in this very place, a fact that clawed at him day and night. "She wasn't afraid to speak her mind. Didn't back down from anything. She was a scrapper."

"She fought, you know."

He looked at her.

"She had a broken hand, broken wrist."

Liam clenched his teeth.

"Sorry." She turned away. "I just thought you'd want to know."

"I do."

They started walking again and reached the hiking trail. After a few minutes they neared the wooden mile marker that was investigators' best guess of the abduction site based on the droplets of blood that had been found there by a canine unit. They stopped at the marker, and Tara glanced around. Her gaze settled on him, and for a moment they stood staring at each other, Tara trying not to shiver and clutching her elbows with those fuzzy red gloves that made her look like a kid.

"Thanks for telling me about Catie," she said.

"You're up to your neck in this thing. You need to know who she was."

CHAPTER FIFTEEN

They were silent on the drive back, and Tara stared out the window at the forest. Did she have it all now, the entire story? Or was he still leaving something out? She might never know, but at least she knew more about it than she had when she'd rolled out of bed this morning.

She looked at Liam. He seemed pensive now, and she was surprised he'd shared so much about Catalina. She could tell it went against his instinct to guard his clients—not only their lives but their privacy. It seemed fundamental to who he was, a protector. He hadn't even been Catalina's bodyguard anymore, and still his failure to keep her safe from harm seemed to haunt him.

Tara watched him. He'd trusted her with sensitive information. He'd trusted *her*, and she felt the weight of it.

"So, what was her thing?" Tara asked. "Come home

from the office to find her husband's 'working late' again and then get blitzed?"

He slid a look at her.

"I'm not judging. It's just something I'd like to know."

"That was it, basically," he said. "She couldn't exactly go bar-hopping." Because she was a public figure, he meant. She had to keep up appearances.

"You know, if she was having an affair, I need to know his name."

Liam looked like he'd been expecting the question. "Jeff Timmons," he said.

"Her business partner."

"Silent partner. He was an investor only. Catie ran everything."

"So, if they had a relationship, I assume you checked him out. What do you think of him?"

"Not much."

"But you don't think he's a suspect?"

"You should look into it." He glanced at her. "I'm sure you will. But in my opinion it's a dead end. They broke things off before the election, and anyway he doesn't fit the profile."

"Why not?"

"He's late fifties, out of shape. From a physical standpoint I don't think he's capable. And then there's motive. If the other murders end up being related, I'm not seeing it."

Tara gazed out the window, thinking about it. She would definitely follow up, even though Liam's logic seemed solid.

She watched the endless wall of pines whisk by and thought of Catalina alone on that wooded trail. She'd probably been out there seeking refuge from the turmoil in her life. She'd probably been focused inward, then suddenly jarred alert at the moment of ambush.

Had she felt the blade? Or been unconscious by that time?

Tara harbored a fear of knives. So much slower than a bullet and likely a more painful death. Plus the terror of *knowing*. Of seeing the blade and realizing what was coming.

As weapons went, she much preferred firearms. Many of the SWAT guys she worked with were gun freaks, and she understood the appeal. Throughout her training she'd learned to confront people with a variety of weapons—guns, Tasers, batons. She'd learned hand-to-hand tactics, too, which had been the highlight. Long ago she'd made a conscious choice not to be helpless, not ever again.

Liam slowed as they neared the sign for Big Pines, and she felt a flicker of regret. His truck was warm and cozy, and now she faced a two-hour road trip with only a temperamental heater and her morose thoughts for company. She preferred Liam's company. Not just preferred—she was starting to crave it.

A troubling sign.

"How are your ribs feeling?"

She glanced across the console. "Okay. Bruised, not broken."

"You sore?"

"I've had worse."

He pulled up behind her Explorer and shoved it into park. He turned to look at her. "The guy you want to talk to at the Delphi Center is Travis Cullen," he said. "He's the best."

"How would you know?"

"I know some people over there. Travis is a good guy, former Marine. Don't let them pass you off to some lab rat." His gaze lingered on the pistol at her hip. "And be careful today."

The protective tone of his voice unsettled her. "I'm always careful."

"I'll be in Houston tonight, the downtown Marriott. Call me if anything comes up. If you need anything here, call Jeremy."

"Look, I appreciate your concern. Really. But I can look out for myself."

He reached out and traced his thumb over the bruise on her jaw, and to her dismay she felt that warm tingle.

"I'm serious, Liam."

He kissed her. It was gentle and warm but over much too soon.

His hand dropped away. "I know you are."

JEREMY MET HIM on the east edge of the tract owned by Corrine Timber. Liam had parked on a ridge, not a high elevation but the highest in the area.

Jeremy slid from his pickup.

"You bring the .300?" Liam asked.

"Yep."

Jeremy took the case from the back of the cab and set it down on the driver's seat. He flipped the latches and pulled out the rifle, which was outfitted with a state-of-the-art 4-12x40mm variable scope.

"This way," Liam said, and they hiked to the top of

the ridge, following a path made by deer and coyotes, judging from the droppings. They trekked in silence a few minutes.

"How'd it go with Tara?" Jeremy asked in an uncharacteristic burst of conversation.

"'Bout how I expected. She's stubborn."

Jeremy grunted his agreement as Liam led him along the ridge.

Liam should stay away, he knew it. But he couldn't stop thinking about her. He liked her determined eyes and her defiant attitude and her lush mouth. She'd become a yearning, a distraction. And in his line of work distractions were never good. They could be fatal.

They walked in silence. Liam kept his pace even as they approached the site to see if Jeremy would spot it on his own. His friend seemed to sense when they neared the place. He slowed, then stopped and did a 180-degree scan of the area. When he spied Liam's find, he gave a low whistle.

"That's it." He met Liam's gaze and handed over the gun.

Liam approached the spot, careful not to mar any tracks, although he hadn't seen any. He hadn't seen much of anything, in fact, except a man-shaped patch of flattened grass and two small indentations in the dirt about half a meter apart.

Jeremy crouched down. As a Marine sharpshooter, he knew exactly what he was looking at. He pointed to a patch of bald soil where two small circles had been made by the feet of a bipod.

"He set up here, facing southeast." He glanced around, looking for the same things Liam had—cigarette butts, food wrappers, dried puddles of chewing tobacco. Sniper work was a waiting game, and guys liked to pass the time. But this one had more discipline than most, from the looks of it. Or he'd cleaned up after himself.

Jeremy stood up and stepped away from the nest. Liam stretched out prone, digging the toes of his boots into the same indentations the shooter had used. He snugged the stock into his shoulder and peered through the scope.

The firebreak formed a perfect treeless tunnel, and Liam quickly found the gate where only a few hours ago Tara had been poking around in the dark. In broad daylight, with some of the most advanced optics on the planet, the view was clear and crisp—even sharper than reality.

It was a straight two-hundred-yard shot, one any sharpshooter could make in his sleep, even in the dark, provided he had a decent night scope.

The setup offended Liam on the most basic level— a trained operator taking aim at an unsuspecting woman from a concealed position. That it had happened only a few miles from Liam's homestead compounded things.

"What's that, one-eighty?" Jeremy asked, looking out over the landscape from his higher-than-average vantage point.

"Two hundred, I'd say." Liam zeroed in on the fence post and the tree trunk where he and Ingram had collected the slugs.

One shot, one kill. A sniper's motto.

Tara was alive right now because the shooter had decided it was more entertaining to spook her than to put a bullet through her head.

Jeremy dropped into a kneeling position. Liam handed the gun over, and with smooth efficiency Jeremy lifted it to his shoulder and aimed it over his knee. The trajectory was ninety degrees south of the shot aimed at Tara.

"Shit, you won't believe this."

Liam would believe it. He'd already put it together when he'd come out here earlier this morning. From this location, the shooter had a view of not only the gate accessing the firebreak but also the public road accessing Corrine Timber, the road that yesterday had been congested with law-enforcement vehicles converging on the scene where two bodies had been dumped.

"I saw it," Liam said. "Looks like he's fixated on the investigation. He was keeping an eye on things."

They stood up and glanced around, looking for any evidence they'd missed that might provide a clue. Their guy had spent some time here, that was clear. Had he spent the night?

Liam walked into the nearby woods and searched the ground. It sloped down abruptly, and the trees grew thicker. He'd been over this area earlier.

"Look here," Jeremy said. "Cooking fire."

Liam spotted the charred patch of dirt. He walked over and knelt beside it. He took out his pocketknife and poked through the ashes but didn't luck into any helpful debris.

"You tell the sheriff about the sniper hide?" Jeremy asked.

"What good would it do?"

Jeremy didn't respond.

"We'll run it ourselves." Liam stood. "I want a

two-camera setup, minimum, motion-sensitive to pre-
serve battery life. And I need it fast. Jim Willet arrives
in Houston in three hours."

Jeremy propped the rifle on his shoulder and gazed
into the woods. "What are the odds he'll come back?"

"Long," Liam said. "But it's worth a shot."

CHAPTER SIXTEEN

The Delphi Center lobby offered a view of the rolling Texas countryside, including a cluster of oak trees that attracted carrion birds. The giant buzzards swooped down from the sky and disappeared into the foliage, probably checking out the lab's latest science experiment.

Tara glanced around the lobby. No sign of Kelsey Quinn or the tool-marks expert who was supposed to meet her here. She tried to make eye contact with the receptionist, but the woman was on the phone, determinedly ignoring the visitor who'd been cooling her heels in the lobby for twenty minutes now.

Tara looked outside and tried to focus her mind on the case. It might have been delayed shock or fatigue, but her brain kept seizing on the events of last night.

She replayed the sounds, the smells, the icy panic she'd felt as she inched her way up the hillside, followed by the hot bolt of fear as she'd thrown her car into gear and sped blindly through the woods.

The next part was blurry, but somehow she'd ended up at Liam's.

It seemed odd to her now in the clear light of day. She hated asking for help, but last night she'd been shaken beyond thinking, and her car seemed to have steered itself to Liam's gate. He'd helped her, and for that she felt grateful. But then he'd gone all alpha male and started bossing her around.

Work was one thing. She had no problem taking orders from her boss or her SWAT commander. But she didn't work for Liam, and the sooner he figured that out, the better.

She caught herself. She was thinking as though they had a relationship. They didn't. He was one small step away from being their prime suspect. And he was still intricately involved in the investigation because of his links to the crimes.

Dunn's Landing was a small town, so small it was invisible on most maps. Tara knew every eye was on her and even the slightest hint of impropriety could cause an uproar.

She couldn't afford an uproar. She had enough to deal with investigating four murdered women and a possible serial killer at work. If it was a serial killer, he was focused on a tight geographic area, which meant he could very well be local—all the more reason to keep every last detail aboveboard with local residents and cops.

Tara was acutely aware that she was the outsider. If anything went wrong, she'd be the first one blamed by Ingram or one of his deputies.

Damn it, why had Liam gone to the sheriff? Her body and her confidence had taken a beating last night, and now she felt embarrassed, too. She wished she'd held on to her phone and called for backup instead of racing out of there like a frightened rabbit. Maybe then they'd have a suspect in custody instead of only a few chunks of brass that were too deformed to yield any clues.

"Agent Rushing?"

She turned to see a man crossing the lobby. Athletic, crew-cut. He wore a black golf shirt with the Delphi Center logo on the front pocket, but everything else about him screamed military.

"Travis Cullen." He shook her hand firmly and glanced at her visitor's badge. "Looks like you're checked in. My lab's in the basement."

"Where's Dr. Quinn?" she asked as he led her toward the elevators.

"In a meeting, I think. We can get started without her."

Tara nursed her irritation as they rode the elevator to one of the lower levels.

He caught her eye in the mirrored doors. "I talked to Kelsey this morning. Sounds like your case is getting complicated."

"Looks that way," she said, although from her perspective the case had been complicated from the beginning. Not just complicated but intense. And with every day that ticked by, Tara was getting more and more anxious. This morning she'd tried to reach Jacobs to voice her concerns. He'd sent her out on this bizarre assignment and acted as though it was high priority. But where the hell was her support? For five days now, she and M.J. had been left more or less on their own to deal with cops, crime labs, and political forces that still remained a mystery. And meanwhile, the media interest was mounting.

Tara was starting to suspect she'd been set up.

They reached the basement, and she followed Cullen down a long corridor. Dull popping noises echoed around her.

"They're test-firing," he explained.

"Who is?"

"Our firearms lab. We share this level with them." He ushered her into a small room with a worktable in the center. "It's not that different, really, and we use a lot of the same equipment. They're examining marks made by gun barrels and firing pins. We're examining marks made by other kinds of tools. Such as"—he stepped up to a counter and tapped a few keys on a notebook computer—"bolt cutters. I just finished analyzing that padlock the fire chief sent in."

A picture appeared on the screen, and Tara stepped closer. It was a close-up image, black-and-white, showing striations in metal.

"See the marks? This lock was definitely severed with a pair of bolt cutters." He looked at her. "You guys recover a tool yet?"

"Unfortunately, no." She dug into her jacket and pulled out the envelope containing the padlock she'd discovered last night. It had stayed in her pocket during her tumble down the hill. "But I have another lock for you. Any chance you can tell me if the same tool was used on both?"

He took the envelope and glanced up at her, a look of keen interest on his face. "Where'd you get this?"

"Near the newest recovery site. We also need to check it for prints and DNA in case it matches anything from the first one."

"Then I'll run it upstairs first, see if they can lift something before I go to work on it. They didn't get anything from the first lock, but you never know." He smiled. "You know what we say around here at Delphi."

"What's that?"

"Every contact leaves a trace."

Travis set the envelope aside. "Here, let me show you what I got from the bones." He tapped the keyboard again, and this time a black-and-white image came up on a display screen mounted on the wall.

"I asked our forensic photographer to give me a hand," he said. "She specializes in microphotography. This thing goes to trial, it's not just about my findings, it's about being able to put it all in front of a jury."

Tara stared at the big screen. "What am I looking at here?"

"The terminal phalanx on the fifth digit."

She shot him a look.

"That's Kelsey-speak. This is the tip of the little finger."

"Whose finger?"

"Jane Doe One."

So they'd started numbering them. God. A weight settled on Tara's shoulders as she stared at the picture.

"What you see here is a defensive wound," he said. "Part of the finger's been amputated—about five millimeters, according to Kelsey. Both of us agree this injury was made by the slash of a knife."

"A parry wound." Tara looked at him. "She was trying to fight him off."

"That's right." He tapped the keyboard, and another image appeared on the screen. Again black-and-white, and again Tara had no idea what she was looking at.

"Here we have a close-up picture of the eighth and ninth thoracic vertebrae. Another knife wound here. So, we can tell the killer penetrated all the way through the torso with a stabbing motion."

Bile rose in Tara's throat. But she kept her focus on the picture and tried to be objective. "Any chance this mark was made later, possibly by scavengers?"

"No. It's what we call a green bone injury. You can see it even better with the ribs." He tapped his keyboard a few times, scrolling through images. "See the way a sliver of bone curls up there? Marks made later, after decomposition, the bones don't respond like that because they're drier, more brittle. Jane Doe One and Catalina Reyes both had bone injuries like you see here. And they have something else in common, too. The knife signature."

She looked at him.

"Every victim so far has injuries inflicted by the same knife," he said. "You can tell from the marks on the bone."

"How?"

He leaned back against the counter. "Every blade is different. The more a blade's been used, the more pronounced the differences. For example, in this case I can tell you the killer used a twenty-degree blade, at least seven inches long, with a microscopic deformity at the tip."

"So . . . can you tell me what kind of knife it is?"

"Absolutely. You want to see?"

Without waiting for a response, he crossed the lab and opened the door to a large storage room, no windows. Tara followed him inside and stood in the center, gaping at the shelves containing all sorts of tools—hammers, axes, saws, shovels. So many weapons, so many ways to inflict pain.

Travis stepped around a worktable and led her to the far wall.

The knives.

A chill came over her. She'd never seen so many in one place. They ranged from switchblades to scimitars, all lined up neatly on shelves. She stepped closer to examine a Samurai sword.

"Jesus." She crouched down and studied the combat knives. Some looked like standard military issue, while others had been customized. "I've never seen so many Ka-Bars all together."

He pulled a knife from one of the shelves and placed it in the middle of the worktable. He flipped on an overhead spotlight as she walked over to take a look.

It was black from hilt to tip, with only a thin sliver of exposed metal along the cutting edge.

"This is a Full Black knife, best in the world," he said. "The brand's a favorite with Navy SEALs, Army Rangers, Recon Marines."

She looked at him. "Full Black as in black ops?"

"You got it. You're looking at high-carbon steel with a twenty-degree cutting edge and a blade hardness of sixty-two. Cuts through aircraft skin like a can opener."

Tara shuddered to think what it could do to human skin.

"It was originally designed for pararescuemen, to help remove pilots from wreckages. Slices through metal, heavy-duty plastic, seat belts. It can also be used as a pry bar, to break a windshield, whatever you need."

"May I?" she asked.

He nodded.

She picked it up. Despite its length, it was surprisingly light. The hilt fit comfortably in her hand.

"How long is this blade?" she asked.

"Seven inches."

"And what's this finish?"

"That's the kicker. Baked-on ceramic coating to protect against wear. Comes in custom colors—black, gray, various camo patterns. The formula for the stuff is patented, only used by one company." He met Tara's gaze. "We found microscopic flecks of it in two of the victims' wounds."

"You're sure?"

"Positive. I had one of our tracers run it through a spectrometer."

She held the knife up and looked at the blade. "You said something about a signature?"

"Here." He carefully took the knife and touched his finger to the tip. "The one used by the killer has a defect, a very slight bend in the tip, probably from being used to pry something. Like I said, it's slight." He set the knife down on the table between them. "You need magnification to see it, but the signature's there."

Tara's pulse sped up at his words. "So if we find the weapon, can you match it to the victims?"

He winced. "You know forensics geeks, we hate

the word *matched*. Defense attorneys jump all over it. But yes, I can tell you the same knife was used on all four victims. Find the knife, and you'll have your smoking gun."

Tara looked at the collection of tools again, all of which could somehow be used to cause pain and death. Sometimes Tara felt physically sickened by the extent of human cruelty. After six years of law enforcement, she should be used to it by now, but she wasn't.

She still remembered the euphoria she'd felt when she'd received her acceptance from the Academy. For days she'd walked around in a state of stunned disbelief. They'd picked *her*, and she'd been determined to prove herself worthy.

Part of her was still that trainee brimming with enthusiasm. But part of her had changed. She could still run a seven-minute mile and do sixty push-ups in a minute. But the job had taken an emotional toll, and sometimes—such as now, as she stood before a vast array of murder weapons and calmly conjured up possible scenarios—she felt a slight withering of her soul. And she had to remind herself that she'd chosen this path.

Was this what disillusionment felt like? The beginnings of burnout? Or had she just become cynical, as Liam had said?

She didn't know, but she felt set apart from normal people, alienated. She always had, but the profession she'd chosen made it worse.

Travis was watching her, probably wondering at her fascination with the weapons collection.

Her phone chimed, and she dug it out from her pocket. "Rushing."

"Tara! Glad I caught you." It was her SAC's assistant in Houston. "Jacobs wants you in a meeting with him at two."

"Not happening," Tara said. "I'm at the Delphi Center crime lab."

"He knows. He's in their first-floor conference room with their forensic anthropologist. Their cyberprofiler's there, too. Jacobs wants you in on the meeting."

Tara shot a look at the clock and bit back a sarcastic comment. The meeting started in three minutes, so including her was obviously an afterthought.

"Tara?"

"Tell him I'll be there in five."

By the time she wrapped up with Travis and hustled upstairs, the meeting had already begun. Kelsey was seated at a conference table across from several men. She wore a white lab coat and had her hair piled up in a messy bun. A video screen on the wall behind her featured a photograph of yesterday's excavation site.

"This just came in this morning," Kelsey was saying. "They haven't even notified the family yet."

"Agent Rushing, glad you could join us." Jacobs nodded at Tara as she claimed an empty chair. Her boss was in his usual suit and tie and had a legal pad in front of him. "Have you met Delphi's chief cyberprofiler, Mark Wolfe?"

Tara's gaze settled on the stranger at the table.

"Special Agent." He nodded at her. "I don't believe we've met," he added, because she couldn't seem to get a word out.

She thought of Liam this morning. *I know some*

people over there. She looked at Jacobs. "I wasn't aware this case had a cyber element to it."

"It doesn't," he said. "But Mark used to work for us in the Behavioral Analysis Unit. We wanted him to weigh in on this."

She glanced at the profiler again, and he was watching her intently. He was tall and broad-shouldered and filled out his perfectly tailored suit.

"So, you were saying?" Jacobs shifted the conversation back to Kelsey. "About the bone database?"

"Not bones, precisely," Kelsey said. "Mitochondrial DNA, which is found in bones and also hair. The database we use is the largest in the world, containing profiles collected from unidentified remains, missing persons, and relatives of missing persons. The hit came late yesterday evening."

"You got an ID?" Tara asked.

"Jane Doe One," she said. "Her real name is Marianna Cruz, and she lived in Dallas. Her sister reported her missing four months ago and provided a DNA sample, but the profile just got loaded into the system." Kelsey tapped a few keys on her laptop computer, and an X-ray image flashed up on the screen. "Here we have her films. She sustained knife wounds to various ribs and vertebrae. She also sustained defensive injuries to her hands. See this? One of her digits was severed. Our tool-marks expert believes the weapon was a knife."

"I just spoke with him," Tara said. "He thinks it's the same knife used on Catalina Reyes."

Kelsey nodded. "And Alyson Hutchison. Her ID just came in yesterday."

"That was fast," Tara said.

"She'd been missing nearly a year," Kelsey said. "Her DNA record was in the system, so as soon as I entered a profile, we got the hit."

"So, now you've got three out of four victims positively identified," Mark Wolfe said. "That makes it easier to get a feel for this UNSUB."

UNSUB, or FBI-speak for *unidentified subject.* Having worked for the Bureau, he knew all the jargon. He was staring at the screen now, which showed a wide-angle photograph of the wooded crime scene where Tara had spent the better part of yesterday sifting dirt.

Tara turned to Kelsey, noting her bloodshot eyes and the supersized coffee at her elbow. She must have been at the lab all night processing bone samples and running queries through the database.

"How long will it take you to get a profile?" Jacobs asked.

Tara glanced back at Mark, who was watching her now with a pensive expression.

"I'll need more on the victims." He turned to Jacobs. "But from what little you already gave me, I can tell you some basics." He paused and glanced down, seeming to collect his thoughts. "These crimes are tremendously violent. And I'm sure you've already picked up on a common theme." His gaze zeroed in on Tara.

"Wooded areas?" Jacobs ventured.

"That." Mark nodded. "And also—"

"He hates women," Tara said.

"Misogyny." Mark nodded again. "That's the overriding motive here. The beating, the strangling, the evisceration. These attacks are up close and personal, demonstrating an extreme anger toward women."

"So we're *not* talking about a political killing," Jacobs said.

"Not in the usual sense, no," Mark said. "Yes, Catalina Reyes was a political figure. But I don't believe she was murdered specifically for her ideology. More likely she was targeted for what she symbolized in the killer's mind. A woman who was successful, powerful, receiving media attention."

"So you're saying he killed her because he doesn't like strong women?" Tara asked.

"He doesn't like any women," Mark said, "most likely as a result of a dysfunctional relationship with his mother. But he wouldn't like Catie Reyes in particular because of what he views as her undeserved success and fame."

Catie again, just like Liam.

Any doubt Tara had that she was sitting across the table from Liam's brother quickly evaporated. At first glance, he didn't look like a man whose father was a mechanic. But underneath the expensive clothes and smooth manners, Tara saw a hardness there that reminded her of Liam.

She wondered if Mark had ever met Catalina personally or if he simply knew her as one of his brother's clients.

"What about the physical evidence?" Kelsey asked.

"You're talking about the knife wounds," Mark said.

"And also the knife itself," she added. "Our toolmarks expert believes some sort of tactical knife was used. Does that mean he's ex-military?"

"Possibly," Mark said. "But I wouldn't rule out nonmilitary professions, such as cops or other first responders. Lots of people use knives like that, including paramedics and SWAT teams." His gaze settled on Tara. She had no idea what Liam had said about her, but clearly he'd told him something.

"What else can you tell us about the UNSUB?" she asked.

"He's strong, for one thing. These victims were deposited deep in the woods. In the case of Catalina Reyes, tire tracks were found half a mile away from her body. The soles of her feet were clean, which suggests he carried her to the final location where he performed the mutilation. In Catalina's case, the posing of the body and the mutilation strike me as ritualistic."

Tara shuddered. "Like this has some kind of religious meaning?"

"No, more like a step-by-step plan that he follows each time, such as a hunter might use to field-dress a deer. He's methodical." He looked at Jacobs. "As for the tire marks, they belong to a pickup truck or large SUV. I'll know more details after I analyze the rest of the reports."

Tara looked at Kelsey. "And what do we know about the newly identified victims?"

"Not nearly enough, but from what I hear, the task force is working on that." She flipped open a folder in front of her. "What I have so far is fairly basic: Marianna Cruz, nineteen, reported missing in Fort Worth in September. Her remains were recovered in November, but we didn't get the hit with the database until yesterday."

"Employment?" Tara asked.

"None," Kelsey said. "She had a criminal record that included several minor drug busts and an arrest for prostitution."

"What about Alyson Hutchison?" Jacobs asked.

"She lived in Texarkana." Kelsey flipped through some papers. "Also nineteen. She *also* had a few minor run-ins with law enforcement. On two occasions she was arrested for solicitation outside a truck stop on Highway Fifty-nine."

"Doesn't sound like these women have a lot in common with a wealthy businesswoman from north Houston." Tara looked at Mark. "Or am I missing something?"

"No, you're right. On the surface at least, they seem different from Catalina."

Tara looked at Kelsey. "What about time of death?"

"I'm establishing that now, but as best I can tell"— she clicked to a new slide, this one showing a time-line—"Alyson Hutchison was last seen eleven months ago, and based on the condition of her remains I would estimate her murder occurred soon after she disappeared. Marianna Cruz went missing in late September, her remains were found in November, and the stage of decomp puts her time of death right around the time of her disappearance. We haven't ID'd the third Jane Doe yet, but I'm estimating she was killed in the summer based on the condition of her remains."

"So we have three murders that happened last year—February, sometime in the summer, and September," Jacobs said.

"And none of them attracted very much attention," Tara said. "Then Catalina Reyes is killed, and suddenly it's all over the news."

"What does that tell us?" Jacobs looked at Mark.

"A lot," the profiler said. "Especially when you consider that Catalina Reyes was found in a setting that was a known hangout for teenagers. I'd say that by the time she was murdered, this UNSUB was getting frustrated."

"'Frustrated'?" Tara repeated. The word seemed much too bland given the magnitude of the violence.

"That's right," Mark said. "He was doing all this work, and he wanted someone to notice."

THE MEETING BROKE up when Kelsey and Mark had to leave, and Tara was left sitting across the conference table from her boss. She watched him jotting notes on his legal pad.

She took a deep breath. "Why wasn't I told about the task force?"

He looked up. "What about it?"

"That it exists, for starters."

He rested his pen. "We're investigating a serial killer. A task force is standard procedure."

"So you mean to involve the locals?"

He nodded. "Sheriff Ingram, Chief Becker. Couple of agents from our office—you, Martinez, Mike Brannon."

Her temper festered. "I'm guessing Brannon's in charge, then?"

"You're in charge."

She stared at him.

"I'm hoping you can provide a bridge between us

and the locals. There are some tricky politics here, as I'm sure you've noticed. Given your background, we think you're the one we need to fill the gap."

Her background. "You mean . . . because I'm from around here?"

"That's part of it. You're one of the few agents in our office who's actually from East Texas. And your background's in policing, which gets us some points with local cops."

"And I'm a woman."

"That, too."

She couldn't believe he'd admitted it. Had he really just put her in charge of an entire task force as some sort of affirmative-action move?

Maybe this was a PR strategy. Maybe he wanted it to look like the Bureau actually gave a damn that some sociopath was going around butchering women, whether or not they happened to be political figures.

Only that wasn't true.

Over the past year, three young women from the same geographic area had disappeared, never to be heard from again. And not one law-enforcement agency, federal or otherwise, had launched a serious investigation until Catalina Reyes's Lexus LS 460 was found abandoned in a park.

The media was going to be all over this angle, if they weren't already, which meant the Bureau was in damage-control mode. It was going to be a firestorm, and Tara was going to be right in the middle of it, taking the heat on behalf of every badge involved.

Well, so be it. She was pissed off enough not to care.

"Are you having second thoughts about taking this case?" he asked.

As if she'd had a choice. "No, but I could use more information."

"Such as?"

"What's Judge Mooring's involvement? Why'd he call us in on this?"

Jacobs leaned back in his chair. "Mooring's politically connected."

"I know, but that doesn't explain why he called us in before the body was even identified."

"He wanted to get ahead of it."

"Ahead of what?"

"Two high-profile politicians from the same county, from opposite ends of the political spectrum. It's no secret their camps don't like each other. Mooring called us as soon as he heard about the abandoned car. He wanted the feds involved early to make sure the investigation was handled right."

" 'Right' as in focused on someone besides him?"

Jacobs just looked at her.

"Has anyone checked him out?"

"Discreetly, but yes," he said. "I put Brannon on it the very first day."

Tara's mind whirled as so many new details—important details—came to light. She cringed to think what else she'd been left in the dark about. She folded her hands in front of her. "Can we talk about the elephant in the room now?"

"What would that be?"

"Liam Wolfe."

"What about him?"

"Why do I get the feeling he's part of the reason I was appointed to head up this task force?"

"Because he is."

Tara tried not to show any reaction. She wasn't surprised, really, that her boss would put her in this position. Jacobs was known to be strategic. But she *was* surprised that he was being so candid about it.

"All of these victims were recovered on or near Liam Wolfe's property," he said. "And he knew one of the victims personally."

"He has an alibi for the night of Reyes's death," she countered. "He was in Aspen, Colorado, with a client, and then he was on an airplane."

"I don't think Liam Wolfe killed her. I don't think he killed any of them. But I do think he's the key to this."

"How?" she asked, even though she figured she already knew. She wanted to hear Jacobs say it.

"We're looking for someone who hates women. Someone who's physically strong, who's skilled with a tactical knife. Someone who drives a pickup and is familiar with the back roads in the area." Jacobs leaned forward on his elbows. "That description probably fits the entire workforce at Wolfe Security. He's got dozens of men working for him, and he trains another hundred each year on his property. Chances are Liam Wolfe knows this UNSUB, whether he realizes it or not. We need his cooperation here."

Tara watched him talk, tamping down her emotions as her boss's real motives became clear.

So, that was the reason he'd put her in charge instead of, say, Mike Brannon. Not because she was a competent agent who showed leadership potential but because she was female. Brannon had much more experience but not nearly as much going for him when it came to getting Liam's attention. And Liam was key.

"I'm sure you're aware," Tara said, "that Liam Wolfe is a former Marine, as are many of the men working for him. The loyalty there runs deep. He's not just going to hand us a list of suspects."

"I know." Jacobs pushed back his chair.

"So what do you want me to do?"

He stood up, effectively ending the conversation. "Do whatever you have to, Rushing. But get him on board."

CHAPTER SEVENTEEN

M.J. pulled open the door to the Cypress County admin offices and was surprised to see Jeremy. He held the door open for her as she stepped in from the cold.

"Thanks," she said.

He gave a brief nod as he walked out.

"Hey, nice talking to you," she called, as the door whisked shut behind him.

She turned to the reception desk, where a woman was shutting down her computer, clearly getting ready to leave for the evening. M.J. walked over.

"I'm here to see one of your dispatchers, Amy Leahy." M.J. cast a glance at the clock. "I think her shift ends at six?"

The woman slung her purse over her shoulder. From the framed photos on her desk, M.J. guessed she was in a hurry to get home to her kids.

"Amy's out."

"Out as in on a break or—"

"She called in sick today. Said she has that cold that's been going around."

"Any idea when she'll be back?"

"No." She pointedly looked at her watch. "You could try tomorrow. She's scheduled for the night shift."

Without further chitchat, she walked past M.J. and pushed through the glass doors, letting in a chilly gust.

M.J. followed her outside, discouraged. Nearly thirty-six hours had passed since an anonymous caller had reported the bones in the woods, and still no one had interviewed the dispatcher who took the call.

M.J. stood on the sidewalk looking out at the square. It was already dark. The shops on Main Street were closing up for the night. M.J.'s gaze fell on a row of sheriff's cruisers parked across the street. Several deputies in khaki uniforms and cowboy hats were milling around shooting the breeze. They made eye contact with her, but they weren't exactly welcoming looks.

She averted her gaze and started down the sidewalk to her car, again wondering why Jacobs had sent her here. She wasn't a fan of small towns. She was much more comfortable working in an urban setting where there was a mix of people and she didn't stand out. Since showing up in Cypress County, she'd seen exactly three other Latinas. Two were maids at the Big Pines Motel, and the other was a murder victim.

M.J. shivered. The temperature was already dropping. She strode past the white gazebo in the town square.

She knew part of the reason the Bureau was here in the first place was to determine whether Catalina Reyes's murder had been a hate crime. M.J. didn't know. But she was well aware of the fact that not far from this place in the not-so-distant past, a black man had been chained to a pickup truck by white suprem-acists and dragged to his death. So maybe M.J. was here as sort of a human weather vane. Maybe Jacobs wanted her to stand in the middle of town and see which way the wind was blowing.

But she honestly didn't know. The place was con-fusing, both friendly and inhospitable at the same time. And as far as the case went, various forces seemed to be conspiring against her, from the shifty-eyed sheriff to the common cold.

As she reached her car, she spotted Jeremy's truck parked in front of Red's BBQ. Interesting that he'd been leaving the county offices right as Amy Leahy's shift should have ended. Coincidence? She decided to find out.

She crossed the square to the restaurant. The smell of barbecued brisket greeted her when she stepped inside. Jeremy was on a corner bar stool watching both the basketball game and the door.

M.J. smiled and walked up to him. "Hi again."

He nodded. His face remained neutral, but she got the tiniest feeling he was glad to see her. Maybe she'd imagined it.

She took a stool and nodded at the menu in front of him. "Having dinner?"

"Picking up."

"What's good here?"

"All of it."

She opened the menu and gave it a quick look. The bartender sauntered over, and M.J. ordered a brisket sandwich to go.

Jeremy was watching her. "What brings you to Cypress?" he asked.

"I need to talk to the emergency dispatcher, Amy Leahy."

"Amy's sick."

"So I hear."

M.J. watched him, waiting for more information. Was Amy his girlfriend? She didn't think so. First of all, he didn't seem like the type to have a girlfriend—too much conversation involved. And if he did have one, he probably wouldn't need some receptionist to tell him she hadn't gone to work today.

M.J. leaned an elbow on the bar. "So, what's the deal with you and Amy?"

His eyebrows tipped up.

"Is she . . . your girlfriend? Your source?"

"My source?"

She shrugged. "We know you and Liam are getting inside information somewhere. Tara was thinking one of the deputies, but my bet's on the emergency dispatcher."

Something flickered in his eyes, maybe amusement. He didn't know what to make of her, but at least he was listening. His gaze hadn't strayed to the TV above the bar, which M.J. considered a victory.

"So which is it?" she asked.

"Amy's a friend."

He held her gaze for a long moment, still looking amused. Did he think she was hitting on him?

The bartender walked over with a pair of to-go bags, and Jeremy seemed to welcome the interruption. They handed over their credit cards. After they finished paying and collected their food, Jeremy held the door for her as she stepped outside. His gaze scanned the streets, the square, the sidewalk in front of the courthouse. The deputies were gone now.

"Where're you headed?" M.J. asked him.

"Home."

"And where is that, exactly?" She was being nosy again, but she couldn't help it. She'd never met a professional bodyguard before, and she was curious how it worked.

"I have an apartment in town," he said. "But when Liam's gone I stay at the ranch."

"To hold down the fort?"

"That's right. Where're you parked?"

"By the admin building."

He started walking, and she realized he intended to escort her all the way to her car. She had no idea why that gave her a little lift, but it did.

"So," she said to fill the silence, "you know, they formed a task force today."

"I heard."

"Tara's in charge."

He didn't say anything, and she couldn't tell whether he'd known that, too.

Did he also know that Tara's first order of business was to take a close look at Wolfe Security? She believed Liam's men fit the profile of the UNSUB, which meant that Jeremy was going to be looked at right along with everyone else.

Given his connection to Catalina, he had to have known this from the beginning. Maybe that was why he was so tight-lipped around her.

They reached her car, and M.J. turned to face him. He towered over her, and she caught something in his look, not amusement anymore but something else. Interest. Butterflies flitted to life in her stomach. The good kind.

She imagined inviting him back to her motel for dinner. Only it wouldn't just be dinner. An invitation like that could only mean one thing.

She stood gazing up at him, heart thudding. Part of her wanted to do it. Another part of her thought she was crazy. She imagined him standing in her room, looking down at her as he was right now. If sex was involved, would he manage some small talk first? Or would he get right to the point?

He glanced around, and suddenly he looked like a bodyguard again, all business. His gaze met hers, and he nodded briskly.

"Drive safe," he told her.

She opened her door. "I will."

THE MEN WERE easy to spot, and Tara watched them, waiting for her moment. They wore suits and holsters and had transparent radio receivers clipped to their ears, and every one of them noticed her—she was sure of it. Lurking near the gift shop and scrolling through her phone, she was just the sort of person they were trained to pick up on: someone trying to blend in, someone doing just enough to look busy but not anything that would attract attention.

One by one, they filed into the elevator. Liam was nowhere, though, and her plan of bumping into him was starting to seem far-fetched. He might have taken the service elevator or the stairwell.

"Hi."

She turned around, startled. "Damn, don't creep up on people like that."

Liam stepped closer. "Why not?"

She looked him over, trying to get her heart rate back to normal. He wore all black, from the T-shirt that stretched tautly over his muscles to the combat boots on his feet.

"Why are you in Houston?" he asked.

"I live here."

"Not lately."

He was right. She'd spent the last five nights at motels, only swinging by her apartment once for necessities. Living out of a duffel was getting old, but she'd just have to deal with it. Liam evidently dealt with it a lot.

"I need to talk to you," she told him. "You have time for a break?"

He held her gaze for a moment. Then his attention dropped to her neck, where the collar of her shirt didn't quite hide her cuts.

He took out his phone and made a call. "What's your twenty?" he asked, then listened a moment. "So, he's in for the night?" He checked his watch. "Okay, you're in charge. I'll check in at 2100." He hung up and looked at her. "You hungry?"

"No, but I could use a drink."

She looked him over as he led her across the lobby. He exuded tension tonight. It was in his shoulders, his gaze, the tight set of his jaw. She glanced down and noticed the talclike dust on his boots.

"Long day?" she asked.

"I was on rooftop overwatch for three hours. Willet gave a speech on the steps of the federal courthouse."

"God, why? It's forty degrees out."

"His strategists wanted the backdrop."

The bar was dark and quiet. He found a corner booth and ushered her in first, then slid around so he had a clear line of sight to the door.

"I'd think he'd want to avoid open-air venues if he's getting death threats," Tara said.

"You'd think."

"Did you try to talk him out of it?"

"I always try." He signaled a waitress. "Sometimes they listen, sometimes not. When they don't, I'm forced to make the best of it."

The waitress stepped up and flashed Liam a smile. "What can I get for you?"

He nodded at Tara.

"Jack and Coke," she said.

The waitress turned to Liam.

"Two Cokes," he said. "And a hamburger, rare, no onions."

The waitress left, and Tara looked at him. His gaze scanned the bar—searching for what, she didn't know.

"So," Tara said, trying to sound casual even though this meeting wasn't. Liam knew damn well she wouldn't come all the way here without a reason. "What was the candidate's speech about?"

"The usual."

"Does he do the same speech, over and over?"

"It varies a little. He switches jokes, depending on the audience."

"You must get bored out of your mind listening to it."

"I don't listen." His attention settled on her. "Listening's a distraction."

"You need to be in the moment, every moment."

"That's right."

He leaned back in the booth, resting his arm on the back of his seat. At first glance, he seemed relaxed, but Tara knew better. There was an intensity to him, always. She studied the lines around his eyes and thought of how unjust it was that men actually looked good with crow's feet.

"You ever get tired of it?" she asked.

"What's that?"

"Looking for assassins all the time."

He lifted an eyebrow. "What's an assassin look like?"

"Don't be glib."

"I'm serious."

"You know what I mean. I'd think it would get tedious looking for bad guys everywhere you go."

"I don't look for bad guys. Or assassins. Fact, I try not to look for anything."

"How do you mean?"

"Looking for something—some specific *thing*, like an 'assassin'—that clutters your mind. It keeps you from seeing what's there right in front of you." He eased forward, seeming to warm up to the topic. "We train our people to be alert and observant without making judgments. If you spend your time making judgments, you'll get sidetracked and miss something."

She frowned. "So when you're watching a crowd, how do you figure out who's a suspect?"

"A suspect is anyone who draws your attention. That's it. You don't need to analyze it. Don't over-think it, just go with your instincts. You want an unfiltered observation."

The server dropped off their drinks. Tara took a sip, watching him.

"So if it's all instinct," she said, "why do your guys need so much training?"

"A lot of the training is about responding to a threat. Most people duck for cover if they hear a gunshot. We train our people to have the opposite response, to move toward danger, not away. That's why we hire so many combat veterans."

Tara's pulse picked up. At last they were getting to what she really wanted to talk about. "What portion of your people are from military backgrounds?" she asked.

"Around seventy percent."

"That's a lot."

"One reason we do so much screening is that the people coming back from overseas, a lot of them have the training, the discipline, and the maturity we're looking for. But some are messed up, and that's the cold, hard truth." He paused. "So, yeah, I screen peo-ple. I'd be irresponsible not to. My business is about people, so I spend a lot of effort making sure I have the right ones for the job."

"But you never know what you don't know about someone," she said.

"True. Sometimes it boils down to a judgment call." He glanced out across the bar. "War changes people. You're never quite the same when you come home." He looked at her. "Everyone comes back with at least some adjustment problems. Unless they were a fobbit, and even then."

"What's a fobbit?"

"A guy who stays on the forward operating base, never leaves the wire. Our unit saw a lot of combat, so we were in the thick of it."

"And that's good?"

"It can be," he said. "Guys who've been in combat, they're used to bullets and explosions and other kinds of chaos. They know how to react in that environment without freezing up."

She thought of her reaction last night. *Freezing up* was an understatement. And she'd had SWAT training. Theoretically, she should be immune to the sound of gunfire, but having live ammunition aimed right at her changed things. Somehow her brain had known instantly that it wasn't a training simulation.

"You're thinking about yesterday," he said. "I can see it in your face."

"Actually, I'm thinking how I don't have combat experience. So if I applied for a job with Wolfe Security, I'm guessing I wouldn't make the cut."

"It's doubtful."

That annoyed her. "Do you hire *any* women? Even veterans?"

"It's not that you're a woman. If anything, that's a selling point."

"Right."

"It is. Women are more in touch with their instincts," he said. "It's a survival thing. What women lack in physical strength they have to make up for by paying attention. How many times have you been in an elevator and some guy steps on and your guard goes up?"

"I don't know. It happens."

"That's because you're paying attention, listening to that faint voice in the back of your head that tells you whether someone poses a threat. Women are hard-wired to listen to that, but men aren't and so a lot of times they don't."

The waitress was back with his food. Tara eyed the mountain of fries, and her stomach rumbled.

"Want some?" Liam asked.

"No."

He chomped into his burger with an energy that appealed to her. He was obviously starving. So much for being craving-free on the job. He was human after all.

"How come you don't have more women working for you?" she asked.

"There are a few. Like I said, being a woman isn't your problem."

She narrowed her gaze at him. "What *is* my problem?"

"Being a cop."

Her eyebrows shot up.

"Cops tend to make crappy bodyguards," he said. "They get bogged down thinking about probable cause and analyzing evidence. That's a huge distraction, takes you out of the moment, makes you miss important details that signal an impending attack." He gave her an appraising look. "Are you seriously considering security work?"

"I don't know." She stole a French fry. "Maybe."

It was a lie. She wasn't considering it at all, but she wanted him on this topic.

"Hate to break it to you, but another problem is your age," he said.

"I'm only twenty-nine!"

"I know. I look for early thirties. Experience counts for a lot. Tackling a public figure to the ground, that's a risk. Me, I've got experience under my belt and I'm ready to weather the shitstorm if I'm wrong."

"So two strikes against me: my job and my age. Do I have anything going for me besides being a woman, which supposedly makes me an expert on body language?"

"There's sex." He smiled. "You've got an edge there."

The warm tingle in her stomach was back. "I'm serious."

"So am I." He leaned closer. "You don't think about it as much, so you're less prone to distractions."

"How the hell would you know what I think about?"

"It's a proven fact, Tara. Men think about sex more than women."

She looked into his eyes, remembering the way his kiss felt. His knee brushed hers under the table, and a jolt of heat went through her. She wanted to look away, but she couldn't bring herself to look anywhere but those green eyes. He was challenging her, and she refused to show weakness.

She thought of what he'd said about being in the moment, every moment. Including this one. She liked that intensity, that mind-body connection that was part of everything he did. He drew her in, and no matter how hard she tried to ignore that, she had a feeling he knew.

"Why are you really here, Tara?" His voice was low and tinged with warning.

"I came to talk to you."

"You want my files."

She held his gaze, trying hard not to bite her lip.

"You bring a warrant?"

"No."

"Then how'd you expect to get them?"

She leaned back, trying to break the spell of his gaze. "I was *hoping* you might do the right thing here. For Catalina's sake, if nothing else." She regretted it the instant she said it. Not because it was a cheap shot but because it would make him dig in his heels.

"Tara."

"What?"

"You're going to have to do better than that."

She took another sip of her drink, hoping to cool her throat. He was really the master of the stare-down. "I met your brother today," she said.

"I heard."

"He's got some interesting ideas about our UNSUB. I assume he's shared them with you?"

"No, but I can guess. You're looking for an ex-soldier or cop who has problems with authority figures."

"He has problems with women," she said.

"Okay, female authority figures."

"Well?" She arched her brows. "Doesn't that concern you?"

He pulled his phone from his pocket and pressed it to his ear. "Yeah." He listened a moment, then squeezed his eyes shut and muttered a curse. "Okay, send Lopez and Chapman over to check it out." He ended the call and slid from the booth.

"Hey, we're not finished."

"Duty calls." He took out his wallet. "You staying here tonight?"

"No." She stood up, irritated that her interview was ending just as she'd been getting to the point. "I'm going back to Dunn's Landing."

"I'll be back tomorrow. The candidate's headed to Aspen."

"You're not going?"

"I've got a team there." He left a few bills on the table. "We'll talk later."

"But—"

"And if you want my help, Tara, you'd better come up with something more compelling than a guilt trip."

CHAPTER EIGHTEEN

Tara had never led a task force, but she'd been on a few and knew the importance of projecting confidence to the team. So she didn't mention to anyone, not even M.J., that she'd started her day with ten minutes of retching in the shower.

It was nerves. Probably. She wasn't sure why she felt so anxious, besides the obvious fact that the responsibility of getting justice for four murdered women weighed heavily on her shoulders.

After Tara recovered from the bout of nausea, she did some PT in her room and then sat at a table with a spiral notebook, jotting down every bullet point she could remember from a seminar she'd taken at Quantico: "Leading with Integrity." She came up with a pretty good list, and when she was finished she crumpled it up and pitched it into the trash.

Forget seminars. She'd rely on what she'd learned during her cop days. She did some quick online research, made a brief detour, and showed up for the task force meeting with an armload of dough-nuts.

Red velvet, apple crumble, chocolate honey-glazed—she had every flavor she could dream of, plus a few she'd never imagined, along with a travel caddy of steaming coffee.

Now, standing in the conference room of the Cypress County Sheriff's Office, Tara knew she'd made the right call. Even Ingram, who had the home-field advantage, was too busy stuffing his face to challenge her agenda.

"That about covers the physical evidence," Tara said. "We have the tire tracks, the anthropologist's report, and the two padlocks, which unfortunately didn't yield prints or DNA." She glanced at the clock. She'd been talking for twenty minutes without inter-ruption. "Any questions so far?"

"What about the glass?" M.J. asked. "Didn't you say a sliver of glass was recovered from Catalina's body?"

"The DNA lab is still working on it," Tara said.

She was hoping the delay might mean they'd found something they wanted to confirm, but Tara kept that hope to herself. Until they knew something solid, the glass was secondary to the other leads they had going.

"Anything else?" She glanced around the room. No questions, not even from the normally vocal Mike Brannon, who'd been silent the whole meeting. Tara figured he was either ticked off that she'd gotten the job he wanted or unhappy about being sent to back-woods East Texas where the chances of getting called in on a SWAT raid were pretty much nil.

"Okay, let's move on to the profile." Tara flipped

open a folder. "This came in late last night, and it's based on all our current information."

Ingram and his deputy exchanged a look, as if she'd just announced she was about to read tarot cards.

"Our UNSUB, or unidentified subject, is most likely a white male between twenty-five and forty—"

Jason sneered. "Where'd they get his age from?"

"I'm not sure," she said briskly. "He's thought to be strong, possibly tall, and drives a pickup truck with oversized tires. He most likely has a background in the military, law enforcement, emergency services, or some combination thereof."

She glanced up, and both Ingram and his deputy were watching skeptically, their arms folded over their chests. With their matching buzz cuts, they looked a lot alike, and she wondered if they might actually be related.

She looked back down at her file. "Given the locations of the crime scenes, it's probable that he lives in the area—"

"What area?" Chief Becker cut in.

"Good question." She thumbed back a page. "Looks like a fifty-mile radius of Dunn's Landing, which includes Cypress to the north and Silver Springs to the south." She glanced up again. "As I was saying, the UNSUB likely either lives in the area or once did, based on the various back roads used to access the crime scenes. This is his comfort zone, in other words."

She skimmed the final page of Mark Wolfe's report. "And . . . that's about all we have so far, but the profiler said he'd have more once he analyzes the victimology."

"The who?"

She glanced at Jason. "The victimology. There could be a pattern that emerges about the four victims. We're still working on that."

She scanned the faces around the room. The sugar-induced alertness seemed to be fading. Time to cut to the chase.

"Let's talk about our current list of suspects," she said. Her goal was to stop wasting time on long shots so they could develop a new list based on the profile, a list they might eventually cross-reference with something from Liam.

Assuming she could get him to cooperate.

She turned to Jason. "You were going to follow up with Donny Price, the short-order cook. How'd that go?"

He shrugged. "Looks like he has an alibi."

"Does it check out?"

"He was on shift at the diner that night. Crystal and Jeannie both vouch for him. Anyway, the aggravated assault charge? It wasn't a woman or anything. He got in a bar fight in Houston, went after some guy with a beer bottle, put him in the hospital."

Tara made a note on her list. "Okay, what about the other one you were looking at, Ross McThune?"

"Still working on him," Jason answered.

"You were right about the plea bargain," Ingram said.

Tara stared at him in shock. Was he actually giving her credit in front of a room full of people? Hooray for chocolate-glazed doughnuts.

"Turns out, he was arrested for aggravated sexual assault," the sheriff continued. "But the girl was his date and it was one of those 'he said, she said' cases. Long and short of it was, prosecutor got him to cop to a lesser charge, kind of a slap on the wrist, it being his first offense."

Tara made another note on her list. "Okay. So what's his alibi?"

"Still checking it out," Jason said. "He claims he was doing a run up to Tulsa."

"A run?"

"He used to be a long-haul truck driver."

That got Tara's attention.

"This was back before his disability," Jason said. "Now he runs a load every once in a while, favor for a friend kind of thing. We're checking it out."

"Sounds like a good lead," she said. "Especially since one of our victims was last seen at a truck stop."

Jason nodded. "I'll keep on it."

Tara glanced around the room. "Okay, let's assign tasks. M.J., I'd like you to follow up on that anonymous call from Monday about the bones in the woods. We're assuming it was from poachers, but we need to nail it down."

"Got it."

"Jason, you handle the surveillance footage from the truck stop where Alyson Hutchison disappeared. Interview the staff, see if you get any hits on Ross McThune. Maybe he's been through there." She looked at Becker. "Chief, where are we on the interviews with people from Silver Springs Park?"

"All wrapped up," he said. "We're still waiting for more forensics on the Lexus, case someone touched anything. Houston PD is giving us a hand with that."

She glanced at Brannon. "And what about our

Houston office? You all have been handling David
Reyes. Are we ready to cross him off the list?"

"That's affirmative," Brannon said, in typical
military-speak. "Our forensic accounting team went
over his financials, nothing suspicious. And his alibi
checks out about ten different ways. I say we table
him for now, focus on other leads."

She looked down at her notes.

"Like Liam Wolfe," Jason said.

"He has an alibi," M.J. put in. "And it's confirmed
by the airline."

"He might be able to help us, though," Tara said.
"I'm hoping to get more info about the men working
for him."

Jason scoffed. "Good luck on that."

Tara ignored the comment, scheduled a follow-up
meeting, and sent everyone on their way. When the
conference room was empty, she blew out a sigh and
stared down at her notes.

Her heart was pounding, and her skin felt clammy.
But she'd made it through her first task force meeting
without any major battles, and everyone had more or
less taken orders.

Or so it seemed.

Whatever resentment was festering beneath the
surface would have to be dealt with later. For now, she
had her own list to tackle, and it was much too long
because she'd never been good at delegating.

Tara gathered up her files. As she left the building, she was smacked by a gust of cold air. Shivering
under her blazer, she made her way to her Explorer
and was surprised to find Ingram leaning against the
door.

A little alarm sounded in her head. He tipped his hat politely, and the alarm got louder. She stopped on the sidewalk and waited.

"Couldn't help but notice something," he drawled.

"What's that?"

"You didn't mention Alligator Joe."

Well, damn. The sheriff was sharper than she'd thought. She'd kept the interview of Joe Giroux for herself because he could very well be a key witness, and she didn't want anyone botching the job.

"Thought I'd talk to him today," she said. "I'm headed out there now."

"You know where you're going?"

"More or less." Which was a crock. She had a vague idea based on a conversation with the manager at Big Pines.

Ingram shook his head. "Outta-towner like you, you're liable to get lost."

"I'll be fine." She moved toward her door, but he didn't budge.

"You should let me take you," he said.

"Not necessary."

"Trust me on this, Agent."

She started to bite his head off, then stopped herself. Why was she turning down help? Besides the fact that she hated accepting it from a redneck good old boy?

But he was right in pointing out that she didn't actually know where she was going. His coming along would save her time, if nothing else.

"Fine," she said. "You can navigate."

He gave an approving nod. "We'll take my truck."

"I'd rather drive."

"And I'd rather be in a county vehicle." He moved for his pickup.

"Why?"

"Because." He looked at her over the hood. "Less chance we'll get shot."

THE SHIMMERY GREEN beauty of forest was marred by the scourge of meth. They bumped along in the sheriff's pickup on a road that was new to Tara, but lined with some of the same eyesores she'd seen on the route she'd taken the first night: boarded-up houses, rusted car hulls, smoke-blackened trailers.

"It started with the house fires," Ingram said, talking around a wad of chewing tobacco. "We got a string of calls, one week after another. At first the fire department didn't know what all was going on, but they figured it out pretty quick."

The road curved east, and the trailers disappeared. Clusters of mailboxes marked dusty turnoffs where modest houses were tucked behind the trees.

"When was this?" Tara asked.

He tapped his thumb on the wheel and seemed to think about it. "Back when some of the paper mills started shutting down. I guess late nineties? I was a deputy back then, Roy Mooring was sheriff."

She looked at him. "Any relation to Wyatt Mooring, the federal judge?"

"First cousins, I think. Anyway, old Roy started making noise about all the problems around here. Him and some other sheriffs got on the task force the DEA was putting together. They went to Quantico, got all trained up, came back down and started doing raids everywhere. Cleared out some of the trash. But then after the new recession, things started back again, worse than before."

Tara looked out the window at the tangle of woods. "We've got it down in Houston, too. It's a cheap high, and times are lean for a lot of people."

"Yeah, but up here it's cultural."

"How's that?"

"Goes back decades. Some of these families, they come from bootleggers. Prohibition made criminals out of a lot of people around here, even churchgoing folks. It created what you might call a contempt for the law. All these years later that's still around."

Tara watched him talk, somewhat surprised that they seemed to be engaged in an actual conversation. In his truck with a spittoon at his elbow, the sheriff seemed perfectly at ease chatting with a female investigator. A federal one at that.

"So, back then it was homemade booze," she said, "and now it's homemade speed."

"That's about the size of it." He glanced at her. "Although I have to say, the speed's a lot worse."

"I know."

"You see signs of it everywhere. Dumped cooking containers and ingredients all over the place. Sheds, car trunks, creek beds. Hell, last year Jason got a call out after some kids found a stash buried behind the elementary school. People call up the office all the time, tell about some neighbor who's cooking up meth. It's gotten better these last few years, but still."

"Is the task force still active?" Tara asked.

"Last year they shut down about twenty labs in

this county. And now we got a hotline for people to call in."

They jostled over ruts, and Tara glanced around. She hadn't seen a house or a trailer in a while, and they seemed to be getting farther away from civilization, not to mention paved roads.

"The task force is helping, but it's still a big problem," Ingram continued. "Filling up our jails, our dockets. I've seen it eat up whole families. Seems like everyone's got someone they know that's on it if they're not on it themselves."

"Joe Giroux?"

"Ah, probably not him." Ingram smiled. "White lightning's more his specialty. Although never say never. That's one thing I've learned over the years, no one's immune. I've seen grandmothers on the stuff."

They dipped over a low-water crossing, and Tara glanced around at the thicket. The sheriff had been right. She never would have found this place on her own, despite having directions.

"Speaking of," Ingram said. "You know, Joe, he's a little rough under the collar."

"I figured. What's he do officially?"

"Officially? I'm not sure anymore. And I doubt you could find it on any tax return. I know he dropped trees for about twenty years before he got laid off. Now he mostly lives off the land."

"Liam Wolfe's land," Tara said, just to see if she could get Ingram's take on it. She still thought it odd that Liam let someone squat on his property.

"He's lived here forever," Ingram said, as if that explained it. "Been through floods and droughts. Old guy's tough as a boot. I don't know what all he does now. Probably keeps the raccoon population down."

He swerved off the road, and Tara braced her hand against the dash as he stopped abruptly.

"Here we are."

She glanced around and didn't see a hint of human habitation, not even a fence post.

Icy fear slithered down her spine, and she looked at the sheriff.

CHAPTER NINETEEN

"**W**here is 'here,' exactly?" she asked, sliding her right hand under the windbreaker she'd foolishly zipped over her holster.

"Joe's." Ingram shoved open his door. "This is where the road runs out."

He hopped out, and Tara watched him, changing her mind again about whether this joint expedition was a good idea.

Liam's words came back to her about warning signals. She'd been lulled into comfort by friendly conversation and a warm truck cab. *Be in the moment, every moment.* She darted her gaze around and unzipped her jacket to provide easier access to her weapon.

Where the hell were they?

Tara saw no sign of a house or a cabin, let alone a person. She slipped her phone from her pocket and checked the bars. Reception looked okay, at least.

"You coming?" Ingram called out.

"Yeah."

He waited a second, frowning, and then turned his back on her and tromped into the woods.

Tara surveyed the area. Her gaze landed on something jutting out from the trees—a truck bed. It was an old blue-and-white Chevy pickup, as Liam had described.

She got out, tucking her hand under her jacket and resting it on her gun. If Ingram thought it was an odd way to walk around, she didn't give a damn. As a backup measure, she dialed M.J. No answer, but she left a long message in a voice loud enough for Ingram to hear as she followed him down a path.

". . . So that's my update. I'm here with the sheriff off Tupelo Road, interviewing Joe Giroux. Call you when I'm done."

Ingram seemed too distracted to notice her conversation as he picked his way through some mulberry trees. "It gets swampy back here," he called over his shoulder. "That's why he parks there by the road."

Before coming out here, Ingram had stopped by the motel so Tara could change clothes, and now she was glad she'd traded her business attire for jeans and all-terrain boots. As she walked past the Chevy, the pine trees gave way to sycamores and swamp hickories, and the red-clay soil of the forest turned to gray sludge that sucked at her feet.

Through the trees she caught a glimpse of something wooden. Too small to be a cabin of any kind.

She stopped in her tracks. It was an outhouse. Complete with the crescent-moon cutout for a window.

"No electric out here. Or running water," Ingram said.

"I can see that."

A squeak of metal had Tara turning. Through some scrub bushes she saw a somewhat larger wooden structure. A short, stocky man with a long gray beard stood in the doorway.

"What y'all want?" he yelled.

"Hey there, Joe." Ingram held up a hand in greeting. "Give us a minute, would you? We got some business to talk about."

Joe scowled at the sheriff, then turned and spit a stream of tobacco juice at the ground. There was indeed something bootlike about him, and it wasn't just his leathery skin. His brown-eyed gaze homed in on Tara. "Who're you?"

"Tara Rushing." She walked over and shook his hand. It was dry and callused. "I'm one of the investigators looking into the recent murders in the area."

"That right?" He squinted up at her.

He wore a canvas jacket over dirty jeans and chunky black boots caked with mud. A layer of brown grit covered him, gathering in the wrinkles around his eyes. Tara guessed him to be five-one, one-twenty, and he seemed accustomed to squinting up at people from beneath the brim of his faded Astros cap. It was the old team logo, from back in the Nolan Ryan days.

Ingram stepped over. "You heard about the bodies dumped out here."

Tara shot him a look. Not *women* or even *victims* but *bodies*.

"What about 'em?"

"We're talking to people who live in the area," Tara said. "I just have a few questions."

He swished his chaw a moment and seemed to consider it. Then he looked her in the eye. "Y'all come on in." He turned around and disappeared into the cabin.

Tara gestured for the sheriff to go in first, and he did, ducking his head under the low doorframe.

It was a one-room structure made of roughly hewn logs, not much warmer than the air outside. The place had a dirt floor. At a glance, Tara estimated it was two hundred square feet, the size of her studio apartment when she'd been a rookie with Houston PD.

A camping lantern hung from a pole in the center. In a corner was a wooden table with a bench tucked under it. In the opposite corner was a narrow cot. The place smelled like bacon and . . . something chemical. She glanced around and spotted a plastic clothes rack, the sort some women used to dry lingerie. This one was draped with animal hides.

"Got you some squirrels, looks like," Ingram said.

"Skinny ones." Joe picked up a wooden stool and set it down beside Tara. "Make yourself at home."

"Thank you." She wasn't ready to sit yet, so she nodded at a set of antlers mounted on the wall. "Nice buck. Is that a twelve-pointer?"

"Fourteen." Joe's voice was tinged with pride. "Got him by Flathead Creek down near the dam. Last buck I'll ever shoot."

"Why's that?" Ingram asked.

"Reached the age. Had my fill of killing things." He looked at Tara. "Nothin' against hunters, though."

She nodded, wondering at the recently tanned animal skins.

Ingram lowered himself onto the picnic bench as Joe dragged over an old ice chest and sat down. Tara took the stool. Her anxiety was lessening now that this seemed to be evolving into a normal interview—as normal as possible given that their host was a cranky survivalist who lived in a swamp.

Joe peeled his hat off and took out a can of Skoal. "What's your questions?" He looked directly at Tara instead of Ingram.

"How long have you been living out here?" she asked.

"Forty-three years."

"And have you always lived alone?"

"Yep."

"Joe, you seen anyone around lately?" Ingram asked. "Anyone who didn't belong?"

He slid the sheriff a look. "Besides y'all?"

"Yeah."

He dug out a lump of tobacco with his finger and tucked it under his lip. "No."

"What about poachers?" Ingram asked.

"Nope."

"How about tracks of poachers?" Tara asked. "Or any tracks that looked out of place to you? Even as far back as, say, September or October?"

"Nope."

Tara watched him. In the lamplight she noticed the threads of silver in his dark gray beard.

She scooted forward on her stool. "Okay, let's talk about more recently. Anything suspicious happen?"

"Not until all you cops showed up—last Thursday, I think it was, when they found that dead gal out there."

"You don't remember anyone unusual before that?" Tara asked.

"No."

"You sure, Joe? Think it over, now."

"What about vehicles or noises?" Tara asked.

Joe looked at her. "Well, now that you mention it. A while back I saw a truck what didn't belong."

"What kind of truck?" Tara asked, thinking about the tire tracks.

"Black Chevy pickup."

Ingram looked at her. "Wolfe drives a truck like that."

Joe shook his head. "No, this one was black head to toe. Nothing shiny anywhere, even the wheel caps."

Tara watched him, soaking up the details. Cops called that kind of paint job murdered out. It was flat and black and dead-looking.

"When was this?" Tara asked. Her fingers itched to start taking notes, but she worried he'd clam up.

He sighed and rubbed a hand over his beard. "First time . . . it was back before that last blue norther. When was that?"

Ingram frowned. "Early October, maybe?"

Tara leaned closer, getting excited. "You saw it more than once?" she asked.

"Couple times. In November, too. Few times lately." He picked up a coffee can and spit tobacco juice into it. "He was through here the other morning. Thursday. I was checking my traps."

"Thursday morning? You're sure?" Tara asked.

"I remember 'cause it was right around sunup. Most folks ain't out yet."

Tara glanced at Ingram.

"And you're sure it was a Chevy?" he asked.

"Two thousand five or thereabouts. Regular cab."

"You get a look at the driver?" Tara asked.

"Nope."

"How about the folks around here, up and down Tupelo Road?" Ingram asked. "Anyone drive a truck like that?"

"Nope."

Tara looked at the sheriff, and she could tell he was excited, too. The timing fit.

Ingram leaned closer. "Listen, Joe, this truck may be important. If you see him again, you give us a call."

Joe spit into the coffee can. "Sure would if I had a phone."

INGRAM GOT BACK on the road but turned in the opposite direction from the route they'd taken before.

"Keep going down this way, you'll get to the fork," he said. "That's where they found the tire tracks off-road, by the path leading to the dump site."

Tara stared out the window, taking in details. Dense tree cover obscured much of the sun. She rested her elbow on the door.

Ingram looked at her. "What'd you think of Joe?"

"His memory seems a little spotty, but it might be a good lead."

"Maybe. Black pickups are a dime a dozen, but a paint job like that narrows it down some."

Tara looked at the mailboxes along the road. They were starting to get to a more inhabited area. Through the trees she saw a few double-wide trailers. They passed a house with several battered-looking pickups out front. Tin foil covered the windows. The place was surrounded by a chain-link fence with a sign tacked to it: BEWARE OF DOG.

"Here's the turn," Ingram said, tapping the brakes.

"Pull over where they found the tire track."

Ingram shot her a look.

"Please."

He turned off the road and drove a short distance, then stopped and shifted into park. Tara climbed out. She'd been here once before, but it was during the dead of night. She and M.J. had stood in the drizzle and watched a pair of CSIs crouched beneath a tarp, hurrying to get a plaster cast of the tire impression.

"It's gone now," Tara observed.

"What's that?"

"The tire track."

"Well, we've had some good rain."

Tara walked off the road into the nearby trees. She glanced up at the leafy green canopy. The air smelled of pinesap, and the staccato tap of a woodpecker echoed through the forest.

"It's pretty here."

Ingram frowned.

She picked her way deeper into the woods. Her gaze caught on something white flapping in the breeze. "Is that—"

"Just a clothesline."

Tara looked at him. "There's a house back here?"

"Jason was there already."

"That wasn't in his report."

"She said she didn't see anything."

"She?"

He sighed heavily. "It's a woman and her kid. Becky Lee Bower. She's been in and out of the system, not the most reliable witness you ever come across."

"Why was she in the system?"

"She was in a meth house we raided back last fall. We collared up six people. The judge let her off with probation so she could keep her kid."

Tara walked through the trees until the structure came into view. It was a small shotgun house, pier-and-beam foundation, chipping white paint.

"Where you going?" Ingram called after her.

Tara ducked under the clothesline, and barks erupted inside the house. The screen door rattled as a big black dog scraped frantically with his paws.

"Earl! Get back here!"

A woman dragged the dog away. She looked gray behind the screen.

"Can I help you?" she called out. The friendly words didn't match her blatantly suspicious tone.

"Ms. Bower? I'm Tara Rushing."

"Yes?" she said through the screen.

"I'm with the FBI." Tara heard footsteps behind her. "Sheriff Ingram and I are investigating the recent deaths that happened not far from here."

"Yeah?" Her gaze narrowed.

"Would you mind talking to us a minute, please?"

She looked past Tara as Ingram clomped up the stairs, sending the dog into a renewed tizzy. "I already talked to the deputy," she said over the barks. "Jason Somebody."

"This won't take long, ma'am."

She looked from Ingram to Tara, then down at her

dog, which was a large mixed breed. "All right, then, come in."

Ingram reached around Tara and pulled open the screen. Tara stepped into the house. Far from the inviting smell of bacon, this house smelled like mildew and wet dog. The floor slanted noticeably, and several of the boards had buckled. A brown rug on one side of the room was littered with toys. A little boy in pajamas knelt there, zooming a truck over a cardboard box. All the sofa cushions had been pulled off and made into a fort.

The woman dragged the dog into a back room, where he continued to bark as she shut the door on him. When she returned, Tara looked her over.

Becky Lee Bower was probably twenty-five or thirty based on her son's age, but she looked fifty. Her cheeks were sunken, her skin sallow, her long hair stringy and dull. Deep lines around her eyes and mouth suggested years of addiction.

Tara glanced around the house. She didn't detect any of the typical sights and smells of a meth kitchen. On the contrary, the woman looked to be cooking actual food, and Tara caught a whiff of burned toast.

"What'd you say your name was?"

"Tara Rushing." She slipped a business card from her pocket and handed it to her. "I'm with the FBI."

The woman darted a look at Ingram, and Tara wasn't sure what it meant. Clearly, she didn't welcome visitors, but she seemed to have some particular beef with the sheriff.

"Relax, Becky Lee. This won't take long. How come your boy's not in school?"

Whatever "relaxing" effect he'd intended his words to have was instantly erased.

"He's sick," she snapped. Then she turned to Tara. "What exactly did you want to ask me?"

Barks and yelps came from the back of the house. Tara forced a smile. "The other night—this would be last Wednesday or early Thursday morning—did you see anyone up and down this road?"

"No." She shot a look at Ingram. "I already told the deputy."

"This was the night before we had that big rain," Ingram said.

"I know what night it was. I didn't see anybody."

"You hear anything at all?" Tara asked.

"No."

Ingram stepped closer. "You sure? Alligator Joe said he saw a truck around sunup that morning."

Tara darted him a look. Talk about leading the witness.

But Becky Lee simply crossed her bony arms over her chest. "I didn't see anything."

"See any tire tracks?" Ingram asked. "Shoe tracks, anything like that?"

She pursed her lips, and Tara could tell he'd hit on something.

"Anything at all you remember might help us out," Tara said.

"I didn't *see* anything, but—" She stopped and turned around as the barking reached a fever pitch. "Damn it, Earl!" She stomped down the hall and opened the door. She took the dog by the collar, pulled him to the back door, and nudged him outside.

"You were saying?" Tara asked. "You didn't see anything, *but . . .* ?"

She leaned back against her kitchen counter and darted a glance at the living room, where her son was still busy with his toys.

"The night you're talking about, Earl woke us up, guess it was about four A.M."

"Who's 'us'?" Ingram asked.

"Me and Corey." She nodded at the boy. "We sleep together with Earl at the end of the bed. That morning you're talking about, he was up barking and carrying on. I don't know what was wrong with him, but I got out of bed and let him out."

Tara exchanged a look with the sheriff.

"You recall which direction he went?" Ingram asked.

"He lit out toward the old smokehouse down by the creek. I figured he smelled a possum or something."

Ingram stepped to the door. He pushed the screen open and looked outside. "That little shed out to the west there?"

"Out behind the septic."

"Show me."

She heaved a sigh and went to the door, and the sheriff followed her outside. Tara stepped to the window and watched them disappear around the back of the house.

Tara glanced at the little boy, still playing with his trucks on the rug.

"Hi, Corey." She walked over, and he glanced up. "I'm Tara."

He wore green and blue Incredible Hulk pajamas,

and his sandy brown hair was tousled from sleep. He didn't look feverish.

"How you feeling?" she asked.

"Fine."

"You making a fort?"

He shrugged.

She lowered herself onto the sagging green armchair. "Tell me about your cars."

He shrugged again.

"What's your favorite?"

He stopped and looked at his collection. Many were police cars, and she wondered if he was reenacting the scene he'd seen the other night. No doubt all the sirens and strobe lights had captivated his attention.

He plucked a red sports car from the shaggy carpet. "This one."

"A Corvette. Nice." She picked up a red fire truck and fiddled with the ladders.

Her presence seemed to make him uncomfortable. He scooted closer to the pillow fort and started playing with action figures.

"You ever notice any pickup trucks around here? Maybe a black one?"

He shrugged. "Just Joe's, but his is white and blue."

"You ever see any people around who didn't belong?"

He picked up two Spider-Man figurines and had them face off on the coffee table.

"Corey?"

"I saw the Hulk down by the creek once. But turned out it was just Joe coming back from his traps." He looked up at her. "You know Joe killed a alligator?"

"I heard."

"He showed me the teeth. They're in a can in his house."

The screen door squeaked open, and Ingram poked his head in. "You want to come see this."

Tara went outside and followed him across the yard. Becky Lee was standing by a rickety wooden shed sucking on a cigarette.

"This is where the dog ran to that night." Ingram pointed back toward the road. "You make a beeline from that tire track we lifted, straight through those trees, you get to the path he took to get to the dump site."

The term *dump site* annoyed her, but Tara let it go. "Okay. So?"

"So, the dog woke everyone up about four A.M. Joe saw the black truck through here when he went to clear his traps. We just whittled our time frame down to two, three hours."

Becky Lee's arm dropped to her side, her cigarette dangling between her fingers. "Are you saying he carried that girl right *through* here?"

Ingram looked at her. "That's what it sounds like to me."

She looked stricken. "But . . . what if he comes back?"

"We'll catch him before then." He gave a confident nod that set Tara's teeth on edge. "Till then, you better lock your doors."

AS THEY MADE their way back to the highway Tara gazed out the window.

"How old is she?"

Ingram looked surprised by the question. "Becky Lee? I'd say twenty-five." He rolled to a stop at the highway and hung a left. "She's been clean about three months now. Probably won't take, though."

Tara looked out the window again, her chest tightening at the thought of Corey in that house.

"You know, it's the kids that get me," Ingram said.

She looked at him.

"Every time we call protective services, it's the same old same old," he said. "No place to put 'em and they end up back in the house or with relatives. Half the time the relatives are just as bad."

Tara looked out the window as a familiar anger gripped her. She thought of Corey in his too-small PJs playing hooky from school. She wondered what his mother was like when she was strung out. And what the men were like, the ones who inevitably came around looking for drugs or sex or maybe even skinny little boys.

Her mind drifted to a crappy little apartment in Nacogdoches. Tara had had her own bedroom and shared a bathroom with her mother and the occasional loser her mom happened to bring home. They were all the same—pseudo-intellectuals with goatees and thrift-shop clothes—and her mom would stay up late with them, drinking Scotch and smoking while Tara lay in bed with acid filling her stomach. Most times she could slip away to school in the morning, but the summers weren't so easy, and more than once she'd awakened to find her mother had gone out on errands and left Tara with some hairy, hungover man in the next room.

Her mother was book smart but unforgivably stupid when it came to men.

Tara thought of Corey again. Not so different from the girl they'd found under the sink last week. Not so different from anyone.

Ingram drove the rest of the way in silence, and Tara spent the time planning. By the time they got back to the sheriff's office, she was ready to get to work and in no mood for bullshit. Ingram pulled up alongside her SUV, probably thinking he was about to be rid of her for the day.

"Guess you're headed back to your office?"

"Actually," she said, "I need a conference room."

He looked surprised. "What for?"

"Work."

Ingram passed her off to a deputy who, after much hemming and hawing about space constraints, finally found her a windowless space that seemed to be a temporary holding pen for obsolete computers. Tara loaded everything onto a pushcart to be relocated and then went about the task of setting up her war room.

She taped a timeline to the wall. Then a list of suspects with notations about where the team was in the process of interviewing each one. She combed through the files and compiled a list of the physical evidence down to the last beer can. It was a long list, and she felt cautiously hopeful as she stepped back to look at it. Any one of the items might be the key that unlocked the entire case. Finally, Tara hijacked a deputy's computer and printed out satellite maps of each crime scene, including the truck stop up on U.S. 59. She'd always been a visual person, and it helped her to see everything laid out in front of her like a giant jigsaw puzzle.

When she had everything listed, mapped, pinned, and displayed, she stepped back to study it.

"Shit, what's that?"

She turned to see Jason standing in the doorway.

"A case board," she said. "You ever use one before?"

"No." He stepped into the room and approached the board, immediately zeroing in on the satellite map of the truck stop.

He tapped the picture. "I just came from there."

"How'd it go?"

"Dead end."

"They don't have security cameras?"

"Nah, they have some. That's not the problem. Problem is, they're run by some outside company and the manager there wouldn't turn the tapes over."

"So get a warrant." Tara's phone chimed and she pulled it out. "Rushing."

"It's Kelsey. We have the report back on that shard of glass."

Tara caught the excitement in her voice. "Did you get DNA?"

"Yes, but only the victim's," Kelsey said. "We got something else, though. Our experts analyzed it and turns out it's optical glass."

Tara thought for a moment. "You mean like glasses?"

"Not eyeglasses, but it's some kind of lens."

Tara looked at the satellite image of the woods where Catalina's body had been discovered with a shard of glass embedded in her hamstring.

"What kind, exactly?"

"That's the interesting part," Kelsey said. "Evidently, it's from a scope such as you would use with a rifle. It's a specialized type of glass and we were able to trace it to a particular manufacturer."

"Okay."

"It's a very small shop and they make all sorts of gear for the law-enforcement agencies, the Defense Department, private companies."

Tara waited, holding her breath. She knew what was coming.

"One of their clients is Liam Wolfe."

CHAPTER TWENTY

Liam loaded the last of the weapons and secured the gun locker at the range. He called Jeremy as he started up his truck.

"I'm on my way in," he said. "How'd it go with the ammo?"

"Everything's here except the long-range tactical rounds," Jeremy reported. "Should be in Thursday."

Liam swung onto the dirt road leading back to the gym, avoiding the ruts to keep from banging up his cargo. Between now and next weekend, every firearm he owned had to be stripped and cleaned for a training session.

"They know we're on a timeline," Jeremy said, predicting Liam's next question. "I told them if there were any more delays we'd cancel."

"Okay, good. Anything else?"

"Tara Rushing."

"What about her?"

"She's here," Jeremy said. "Tailgated me in."

Liam felt a buzz of excitement. "What's she want?"

"I don't know, but she looks pissed. I told her to wait at your house."

Liam reached the training center, and the floodlights flashed on as he pulled up to the door.

"Want me to get rid of her?" Jeremy asked.

"I'll handle it."

"That case, I'm heading out."

"See you at 0800."

Liam climbed out and went around to the tailgate. He unloaded the guns and crossed the darkened gym to the armory. On his way back out, he switched on some lights in the weight room. He stepped outside and nearly bumped into Tara.

"Where have you been?" she demanded.

He looked her over and decided *pissed* was an understatement. Her cheeks were flushed despite the cold. Dressed in jeans and assault boots, she looked ready to kick down a door.

"Working." He stepped around her.

"I've been trying to reach you all night."

"Well, you've reached me now. What do you need?" He unloaded another two guns, and she followed him into the gym.

"I need you to cut the crap. No more stalling. I want a list of your employees, past and present, along with a list of every man who's ever been through one of your training camps."

He stowed the rifles in a cabinet and glanced up at her. She was standing in the doorway gaping at all the weapons.

"That all?" he asked.

"No. I also want those psych evaluations."

He squeezed into the doorway, forcing her back against the jamb. "And I assume you have a warrant signed by a judge?"

"No, but I can get one."

"How?"

"A shard of glass recovered from one of the victims' bodies has been traced back to your rifle scopes."

"Mine?"

"A scope like the ones you own, yes."

He stared down at her for a long moment, trying to read her expression. He could tell she was dead serious. "I own a lot of stuff." He squeezed past her and crossed the gym again. "What makes you think some judge is going to sign off?"

"Because this piece of evidence traces back to a certain manufacturer that only does business with a handful of companies, and one of those companies is yours."

"So?"

"*So?*" She stalked after him. "Don't you get it? How many more ways does this UNSUB need to link back to you before you admit that it's someone you know?"

He picked up two more rifles and tucked a third under his arm. "Grab that last one, would you?" He walked back to the gun room and stowed the weapons, then took hers off her hands because she seemed distracted by something in the other room.

"What the hell is that?" she asked.

"Boxing ring."

"Why do you have a boxing ring?"

"Because we do boxing, defensive tactics. Sometimes Ultimate Fighting when the men are bored."

At the mention of his men, her gaze snapped back to his. "Why do you keep doing this?"

He walked over and leaned a palm on the doorframe. "What, exactly?"

"Stonewalling. Doing everything possible to impede this investigation. I could have you arrested for obstruction."

"You could try."

"Liam . . ." She squeezed her eyes shut and rubbed her forehead.

"Hey. Look at me." He pulled her hand down. "What's got you so wound up?"

"*You*." She snatched her hand away. "Do you realize how much trouble you're causing me?"

He'd been enjoying her little temper tantrum, but now he was starting to get annoyed. "By insisting you do your job?"

"By refusing to cooperate!"

He looked her over and noticed the deep furrow between her brows. She was really stressed about this.

She darted a glance at the sparring ring again, and something came into her eyes. It looked a whole lot like lust, and Liam's pulse picked up.

"Come here," he said, taking her hand.

"What?" She jerked free of him but followed him across the gym.

"You look like you want to smack somebody. Why don't we climb in, go a few rounds?"

"Liam, I'm being serious."

"So am I. Sounds like you've had a shit day, and I have, too, so let's blow off some steam."

She shook her head and muttered something, and

he stepped closer until he was definitely invading her personal space. She glared up at him.

"Come on," he said. "Sometimes you just need to pound it out."

Her eyes sparked, and he could tell she liked the idea even if she wouldn't admit it. She glanced at the ring again. He could see it in her face. She wanted a fight. It was something primal, something she needed. He didn't know why. But he understood it completely.

"I'll make it interesting," he told her. "How 'bout we fight for it?"

"Fight for it," she repeated.

"You want something from me. I want something from you. Winner gets what they want."

SHE GAZED UP at him, heart pounding now. She knew what he wanted. She'd known since the very first day. And she'd steadfastly resisted him, at first because he was a suspect and later because he was so involved in the case. He was even more involved now.

"I'm making you an offer." He eased closer. "Take it or leave it."

"You're crazy."

He smiled and crouched down, and her heart lurched as he started untying his boots. "You know you want to."

She sneered. "I'm not fighting you."

But he didn't seem to be listening, and she watched, speechless, as he got rid of his boots and socks and tossed them beside a weight bench. And then he was standing there barefoot, in only his black cargo pants and an olive-drab T-shirt that molded to his pecs.

Tara's pulse thrummed. She darted another look at the ring and felt the sharp pull of temptation.

"Man up, Rushing." He stepped closer, and she forced herself to keep her feet planted right where they were. "Or are you afraid you'll embarrass yourself?"

Her gaze narrowed. "You're really cocky, you know that?"

"Not cocky, confident."

"I've taken down bigger men than you."

"See? You're competitive. You want to try, even with the odds stacked against you."

She looked up at him. Her pulse was racing now, and her fingers itched because he was right about one thing: she did want to smack him.

He eased closer. "Take me on," he murmured. "I know you want to."

She gazed up at him. Warnings were going off in her head, and she was about to ignore all of them.

"Not for the case." She peeled off her jacket, and his eyes heated as she reached for her holster. "This is off the clock."

He watched her drop her holster onto the weight bench, and she felt the tension in the room kick up a notch. She'd done it. She'd taken the bait. Before she could give herself a chance to back out, she pulled off her boots and ducked into the ring.

The floor was springy. She bounced on the balls of her feet, testing it, as adrenaline surged through her system. She loved sparring. But as Liam climbed into the ring, she felt a hot flood of apprehension, because he wasn't like any sparring partner she'd ever had. He was dark and intense, and she was about to have all that intensity focused solely on her. His sheer size caused a flurry of nerves in her stomach. He outweighed her by probably eighty pounds, so she'd have to rely on speed and strategy.

"I don't want to hurt you," he said, and he had a wary look in his eyes now, as if he couldn't believe she'd agreed to this.

"No holds barred," she said crisply. "First one pinned loses. Got it?"

"I—"

She lunged in low with a side kick designed to take out his feet. He jumped sideways and quickly responded with a side sweep of his own. Tara leaped back, evading him, and smiled as he recovered his balance. "Size isn't everything," she said.

He paused for a moment, and she used the time to plan her next strike. He was left-handed, so she faked a left-side kick, then jumped back and spun around to the right, sweeping his legs out from under him and dumping him on his ass. He sprang to his feet, but the damage was done.

Her victory was short-lived, though, as he stepped back a few paces and gave her a hard look.

"Not bad." He prowled back and forth, eyeing her like a predator sizing up his next meal. Then he approached her straight on, probably hoping to intimidate her with his bulk.

She ducked under his arm with an elbow jab and realized he'd predicted the move when he did a quick spin that took her legs out from under her. She pitched forward, then rolled sideways as she caught him coming at her in her peripheral vision. She leaped to her feet and danced backward across the ring.

"You're quick." He nodded approvingly, and she felt a stab of irritation.

"You're condescending."

The corner of his mouth curled up. "Honey, you're about to get your ass handed—"

Her lightning-fast kick caught him in the chest, but he grabbed her ankle and jerked her off balance. She landed on her butt and rolled left, but he was on her in a heartbeat, caging her in beneath his big chest, with his palms planted on either side of her head.

She stared up at him, chest heaving. She dug her heels into the mat and tried to lever him off, but it was like pushing a tree.

"Nice try." He grinned down at her, and she had the satisfaction of seeing the sheen of sweat on his brow.

She made herself go limp for a moment, huffing out a sigh. When his shoulders relaxed, she slid down and rolled out from under him. As she jumped up, she knew he'd let her go. Getting free had been far too easy.

He got to his feet, smiling, and she went at him with a 360 spin kick that caught him off balance and landed him on his butt. She jumped on him, pinning his arms beside him, and she felt a surge of triumph, but it vanished as he heaved himself up and tossed her onto her back. Before she could get a breath, he was between her legs, pinning her to the mat with his hips and clasping her wrists beside her head.

"Give?"

"No."

He ducked his head down, catching her lower

lip in his teeth. She bit back, and then his mouth crushed against hers as his pelvis ground into her. She squirmed and bucked until he pulled away. Heat glittered in his eyes as he gazed down at her. "Now?"

She gave a slight nod. When he released her wrists, she took his head in her hands and pulled him down. The kiss was hot and urgent, and she wrapped her legs around him, squeezing him against her as she dug her fingernails into his scalp. He rolled onto his back, hauling her on top of him with a low groan and shifting her hips so she straddled his lap. She leaned back, panting, but he cupped his hand behind her head and pulled her down for another kiss.

Her breasts settled against his chest. He was huge and strong beneath her, and she rubbed against his body, loving the hardness of it and getting dizzy from all the friction points.

A noise had her jerking back, suddenly alert. "Who's here?" she asked.

"No one."

She looked at him as he shifted to prop himself on his elbows, chest heaving. "Liam, we can't—"

He cut her off with another kiss and rolled her onto her back again, easily trapping her with the weight of his body. She kissed him, letting herself get lost in the heady flood of lust coursing through her system—just for a moment, because they were in a *gym*, for God's sake, and she was going to have to put a stop to this. Soon. Very soon. He ground his hips against her and she whimpered into his mouth, and he did it again and her entire body started to throb. A warm ache spread through her as the kiss went on and on until finally she pulled free.

"Stop."

He leaned back, looking slightly dazed.

"We can't do this here, Liam."

He stared down at her a moment. Then he got to his feet and pulled her up by the arm. "You're right." He ducked under the ropes, pulling her with him. He grabbed her holster off the weight bench and pushed it into her hands.

Tara glanced around, suddenly one-hundred-percent certain she was being watched. She spotted a security camera up by the ceiling, and it was like a bucket of ice water on her overheated body.

Liam grabbed her boots off the floor with one hand and caught her arm with the other. She managed to snag her jacket as he propelled her past another weight bench and to the door of the gym.

A wall of frigid air met her at the threshold, and she stopped short.

"Don't." He pulled her against him and kissed her, hard. "I know what you're going to say, but don't, okay?"

She blinked up at him, heart pounding, and she had no idea what he thought she was going to say because she didn't know herself. She only knew that she wanted to go to his house right now, this minute, so they could be away from people and cameras and God only knew what else.

She went up on tiptoes and kissed him, and he took that as the answer it was and practically dragged her across the cold, damp grass toward his cabin. Instead of leading her up the front steps, he steered her to a side entrance that had to be his bedroom. She tripped going up the stairs, but he caught her arm.

"You okay?"

She nodded. And then she stood shivering beside him on the cold planks of the deck in her bare feet. His were bare, too, but he didn't seem to notice as he tapped a code into a panel beside the door. A quiet *snick*, and he pushed the door open and hauled her inside. He dumped her boots onto the floor and took her holster and dropped it onto a counter. She glanced around the dark little space, but before she could get her bearings, he pushed the door shut and backed her against it.

His mouth was hot and insistent, and lust rippled through her as she kissed him in the confines of the cramped little room.

The wall against her back felt hard, and the tile under her feet felt cool. But his body was warm and solid, and he surrounded her with his musky scent. She licked into his mouth, loving the taste of him and the fierce energy of everything he was doing. She glided her fingers over the contours of his shoulders, and it hit her. This was happening. Now. And the undeniable, rock-hard reality of it was pressed against her waist.

He tugged her shirt from her jeans, and then his hands were sliding over her skin, pushing aside the thin cotton layer of her bra. He rubbed his thumbs over her nipples, and warm, tingly shudders moved through her body. Her breasts were small but very sensitive, and he homed right in on her body's reaction to what he was doing, and he kept doing it until she was so dizzy with desire she could barely think.

He pulled back and gazed down at her in the dimness. "Why are you shaking?" His voice was low and husky.

"I don't know. Nerves."

"Relax."

She closed her eyes and tipped her head back and felt the tension draining away, replaced by a pulsing heat. He pushed her shirt up, and she felt the hot pull of his mouth. She made a sound in her throat and he pulled harder, and she arched against him and combed her fingers into his hair.

Something scraped against the floor, and she opened her eyes.

"Where are we?" she whispered.

"Mud room. Sorry."

He took her hand and pulled her down a narrow hallway and into a room that felt bigger, but it was hard to see in the nearly pitch black. The only light came from gaps in the blinds that cast parallel stripes over a king-size bed. Tara's stomach fluttered, but she had no time to think as he came up behind her and pulled her shirt off, his fingers caressing her skin as they slid up her arms. He turned her to face him, and she slid her hands under his shirt, exploring the smooth, hard shape of his muscles. He felt so solid and tantalizingly male, and her pulse thrummed with anticipation.

He pulled his shirt off. She reached back for her bra, but his hand was already there, popping the clasp, and then his palms surrounded her breasts again. He dipped his head, licking her nipple into his mouth as one of his hands slid inside her jeans. He tugged at the snap, and she heard the rasp of the zipper. He knelt down, sliding her jeans down her legs, then looked up at her as he hooked her panties with his fingers and slid those down, too. He nuzzled her navel, and hot shivers raced over her skin as he stroked his hands up the sides of her body and stood up.

She kissed him, pulling at his belt and refusing to break the contact as she hurried to get his clothes off. He pushed his pants down and tipped her back onto the bed, and then their skin touched and everything ignited.

She rolled him onto his back and felt a flood of triumph as she captured his wrists against the bed. He wrestled his hand free so he could reach up and pull her down for a kiss, and she kissed him back, hard, rocking her hips against him as his fingers tangled in her hair.

They moved together, kissing and struggling for control, until he suddenly rolled her onto her back. He stretched out over her and hitched her leg up to his waist, and she squeezed him in close as he pressed into her.

"Condom," she gasped, and he pulled back, then lunged for the nightstand. She heard the drawer scrape open and waited, gripping the bedspread in her fists, and then he was back, pushing her thighs apart.

"Hold on," he said, bracing his hand against the mattress as he positioned himself over her.

"Hurry."

He drove into her, and she cried out, wrapping her legs around him, trying to hold him there as he pulled back. His gaze held hers, hazy with desire, as he took her hands and flattened his palms against hers, pinning them to the bed and making her helpless to do anything but go along with the rhythm he wanted.

She thought he might be gentle, but he moved roughly, ruthlessly, pushing her body to the limit as the tension built, and she knew *this* was the competition she'd been looking for all along—not the sparring but this—and she wrapped her legs around him and pulled him in close and kissed and kissed him until her entire body ached and burned. She felt the power of his muscles, saw the tendons in his neck straining. She surged against him, over and over, as he pushed and pushed and pushed and her vision started to blur. Finally, he released her hands, and she twined her arms around him.

"Tara—"

"*Yes.*"

The next thrust brought a blinding flash of pleasure, and she cried out, arching against him. His body bucked. She clung to his shoulders as he drove himself into her one more time and collapsed against her.

For a moment, nothing, not even a sound.

She lay there, cemented in place by his weight. His breath felt warm against her hair. Her eyes drifted open, and she was staring at a shoulder.

He pushed himself up on his hands and gazed down at her, but she couldn't read his expression in the dimness. He flopped onto his back.

"Damn." He turned to look at her, and the reverence packed into that one little word brought a wave of giddiness.

She took a deep breath, filling her lungs as her thoughts drifted back to earth. She felt limp. Boneless. Even with his weight gone, she wasn't sure she could move. She gazed at the ceiling, making out dark rafters high above her head.

Her clothes were scattered. Her emotions, even more so. Everything felt too strong, too intense. She'd known it would be like that since the moment she met him.

She turned to look at him beside her, still catching his breath as he gazed up at the ceiling.

Panic flitted inside her. She sat up and looked around. Where *were* her clothes? Her boots?

Jesus, where was her gun?

She slipped out of bed and glanced around, trying to get her bearings.

"Holy crap, is that a fireplace?" She stared at the huge maw in the middle of the room.

She glanced over but got no response from the immobilized body on the bed. She snatched a shirt off the floor and looked around for a bathroom.

"On your left," he said in a rusty voice.

The soft carpet under her feet gave way to cool tile. She shut the door and found a light switch that illuminated a huge bathroom with lots of glass and black stone surfaces. She tapped at the panel of switches until she got it down to one light glowing over a spacious shower. Then she hazarded a look in the mirror.

Even in the dimness her reflection shocked her. Her hair was a wild mane. Her lips were swollen. She leaned in to examine the dark hickey that was already forming beneath her nipple. Then she studied her eyes.

What had just happened? This wasn't just sex. More like a full-on, no-holds-barred battle. It had been all-consuming.

She cupped her hand under the faucet and gulped down some water. She smoothed a hand over her hair, which didn't help at all, and picked up the T-shirt she'd carried into the bathroom. It was his, not hers. Should she get dressed and drive back to her motel? Or should she slip back into bed with him?

A surge of heat swept through her at the thought.

Staying was a bad idea. She should go home and regroup.

She crept back to the bedroom and found him kneeling beside the fireplace as he struck a long match. He held it under the logs until the flame caught. Then he stood up, and her nerves skittered at the sight of his huge, muscular body in the firelight. He was completely, gloriously naked, and his gaze settled on her.

So much for leaving.

"What's wrong?" He took his T-shirt from her hand and tossed it onto a leather chair.

"Nothing." She gave a careless shrug as his hands stroked over her shoulders. "The whole firelight thing. It's kind of . . . I don't know."

He pulled her toward the bed. "Sexy?"

"Unnecessary," she said, as he leaned her back onto the mattress. "I mean—news flash—I'm already naked."

"I noticed." He slid his knee between hers, and she felt the friction of his thigh.

"So, you can quit trying to seduce me. You won. You got what you wanted."

He stretched out over her and caged her in with his big arms, like he'd done in the sparring ring. He leaned down and nibbled her lip.

"Maybe I want it again."

CHAPTER TWENTY-ONE

Tara awoke alone in his bed and immediately knew that staying had been a mistake. Sunlight filtered between the blinds. The smell of firewood hung in the air. The night came back to her in a barrage of images, and she lay on the ocean of his sheets feeling faintly embarrassed and wishing she'd made a cool exit while she had the chance.

She sat up and rubbed her neck as she looked around the room. Her eyes were heavy from lack of sleep, and her limbs felt sore. Not just her limbs—her mouth, her breasts, her everything.

She darted a look toward the bathroom, then slipped out of bed and retrieved her clothes from the floor. His bedroom was impressive in the light of day, with sleek dark furniture and plush gray carpet, and she skimmed her gaze over everything, taking in the details she'd missed before. No photographs, she noted, or artwork or books. Nothing on the walls or the surfaces that revealed anything about Liam's personality beyond a fondness for wood and stone.

She followed the sound of thunking cabinets and found him in the kitchen with his cell phone pressed to his ear. He looked her up and down as he continued his conversation, which seemed to be with one of his men and seemed to concern a shipment of ammunition.

His hair was damp from the shower, and he was in commando gear again. His laptop sat open on the counter and an Army-green duffel was parked beside the door. Tara glanced out the window and saw his truck pulled up to the house beside her SUV, meaning he'd moved it since last night. How long had he been up? And why hadn't she noticed?

She dropped her boots onto the floor and bent down to put them on.

"Okay, later," he said, ending the call. He shut down his computer, and then his gaze settled on her. "Hi."

"Hi." She eyed his fresh black T-shirt with envy. He was all cleaned up, and she looked like a pile of laundry.

"I'm out of coffee."

"It's fine."

"Cereal's about it," he said, carrying a bowl to the sink.

"I'm good." She glanced at her watch. "I need to get going, actually."

He leaned back against the counter and looked at her.

She held his gaze, hoping she projected more confidence than she felt.

He nodded at her mud-caked boots. "Where'd you go yesterday?"

"To interview Joe Giroux." She hooked her thumbs into her pockets. "He's quite a character."

"You shouldn't go into the woods alone."

"I was with Ingram."

He lifted an eyebrow. "You trust him?"

She started to respond, then caught herself. "I don't know. He seems . . . manipulative."

"He is."

He turned and dropped his cereal bowl into the sink as Tara's phone vibrated with an incoming text. She pulled it from her pocket and read a message from M.J. She was already at the diner waiting, which was not good news because Tara desperately needed a shower.

"You ready?"

She glanced up. "Yeah."

He stepped past her and grabbed the duffel off the floor. From the way his muscles bunched she could tell it was heavy, and she wondered where he was off to today. He opened the door, and they stepped into the cold morning air.

"You in town all day?" he asked, walking her to her SUV.

"Yes. Probably." She pulled open her door and turned around, feeling flustered. "Actually, I don't know. It depends."

He slid an arm around her waist and kissed her. It was brief but warm, and she had to resist the urge to wrap her arms around him.

He nodded at the holster on her hip. "When's the last time you practiced?" he asked.

"I don't know. Three weeks?"

"That's too long." He opened the door of his truck and retrieved something from the console. "Here," he said, handing her a black device the size of a key fob.

"What's this?"

"Gate pass. You can come in and out, use the range whenever you want."

"It's fine. I use the range near the office." She handed it back.

He looked down at her a moment, then tossed the device back into his truck. "Don't go in the woods alone." He unlocked the toolbox behind the cab as she watched him with a prickle of annoyance. "You need someone to go with you, call me. Or Jeremy. Or Lopez should be here, too, if we're gone."

"I don't need a babysitter."

He hefted the duffel into the toolbox. "Not a babysitter, a guide."

"I don't need a guide, either. I don't need—"

"You don't need anything from me! I know."

She blinked up at him, startled.

"I know you don't *need* me, Tara." He huffed out a breath and glared down at her. "I want you to want me anyway."

She opened her mouth to speak, but nothing came out.

He slammed the toolbox shut and got behind the wheel. He gave her a hard look as he fired up the engine.

She stepped back from the door.

"Be careful today," he told her.

"I will."

• • •

M.J. WAS AT the diner's crowded counter, where she'd managed to save Tara a seat. A hot cup of coffee was already waiting there, and Tara picked it up as she claimed the stool.

"Check it out," M.J. said cheerfully, sliding a stack of papers in front of her.

"What's this?"

"A little court order to go with your morning java."

Nerves flitted in Tara's stomach as she skimmed the document, which had Liam's name on top and had been signed by a judge. Tara hated writing up warrants. M.J. had offered, and considering her legal background, Tara had been more than happy to let her take a crack at it.

"You decided to go for everything," Tara said.

"I figured why not?" M.J. flagged the waitress. The restaurant was packed with out-of-towners, and Jeannie looked overwhelmed. "We may not get another shot at this. And I wanted access to everything we could get in case what we need isn't in an obvious place. Plus, there's always the possibility someone's gone in and tried to erase records. Our guys can recover anything as long as we have the hardware."

Tara read the document, sipping the coffee that would do nothing to settle her stomach. Seizing Liam's computers, not to mention scouring them for deleted files, sounded so adversarial. Tara had really hoped to go over there and sit down at his desk and let him simply pull up the personnel records for her to examine.

"Excuse me?" M.J. waved down the waitress. "I ordered a bagel a while ago and—"

"It's coming, hon." She stopped to top off the coffees. "We got a waitress running late and an oven on the fritz. And today of all days—we're stuffed to the gills." She looked at Tara. "What about you? You want a muffin? A biscuit?"

"Just coffee for me, thanks."

"So, what's wrong?" M.J. asked Tara. "You don't agree with my strategy?"

"No, this is good." For the case, at least.

"I thought better safe than sorry, right?"

"You're right," Tara said. "I'm just surprised a judge went for this. You used the criminal profile as part of the probable cause. Not exactly standard procedure."

"I know." M.J. smiled, and Tara could tell she was proud of herself. "I'm glad it worked, too. The word *profile* sends a lot of judges running for the hills. Thing is, this guy's local and he wants to see this case solved, like everyone else. If you believe the media hype, we don't even have any suspects yet."

It wasn't the truth, but it wasn't far from it, either. Their suspect list was alarmingly short, but Liam's personnel records could yield a treasure trove of new leads.

Or so Tara hoped.

"Then what's the problem?" M.J. asked. "You're holding something back."

Tara looked at her. "It's just—what if he's right?"

"Who, Liam?"

"Yeah. He insists he really knows all these men. You think he hasn't been through the possibilities on his own?"

"Yeah, but that's the whole point," M.J. said. "He *knows* them. Probably knows them personally in a lot of cases, especially if they served in the military together. That gives him a blind spot. No one wants to think they made a mistake, had bad instincts about people. I mean, the man commands big bucks to provide security. You think he wants to believe he could have hired some psychopath? Just the press coverage alone would crush his business." M.J. paused, searching Tara's face. "Look, if you're afraid to serve him, I'll do it."

"No, I'll do it." Tara slid the paperwork back.

"You sure? I've served papers before. I really don't mind." She gave Tara a pointed look. "I don't have quite the same *personal* connection, so—"

"I'll do it," Tara said tersely. "It was my idea anyway."

M.J.'s food arrived, and Tara sipped her coffee, trying to ignore the queasy feeling in her stomach. M.J. was right. She was letting personal feelings get in the way of her professional responsibilities.

Was that what Liam had intended all along? Was everything between them just some grand manipulation?

She didn't want to think that way, but she couldn't help it—it was how her mind worked. Distrust was deeply ingrained. Liam had said himself that sex was the mother of all distractions, so maybe last night had been about distracting her from her objective.

Her phone chimed, and she dug it out of her pocket. Not Liam, but almost.

"I have some updates," Mark said. "You have a minute?"

"Yeah." Tara slid off her stool. She motioned to M.J. that she needed to take the call and then squeezed her way through the breakfast crowd and stepped into the chilly air.

"What's up?" she asked, her gaze automatically scanning the parking lot for a black Silverado.

"I've been fleshing out the profile."

"Okay."

"Are you familiar with the concept of high-risk versus low-risk victims?"

"I think so. Refresh me."

"The higher-risk a victim's lifestyle, the lower-risk she is to the offender who targets her. In other words, he can more easily carry out the crime and get away with it. So in the first two instances the victim's lifestyle made her a relatively easy target for a predator. Drug use, criminal activity, prostitution. All of those are risk factors that tell us something about the UNSUB," he said. "These victims are easy targets, and I believe he considers them disposable women."

"Disposable." The word put a burn in her throat.

"That's the way he thinks," Mark said.

"Yeah, well, we'll see who's disposable. He's doing this in a death penalty state."

"The point I'm making is his MO is shifting. Most recently he picked Catalina, a victim who didn't have those risk factors at all. It shows an important shift. We're not sure why the change, but my theory is he wasn't getting the attention he needed from the first victims."

"He had to up the ante."

"Right," Mark said. "We also need to focus on the timeline. That could provide a significant clue to the investigation."

"How?"

"Well, we have to start with the assumption that we've recovered all the bodies," he said. "Which may not turn out to be the case. But we're limited to what we know, which is that a forensic anthropologist looking at all the known remains puts the first murder back last February. That could be important."

"Because it's when he started?"

"Exactly. These types of offenders, the impulse to kill, to hurt, is something that's been inside them for years. Often it starts in childhood. It builds over time and by the time one of these offenders graduates to murder you can bet he's already got a history of violence, either reported or unreported. But what prompts that leap? The leap from, say, assaulting his wife or some guy in a bar to actually picking up a woman with the intent to kill and mutilate?"

"You're talking about a triggering incident," she said.

"In this case, I can guarantee you it's some sort of rejection. It could be a layoff, a divorce, a breakup. The point is, something happened that set him off, and you need to keep that in mind as you work through your suspect list. There's always a stressor."

Tara stood on the busy sidewalk, her hair whipping around her shoulders, as she digested everything he'd said.

"Jacobs told me he put you in charge of the task force," Mark said. "Congratulations."

She scoffed. It didn't seem like something to celebrate.

"Have you convened your team yet today?" he asked.

"We plan to meet at ten."

"If you can make it eleven I'd like to be there. I'd like to talk to your team. I believe this UNSUB is going to try to insert himself into the investigation somehow, if he hasn't already. He needs the attention. It's part of what drives him. Your people have to be prepared."

She didn't respond. She didn't know how her team would feel about some profiler sitting in on their meeting. She didn't even know how *she* felt about it.

"It's important they understand who this is if they want a shot at finding him, Tara. This UNSUB is evasive and exceptionally brutal. And we don't have time to waste here. None at all."

"You're saying—"

"He's escalating. The gap between victims is closing, and he's becoming fearless. His first few kills went virtually unnoticed, but with Catalina Reyes he accomplished something important—he attracted media attention. Now all the press he's getting is just feeding his ego. He thrives on it."

"I know." Tara understood it instinctively, without having to be told. It was why she'd been determinedly avoiding the media and instructing everyone on the task force to do the same.

"What that means for you," Mark continued, "is you need to double down your efforts, be aggressive, don't get bogged down with red tape."

She bristled. "I'm doing my best."

"This requires a new best."

"I don't need—"

"You're wrong," he said firmly. "You need all the help you can get, from anywhere you can get it, so lose the pride, all right? I was in your shoes once, Tara. I understand what you're up against."

Her throat felt tight. Her shoulders, her stomach. She could feel the tension coursing through her body.

"Every now and then a case comes along and it requires you to work faster and smarter than ever before," he said. "It's a push."

"I realize that."

"Good. You all need to realize it. Because now that he's done this, it defines him. He's got a taste for it now, and he's not going to stop."

LIAM'S GATES SLID open when Tara arrived. She didn't see his truck around, but Jeremy met her on the front porch with what passed for a friendly nod.

All trace of friendliness evaporated when she produced the search warrant.

Without waiting for a reaction, Tara strode past him and went to work in Liam's office. The paper files were surprisingly minimal, mostly invoices related to improvements around the ranch. But she found three thumb drives, which she collected in evidence envelopes as Jeremy watched her from the doorway with cold, flat eyes.

Next, the CPUs. He had two systems, and she loaded both into her backseat, leaving the monitors behind. She returned to the desk and checked the drawers again to make sure she hadn't missed something.

"Anything else?" She stood up and looked at Jeremy.

No answer.

She walked past him, stopping in the kitchen when she noticed the silver laptop on the counter. Liam had been using it that morning. Should she take that, too? Computer analysis could take days or even weeks. She intended to copy everything and bring it all back, but what if something got delayed? Leaving Liam with nothing could paralyze his business.

"Thunder ain't rain," Jeremy said from the doorway.

She looked at him. "What's that supposed to mean?"

But he didn't say, and she returned her attention to the laptop.

Screw it. Liam was a big boy. He'd just have to handle it. Tara had dealt with pissed-off men before, and no doubt she'd have to do it again.

Tara snapped shut the computer and tucked it under her arm. Then she filled out an evidence receipt, and dread expanded inside her as she listed all the items she'd taken. With a quick flourish, she signed her name at the bottom of the receipt.

"Give this to Liam," she said, holding it out to Jeremy.

He remained stock-still. "Give it to him yourself."

CHAPTER TWENTY-TWO

"**A**nd . . . you're in."

The techie from Tara's office rolled back in the desk chair and gestured to the screen.

"That was fast." Tara peered over his shoulder. She and M.J. were crowded behind their visitor in the makeshift war room at the sheriff's office.

"I wouldn't say fast," he told her. "Usually I can do it in fifteen minutes. This guy's pass codes were harder than average."

"So I've got access to everything?" Tara took a seat beside him.

"On this you do. I'll need some time with those thumb drives."

"Have at it."

Tara took off her blazer, rolled up her sleeves, and got to work. M.J. joined her, and within minutes it became clear why Liam had been so protective of his records.

They were a gold mine of information, both sensitive and highly personal, including detailed dossiers on every person who'd ever hired Wolfe Security. His master client list read like a who's who of Texas VIPs, from politicians and singers to NFL athletes who probably didn't want it made public that they'd ever felt the need to hire a bodyguard.

Catalina Reyes had a folder, and Tara dragged it onto the desktop but decided to save it for later. Liam certainly would have already reviewed it for clues, and the more urgent matter right now was the suspect list.

Tara started with the personnel files. There were a daunting 112, all current or former employees of Wolfe Security.

"One hundred and twelve employees? In three short years?" M.J. asked. "We'll be here all week."

A spreadsheet file caught Tara's eye, and she clicked it open. "Maybe not."

"What's that?"

"Shortcut." She breathed a sigh of relief. "Looks like a list of everyone working for him since, let's see, his first year of operation."

"Let's start with recent."

Tara clicked open a spreadsheet for the current year. "Okay, forty-six. That's a more manageable number."

"That's how many he has working for him now?"

"Looks like."

"Damn, can you imagine his payroll?"

Tara couldn't imagine it. And she really didn't want to. Thinking about Liam's financial success made her antsy for some reason, and it wasn't something she wanted to analyze now. Instead she focused on the spreadsheet, paying close attention to column labels across the top.

"Hey, look." M.J. tapped the screen. "Past military service. He did our homework for us."

"It's broken down into branches and even units." Tara's pulse picked up as she scanned the list. "Here's a guy from DEVGRU. That's SEAL Team Six."

He also had columns for law enforcement, emergency services, and private security.

"Not a lot of women on this list," M.J. muttered.

"Nope."

"I don't see any, in fact."

"Whoa, look at this." Tara clicked on a cell that contained an acronym she recognized. "CQC."

"What's that?"

"Close-quarters combat. There's a whole category here for what he calls 'special skills,' including CQC, sharpshooting, pararescue training."

M.J. leaned closer. "Didn't you say the weapon used, the Full Black knife, was originally designed for pararescuemen?"

"Yeah, I'll look at those guys first," she said, leaning closer to study the PT column. Everyone had three scores listed: speed, strength, and agility.

"That might be useful," M.J. said. "We're definitely looking for someone strong enough to carry a hundred-twenty-pound woman more than half a mile."

"Thing is, these men aren't your average Joes. I'd bet everyone on this list could do that. Did you see Liam's PT course?"

"No."

"Well, I did, and it's no cakewalk."

M.J.'s phone beeped with an incoming message, and she muttered a curse.

"What is it?"

"Sorry, but I have to go do an interview." She stood up and gathered her purse to leave. "What are you going to tackle first?"

"I'll run a detailed criminal history on this entire list, starting with the current year," Tara said. "That's a hundred and twelve men."

"He's bound to hire at least some women, don't you think?"

"Yeah, that'll help a lot. I can probably whittle it down to a hundred ten."

Tara settled in and got to work, and she soon discovered her estimate wasn't far off. Of the complete roster of employees, past and present, there were only four females. Everyone else had to be systematically run through the database, which resulted in some interesting discoveries.

First off, Liam seemed thorough in his background checks. Only a handful of the men he'd hired had criminal histories at all, and those who did had offenses that were either minor or so far in the past that they didn't seem relevant. One guy had been busted for drugs his senior year of college, which had resulted in him getting kicked out of school, joining the Marines, and ultimately ending up in an elite unit in Afghanistan. The man was one of Liam's first hires. Another guy had a DUI conviction in his early twenties, but when Tara opened his individual file, she discovered detailed notes about the treatment program he'd gone through prior to joining the Army.

And it wasn't just military guys who seemed attracted to Wolfe Security. Liam's workforce included ex-cops, ex-DEA, ex-ATF, even a former FBI agent.

After the criminal histories were completed, Tara went through the list again, this time adding men whose special skills included anything related to knives.

That finished, she clicked open the file that contained the other list she wanted to check: trainees, the men and women who had been through one of Liam's intensive boot camps. Tara scrolled through the spreadsheet, letting out a moan as it kept going and going.

Tara's phone chimed. The Delphi Center. Her heart did a little dance as she answered it. "Rushing."

"It's Mia Voss at the DNA lab. Do you have a minute?"

"Absolutely."

"I have good news and bad."

Tara held her breath.

"You recall the tooth we were examining in the Catalina Reyes case?"

"The right first molar that was inside her throat. Yes, I remember." Tara's pulse sped up. "Did you get DNA?"

"As a matter of fact, we did. We have two separate profiles, one from the victim and then a second profile. That's the good news."

Tara leaned back in her chair. DNA evidence was huge. The second profile would be her attacker. Possibly blood from his fist when he knocked out her tooth.

"What's the bad news?" Tara asked.

"Unfortunately, the profile doesn't match anything in the Offender Index. Or even the Forensic Index."

"You mean—"

"The Offender Index includes convicts," Mia said, "along with various arrestees, although not every arrestee who has had a sample collected has been entered in the system yet. The new rules requiring DNA from *all* federal arrestees has created a tremendous backlog."

"I've heard," Tara said. "What about the Forensic Index? That's un-ID'd DNA from crime scenes, right?"

"Correct. No match there, either," Mia said. "So, the good news is we have DNA that I believe belongs to the perpetrator. However, he's not in the system, so you're going to have to come up with a suspect before we can run a comparison."

Tara's mind was spinning. "What about military?" she asked.

"How do you mean?"

"We have reason to believe the UNSUB might have a military background. The military keeps DNA samples of everyone on file, right?"

"That's true," Mia said. "Ever since Desert Storm."

The next few seconds were filled with silence.

"I know what you're thinking," Mia said. "My husband's a homicide detective, so I know just what you're going to ask, and the answer is no. Those records are for ID purposes. Human remains. The Department of Defense won't permit me to run a blind search of their database. They're very protective."

"What about—"

"If you had a particular suspect developed you *might* be able to get a court order," Mia said. "But I'd say that's a long shot, not to mention time-consuming. If you zero in on a suspect, it would probably be easier to collect a DNA sample surreptitiously. You know, tail the guy around and collect a discarded cigarette butt or drinking cup or something."

"I can tell you're married to a cop," Tara said.

"Yes, well. The thinking rubs off. Listen, I know you're frustrated. But keep me posted, all right? If you come up with a viable suspect—"

"You'll be the first to know."

They ended the call, and Tara stared at her list again. DNA evidence was huge, but now more than ever she needed a suspect. And the fact that the DNA profile didn't match anyone already in the system meant that several of the suspects they had—the ones with criminal records—were most likely dead ends.

Back to Liam's database. Tara stared at the list on the screen, hundreds and hundreds of names. She ran a hand through her hair. "Damn it."

"What's that?"

She glanced up to see Brannon standing in the doorway. "I'm drowning here."

"You look like it." He stepped into the cramped room and had the nerve to smell like aftershave instead of BO and frustration. He leaned close and looked over her shoulder. "Looks tedious."

"It is."

"How about a break?"

"I already had a sandwich."

"I meant dinner. It's almost five."

Tara blinked up at him. She checked the clock on

her computer and realized she had, indeed, spent four hours in front of the screen.

"Okay, but I'm driving." She got up and grabbed her blazer.

"Then I get to pick the place," Brannon said.

Five minutes later, they were in her Explorer and headed toward Dunn's Landing, where Brannon had heard the diner served up an unbeatable meat-loaf-and-macaroni special on Thursday evenings.

Tara felt dazed as she drove. Too little sleep, too much computer time, and the hypnotic *swish-swish* of the wiper blades threatened to put her out. No meat-loaf-and-mac for her. She'd be better off with a crisp green salad and about three Cokes to wake her up.

Brannon fiddled with the knobs on her dashboard. "When are you going to get rid of this thing?"

"What, the Beast?"

"You've got to be approaching two hundred thousand miles by now."

She snorted. "Passed that years ago."

He managed to get a breath of warm air going and settled back in the seat. "So, how does your boyfriend feel about you seizing his computers?"

She glanced at him, surprised. Had M.J. said something? "He's not my boyfriend."

"Whatever he is, I'd think he'd be pissed."

Tara gritted her teeth. She didn't like being needled on this topic. She didn't like that it was a topic at all when they were supposed to be concentrating on a case. Did she go around asking the men she worked with about their personal lives? No.

But then, Brannon was different. They had a past together—shallow and infrequent, yes, but still a past—so maybe he thought he was entitled to some sort of status update.

He wasn't.

She focused on the road, trying not to think about Liam, which was impossible now that Brannon had brought it up. What *was* Liam? She didn't know. She had a sudden memory of him looming over her in the sparring ring, and she felt her cheeks heat. Was he simply a man she'd had scorching-hot sex with? Or was there more going on? She pictured the look on his face when he'd given her his gate key. He'd downplayed the gesture, but it had been symbolic. She knew that now—hell, she'd known it at the time.

Guilt gnawed at her. The crazy thing was that she'd *wanted* to take the key. She'd felt this little burst of joy when he'd handed it to her, like he was asking her to go steady or something. Like she wasn't merely some woman he'd shagged on the floor of his gym and then sent home without breakfast. And how had she responded to that rush of giddiness?

She'd rejected him.

Really, it was no wonder she couldn't maintain a relationship. Or even start one in the first place. Somehow she always sabotaged herself.

And although Tara didn't like Brannon's needling, he brought up a good point. How did Liam feel about her seizing his computers? She didn't know. After delivering the warrant, she'd left him three phone messages, and he hadn't answered a single one.

"So, boss, don't you want to hear what I did today?"

She shot him a look. "I thought you were helping Jason with the tapes."

"No, Ingram was helping Jason. You should keep better track of your minions."

She ignored the comment as a sheriff's cruiser rode up on her bumper. She moved into the right-hand lane to let him pass.

"I went through some ViCAP records," Brannon said.

Tara had already tried the Violent Criminal Apprehension Program. "I checked," she said. "Nothing with the same MO."

"Yeah, but what about a broader MO? You heard the profiler this morning. Our UNSUB most likely built up to this gradually. So I was checking older crimes, anything involving strangulation."

"And?"

"I got a ton of hits," he said. "Hundreds. After I wade through everything, I'll let you know."

It sounded like a long shot, but Tara was glad he'd taken the initiative.

"When I get my list together," she said, "we can cross-reference, see if any common names pop up." She looked at Brannon. "The Delphi lab came through with a DNA profile and they think it belongs to our UNSUB."

"You're kidding. Why didn't you tell me?"

"I just found out. Problem is, the profile isn't in the database."

"So we need to come up with a suspect," Brannon said.

"Exactly."

"Shit, that's a good idea. Why didn't I think of that?"

Another sheriff's cruiser blew past doing at least

ninety. Tara's stomach tightened, and she glanced at her phone in the console. No missed calls. She checked her mirror to switch lanes just as a sheriff's SUV raced by.

"Damn it." She changed lanes and floored the gas. "Something's going down. You miss any calls?"

"No."

She caught up to the SUV as it exited the highway. She thought she recognized the guy behind the wheel—one of Ingram's men but not someone on the task force. And that was good, because whatever this was, it could be unrelated.

But then the deputy put on his turn signal, and Tara's stomach plummeted. She gripped the wheel and followed him.

"Hey, isn't this the way to—"

"Silver Springs Park," she said.

Tara glanced around at the thick woods. Yesterday morning she'd driven this road with Liam, and the sky overhead had been a vibrant blue. But now it was lead gray, and the gravel road to the parking lot was dark and wet. A cold trickle of fear slid down Tara's spine as she turned into the parking lot and spotted the mute ambulance.

"Oh, God," she murmured.

"Don't jump to conclusions. Some jogger could have had a coronary."

Tara pulled over beside a row of police units and got out. She spied the cluster of cowboy hats near the trailhead, Sheriff Ingram's towering above them all.

Tara walked straight up to him. He glanced over, and she knew the second she saw his eyes.

"Why wasn't I called?" she demanded.

He looked across the crowd. "Jason was supposed to call you."

The deputy met Tara's gaze, his expression tight. "Sent you a text message."

It was an outright lie, and Tara felt her face go red with outrage, for all the good it did her. She glanced around the scene, which had already been cordoned off with yellow tape. Deeper in the woods was another huddle of men. She recognized Dr. Greenwood's bald head.

Tara's gut clenched. She looked at Ingram as everyone watched her reaction.

"Same MO?"

He nodded.

She turned to Brannon. "Call Jacobs. We need an evidence response team here immediately. Then secure this perimeter. No deputies, no cops, no EMTs. No one goes back there besides myself, the sheriff, and the medical examiner's people. Got it?"

Brannon nodded.

Tara sidestepped Ingram and set off down the path, careful to keep away from the trail itself. Greenwood, dressed for the weather in a gray raincoat, peeled away from a trio of uniformed police officers.

"Agent Rushing." He gave her a nod.

"What do we have?"

"I'll show you."

She followed him into the woods, pushing through the foliage to avoid trampling the hiking path. Dread filled her as he led her deeper into the dank, dark forest. The air was cold and gloomy, and she could feel something terrible lurking in the shadows. Panic bubbled up inside her as she thought of what lay beyond the trees. Her palms felt clammy. She didn't know if she could do it.

This requires a new best.

"Again this time, they found no car, no clothing," Greenwood said. "He deposited her in a clearing."

Tara picked her way through the leaves, ducking under low-hanging limbs. "Who found her?" she asked.

"You'll have to ask Chief Becker. I received the call"—he halted and looked at his watch—"forty-six minutes ago and got here as fast as I could. Based on a cursory examination I'd estimate a postmortem interval of eighteen hours, possibly twenty."

Tara checked her watch. "So she was killed between ten and midnight?"

"It's an estimate."

"We need to get the autopsy scheduled as soon as possible so we can get an ID."

He stopped and turned around. "I believe they already know her."

Tara stared at him. He started down the path again, and she followed, heart pounding now as she pushed through the branches. Her mind raced. She held her breath as they stepped into a clearing.

She was sprawled on a bed of leaves, another horrific tableau. Legs spread apart, arms outstretched. Viciously mutilated beyond recognition.

Except for the scarlet curtain of hair over her face.

Tara's breath hissed out as she knelt beside her. "Oh, God. Oh, Crystal."

CHAPTER TWENTY-THREE

Crystal Marie Marshall was last seen by her coworkers at the Waffle Stop at 10:15 the previous night when she punched her time card at the end of her shift. Jeannie Wharton told investigators she'd been closing up the kitchen and helping Donny clean the griddle when Crystal left the diner wearing only a blue fleece hoodie over her yellow waitress uniform.

Silver Springs police found Crystal's Toyota Corolla in the parking lot behind her two-story apartment complex on the east side of town, but they found no indication that Crystal had been inside since she'd left for work. Her mailbox was full, a pizza coupon was tucked into her doorjamb, and a hungry tabby cat greeted the landlord when he unlocked Crystal's door for investigators.

Had she been abducted from her parking lot? Had she dropped off her car after work and gone out with someone she knew?

These and other questions remained pathetically

unanswered as Tara scoured the hiking trails of Silver Springs Park alongside some of the Bureau's top crime-scene technicians.

After hours of searching in the freezing drizzle, they'd bagged up every food wrapper, water bottle, and cigarette butt they could find. CSIs had collected soil samples, leaf samples, and blood samples from on and around the body, hoping something might offer a clue. The rain had all but obliterated any tire tracks, but an alert SSPD officer—a rookie, no less—had noticed a deep tire rut on a back road not far from the body, and he'd had the sense to peel off his poncho and erect a tarp over the impression while the FBI's evidence response team was en route to the crime scene.

Tara crept through the forest now, shining her flashlight over every limb and tree root, searching for the slightest shred of missed evidence. Beside her, an FBI crime-scene tech did the same. This was their fourth sweep. The first had been conducted on hands and knees, as workers combed every inch of the park within a hundred-foot radius of the body. The crawling search had been followed by foot searches covering the entire park.

Water seeped into Tara's eyes, and she blinked it away. Her nose felt raw, and her ears ached with cold. Inside her gloves, her fingers were stiff.

The CSI switched off her flashlight. "Okay, that's it," the woman said.

They'd reached the trailhead again. In the nearby parking lot, giant white klieg lights illuminated the scene as the last members of the evidence response team packed their kits into vans and collapsed the open-sided tent that had served as their temporary headquarters.

"Agent Rushing?"

She turned around to see the team leader, a lanky forty-something who looked skeletal in the glare of the lights.

"We'll start with that tire impression."

Tara looked at him numbly.

"I should have something for you by late morning," he added.

Something, such as a vehicle. Likely the same pickup truck the UNSUB had used before. Tara wasn't sure what good it would do, but she nodded anyway. "Thanks."

"And let me know if you recover anything new at autopsy, trace-evidence-wise," he said. "I have some pull at Quantico, so I can put in a call, speed things along for you."

"I appreciate that."

He gave a crisp nod. "No problem. Good night."

It was a pointed statement, and she knew what he really meant was that she needed to leave now. It was after two, and she'd been testing the team leader's patience by hanging around until the bitter end, as if she might be able to show some of the world's most highly trained crime-scene technicians a thing or two.

Tara trudged to her SUV just as the lights went out, throwing the parking lot into darkness. She climbed behind the wheel and looked around. Everyone was gone—the police, the sheriff's deputies, the other agents, including Jacobs with his grim mouth and disappointed eyes.

Tara navigated her way back to the main road and

saw that even the last pushy reporter had packed it in
for the night. Only a lone police unit remained stationed at the park entrance. The officer sat in his vehicle, his face aglow as he gazed down at his cell phone.

The rain picked up. Tara adjusted her wipers.
She headed back to town with her fingers frozen on
the steering wheel. Several rigs passed her, splash-
ing copious amounts of water at her windows as they
roared by.

She took the exit for Dunn's Landing and drove
through town. The gas station was dark. The Waffle
Stop. The motel. Even the neon sign was off, probably because no one at Big Pines had given a thought
to turning it on after the sheriff pulled up to break the
news.

Tara parked at the edge of the motel lot and sat
there in the dimness. She pictured Leo Marshall in the
interview room at the police station. He'd looked pale
and wet and stricken, as though a lifetime's worth of
grief had rained down on him in the few short hours
since he'd learned of his daughter's death.

Tara pushed her door open and leaned out, sure
she'd be sick. But it wouldn't come.

She crossed the parking lot, not bothering to bow
her head against the rain as she was already soaked to
the skin. M.J.'s room was dark, but a light glowed in
Brannon's window.

"Hey." She turned to see him stepping out from the
vending-machine alcove. He still wore his suit, but
the tie had disappeared. He held up a bag of Cheetos.
"Join me for dinner?"

She stepped beneath the overhang, which offered
only slight protection from the drizzle.

"No. Thank you."

"You okay?" He walked closer.

"Fine. Just tired."

"You sure?"

It was a loaded question, and they both knew it. This was a familiar setup for them. All that pent-up tension after a raid or a takedown, all the suppressed energy that wanted release. But the thought of touching another person right now made Tara's skin crawl.

"I'm sure." She turned around and dug for her key card, hoping to hear receding footsteps as he returned to his room. All she heard was rain on the blacktop.

"Tara."

She turned around.

"There was nothing you could have done."

Her stomach tightened as she looked at him standing there in the light of the Coke machine. "Good night," she said, and let herself into her room.

She shut the door and leaned back against it. The room was cold and silent. Wan light from outside seeped through the gap in the curtains, casting a band of gray over the bed and the wall. Tara tipped her head back and stared up at the water-stained ceiling. She felt wet and frozen to her very bones. Her gaze drifted over the dismal space, and she remembered another cheap room and another cheap dresser with a yogurt cup sitting on top of it. Her mind flashed back to a pair of wide, dark eyes.

Where are they? You can tell me. Where are all the girls?

They're gone.

Tara bit her lip. Too late that day and too late now.

Her chest squeezed, a tight fist of panic. She pushed away from the wall and stripped off her windbreaker. It was drenched. Her blazer, too. She pulled off her shoes and her holster, her shirt and her pants and her bra and her panties and her sodden socks. And then she stood naked in the frigid room, engulfed in silence except for the drumming rain and her own chattering teeth.

In the bathroom, she turned on the shower. Before it could heat, she stepped into the stall and stood under the spray as the water went from cold to cool to lukewarm. Her legs quivered. Her stomach roiled. She leaned her forehead against the stall and squeezed her eyes shut as the fist in her chest tightened again. She slid down to the floor, pulling herself into a ball as the spray pummeled her back, but the tremors wouldn't stop. Finally, she reached up and turned the knob. The bathroom went silent, and she huddled in the darkness in a cloud of steam. She wanted to retch. Or cry or punch or scream, but all she could do was clutch her knees to her chest and shiver, and she felt like the girl, the one she'd found beneath the sink, and she knew she *was* that girl, at least sometimes, more often than she could stand to admit. And she felt like her now, small and shaken, without the faintest spark of will left to overcome the dark.

This requires a new best.

Mark was right. And there was nothing she could do besides get up in a few hours and throw herself into the work and try to do what she'd failed to do today. And the day before. And the day before that. And she didn't know whether she had it in her. She felt so alone—all her life she'd felt it, the deep chasm that separated her from other people.

She squeezed her eyes shut against the burn of tears. They came anyway, sliding down her cheeks and chin and neck as she hugged her knees and felt the sobs well up in her throat, great heaving sobs that made her ribs ache as she fought to hold them in.

Something pounded.

She lifted her head and blinked into the darkness. It came again, a persistent thud from the other side of the room.

She closed her eyes again, futilely wishing it away, but it didn't stop. It grew louder as she climbed to her feet and fumbled for a towel. She wrapped it around herself and padded across the carpet.

She stood at the door swiping the wetness from her cheeks, and she knew it didn't matter at all.

"Tara." His voice was muffled.

She pulled the door back, and Liam stepped inside, bringing about five gallons of rainwater with him. He turned on the light, and she flinched.

"Shit," he said, gazing down at her.

She switched off the light, and those big arms came around her, wrapping her in the cold leather of his jacket. She tried to pull away, but he squeezed tighter.

"Hey."

"I want to be alone," she said against his shoulder.

"Bullshit."

Her knee came up fast, and he turned, shielding himself even as his arms trapped her.

"Let me *go*." She pushed against him, but his arms tightened until it wasn't an embrace at all but a hold. "I *mean* it, Liam."

"Just calm down a minute." He loosened his grip a fraction. "Okay?"

She closed her eyes and stood rigid as the cold wet of his jacket saturated her towel. He tucked her head under his chin.

"It's not your fault."

She jerked away from him and punched his shoulder. "Stop *saying* that!" She swung again, but he caught her fist.

"What, you think you're the only one trying, Tara? Win or lose, it's all on you?"

"It isn't a game."

He forced her arm down to her side and pulled her in close again, and the tears were back, mixed with fury now because she could practically feel the pity emanating from him. He was here out of sympathy, and it ticked her off, and she tried to pull away, but he kissed her.

He smelled like rain and wet leather. His clothes were freezing. But his lips were warm, and she kissed him back, wishing she didn't want what he was offering, wishing she didn't *need* it, but she did. He'd called her a liar, and he was right. For once in her life, she didn't want to be alone. She wanted *him*, and the sharp intensity of it scared her. He smelled so good, and she was so tired of feeling alone all the time. She needed the connection with him, however brief, even if it was only about lust or tension or pity. She needed it anyway.

She kissed him deeper, and his arms loosened as if he sensed she was done resisting. His hands slid down to splay across her back, pulling her close, and she felt the cold pressure of his jacket through her thin towel.

She slid her arms around his waist, feeling the warm flannel of his shirt and the hard body beneath. She felt cold to her core, but he was vital and alive, and she wanted to burrow against him and absorb his heat until the shivers went away for good.

He pulled back and looked down at her, breathing hard, and she saw the tense outline of his jaw in the dimness. He caught her hand and pulled her to the bed. The old mattress gave a loud squeak when he tipped her back and hovered over her as he struggled out of his jacket and threw it aside.

And then he was kissing her again, only it didn't feel like kissing but a feverish fusion of mouths and bodies. She twined herself around him and let her hands run over all the warm flannel. The space between them seemed filled with humidity as they kissed and groped, and then he pushed her towel away and she felt a rush of cool air against her skin. He stroked her breast, gazing down at her, then dipped his head down to kiss her with his hot mouth. She wrapped her legs around him and pulled him in. There was something thrilling about being completely bare under him while he was fully dressed, and the cold denim of his jeans rasped against her thighs. His hands glided over her breasts, her hips, her knees, rubbing warmth into everything as she struggled to pull him closer, as close as she possibly could.

He leaned back again, and her fingers worked the buttons of his shirt until her hands could access the firm planes of his torso. His skin was damp—from rain or exertion, she didn't know—and she leaned up to lick the column of his neck. He tasted salty, and she nipped him there. He reared back.

"Hey, now." He clamped her wrists beside her head and smiled down at her in the dimness, and she pushed against the heavy weight pinning her. "Wait."

"No." She arched against him again, and his smile fell away, replaced by a determined look. He dipped his head, and the stubble of his jaw scraped against her sensitive skin as he kissed her and teased her until her body started to throb and she felt the tremors coming.

"Liam." Her hands were trapped, and all she could do was arch against him. "*Liam*."

He pulled back and seemed to read something in her face. He released her hands and tugged the wallet from his jeans, taking out a condom as she hurriedly went to work on his belt.

"Wait," he said tightly.

She heard the rasp of his zipper as she waited, breathless and dizzy. He planted his knee between hers and wrapped his arm around her waist, shifting her back on the bed. She pulled his head down to kiss him as he pushed roughly inside her.

She clutched him as hard as she could, pulling him in closer as he struggled to pull back. He won the battle again and again, but the fight kept going as the tension built. He made a low moan deep in his chest, and she felt a sudden swell of relief because however this had started, all trace of pity was gone now, and what she felt from him was pure male desire as he drove himself into her over and over until his powerful body quivered under her hands. And she felt a rush of excitement knowing that she could push him to the breaking point. She surged against him even harder and felt his control snap, and they both went over the edge together.

He fell against her, crushing her under him. But it was a blissful crushing, and for a moment she lay utterly still, not even breathing.

He pushed himself up on his elbows and gazed down at her, letting a cool draft of air between them.

The bed creaked as he climbed off and the two sides of his shirt fell together, making him look totally clothed as he gazed down at her naked body. He combed his hand through his hair, then turned and stepped into the bathroom.

She lay there, catching her breath and listening to the rain thrumming outside. She gazed up at the ceiling as a chill swept over her skin. The warm oblivion was gone almost as quickly as it had come, and she was once again by herself in a bleak hotel room with the sadness bearing down on her. She closed her eyes and felt the searing guilt and knew nothing would fix it. No distraction was big enough.

Tears welled again, and a lump of frustration lodged in her throat. Would it always be this way? Being a woman and a cop? She tried so hard to be like the men, who could brush off catastrophe by pounding back a few beers or hitting the range or having sex. She could do all those things, and she did, but at the end of it all she still wanted to cry.

She rolled onto her side and listened to the faucet go off. Then he was back again, and she heard him picking up his jacket from the floor. He was leaving now. Which was good. A relief, really, because she didn't want to hash it all out.

She heard a dull *swoosh* as his jacket hit the chair. The sound was followed by a high-pitched clatter and then a low rumble as the heater switched on beneath the window. He stood beside the bed and stripped off his shirt.

She sat up on her elbows. "What are you doing?"

"Getting some heat going." The bed squeaked as he sat down to take off his boots. "It's a damn icebox in here."

She watched him undress, slightly shocked to realize he'd made love to her with his boots on.

Made love. She felt a dangerous flutter in her heart. What the hell was this? She never used words like that, not even in her own head.

His gaze settled on her. She watched him, heart pounding, hoping he didn't share his brother's seeming ability to read minds.

He scooped up her legs and pulled down the covers. He slid into bed beside her, and she felt a pinch in her chest. He was staying. And she wanted him to.

She turned to look at him as he eased onto his side, propping himself on his elbow. He rested his palm on her stomach, and she felt a warm shiver.

"You want to tell me about it?"

She didn't have to ask what he meant. "No."

She shifted her gaze to the ceiling, and the goddamn tears were back. She closed her eyes and fought against the burn, concentrating on the rain outside as she waited for the knot in her chest to loosen. After a few moments she was pretty sure she had control.

She avoided his gaze and rested her hand on his chest. It was beautiful and sculpted, the obvious result of hours and hours of work. She traced a finger over his shoulder and the raised welt on his deltoid. An entry wound. Brannon had one, too. A souvenir from Iraq.

She felt guilty for thinking of someone else while Liam was naked beside her.

"Is this why you took a medical discharge?" She looked at him in the shadows, and his eyes were dark and luminous.

"You've been checking up on me."

She didn't respond. She wanted him to talk so she could hear the low timbre of his voice.

"It was Afghanistan." He folded his arm behind his head and seemed to settle in for the story. "I was on PSD for a visiting congressman. We were ambushed by some local police."

It was years ago. She remembered seeing the event in the news.

"Basically I'm alive because Jeremy was on over-watch that day. He's a crack shot. Never misses."

A chill skittered down her spine. "So Jeremy killed him?"

"Took out both of them, two shots. But not before they got off a few dozen rounds. There were civilians everywhere, lots of injuries." He paused. "It was a bad day."

His tone was solemn, as though it was still hard to think about all these years later. And yet here he was telling her about it, opening up as though . . . as though what?

Tara wasn't good at these kinds of exchanges— pillow talk where people bared their souls. But she'd asked him. So maybe she wanted more from him, more than she dared to admit to herself. She wanted to know about his scars, his fears, what made him tick. She knew some things, but now she was deeply curious.

She looked at his strong profile in the dimness and felt his fingers tracing gently over her arm.

He turned to look at her. He brushed a curl away from her eyes and kissed her forehead. His gaze on her was dark and intent. She could see the concern there, maybe even tenderness, and it sent her mind in wild directions. This wasn't what she'd thought or expected. She didn't have a playbook for this.

And only hours ago he'd been dodging her calls. She'd thought he never wanted to speak to her again, and she'd actually been fine with that.

Or at least she'd told herself she was.

"What?" he asked.

"I thought you were mad at me," she said softly.

He slid his hand around her waist and pulled her close. "I was."

CHAPTER TWENTY-FOUR

Tara bolted upright in bed.

"What is it?" Liam sat up, blinking at her in the darkness. "Tara?"

"Nothing."

He listened. The rain outside had ceased. The motel room was dead quiet.

"It's just a nightmare. Sorry." She swung her legs out of bed. "Go back to sleep."

She grabbed a T-shirt off the chair as she walked to the bathroom. He glanced at the clock. Already 0500.

He got up and snagged his jeans off the floor. They were cold and damp like the rest of the room. The heater had crapped out sometime during the night.

Liam watched her in the bathroom mirror as he zipped up. Her hair was wild. Her eyes looked swollen and pink from crying—either last night or in her sleep or both.

He walked over and propped his shoulder against the doorframe as she rummaged through a makeup bag.

"Sorry." She met his gaze in the mirror. "I'm coming off something at work. It's been a hard time, even before this."

"The child sex ring?"

She looked surprised. "You know about it?"

"Saw something on the news. That must have been bad."

"It was."

Liam looked her over. Standing there in her T-shirt and bare feet, she didn't look the part of a SWAT jock. She shook an aspirin from a bottle and swallowed it down with a handful of water. "They have someone you can talk to about that, don't they?"

She didn't respond.

"Tara?"

"Is that what Marines do?" She took out her toothbrush. "Go running to a shrink whenever it gets bad?"

He folded his arms over his chest. "You know, you're not alone in this. You don't have to be tough all the time."

"Actually, I do." She ran her toothbrush under the faucet. "I'm head of a task force. If I burst into tears at the drop of a hat, it doesn't exactly inspire confidence."

The faucet started coughing and spurting, and the water ran brown.

"Ew!" She jerked her toothbrush away. "Jesus Christ!"

Liam huffed out a sigh. "How much longer you plan to stay in this dump?"

She turned off the faucet. "As long as I need."

"Why don't you stay with me?"

She stared at him in the mirror.

"You want me to—"

"Come stay at my house. Yes."

She turned to look at him. "I can't just shack up with you."

"Why not? This place is a rathole. And the security sucks."

"You're just being protective."

"Right. I'm protective of people who matter to me."

That got her attention. Her jaw dropped slightly, and she had the same deer-in-the-headlights look he'd seen when he tried to give her his gate key. Again she looked scared, but there was something else there, too, and damned if he didn't need to make her admit it.

He stepped closer. "Is this how it's going to be again? I reach out to you and you stare at me?"

Panic flickered in her eyes. "I'm not good at this stuff, Liam."

"What stuff?"

"*This*. Relationships."

He knew the instant she realized what she'd said because her cheeks flushed. He smiled, which only made her look more upset.

"What are you grinning at?"

He cupped her face. "Progress." He kissed her, tangling his fingers in her hair, and he could feel her frustration as she kissed him back. She didn't want to, but she was doing it anyway, and he knew he'd found her Achilles' heel. Sex. Never in his life had he met a woman so physical, and he couldn't get enough of her.

He forced himself to step back before he got carried away. He checked his watch and retrieved his shirt from the floor.

"Where are you going?" she asked as he buttoned up.

"Meeting Jeremy."

Her gaze narrowed. "Why? It's five A.M."

He pulled on his boots. Then he grabbed his Sig from the dresser and tucked it into the back of his jeans. "I'll call you later, after you're done with the autopsy."

"That's not what I asked."

He shrugged into his jacket, then walked over and kissed her one last time. "Be careful today."

"Liam—"

"And don't ask questions you don't really want the answers to."

FIRST LIGHT CAME slowly because of the cloud cover, and when Liam arrived at the designated location it was barely gray. He parked beside the F-250. Jeremy had the tailgate down and was bent over a map.

"What do you got?" Liam asked.

He glanced up. "I did some tracking. Covered about four square miles due east." He tapped the map, and Liam leaned in to look.

It was a detailed topographical rendering of the area with extensive detail about trees. Liam figured the map had come from the timber company that owned the land they were standing on, which abutted Silver Springs Park.

"When was this?" Liam asked.

"I started before dusk, just after we got word of the body. Packed it in about 2200 because of the rain."

That was about the time he'd sent the text asking Liam to meet him here at dawn.

"I figure he likes to watch," Jeremy said.

"He does."

"Found something else. Took me a while to get there last night, but looks like we can cut through."

"Lead the way."

Jeremy checked his handheld GPS, and they set out for a nearby dirt road. A NO TRESPASSING sign was hooked to the gate. They ducked through the barbed-wire fence and headed into the forest.

The air was cold and misty, but the rain had let up. Jeremy had on a lightweight jacket in woodland camo, and he carried his .300 on a leather strap slung over his shoulder. Liam wore a brown canvas jacket and was armed with his Sig plus a Ka-Bar knife. Out of habit, they took care to leave no trace as they moved through the foliage.

Liam scanned the ground for evidence—footprints, food wrappers, signs of recent traffic. The sky was brightening by the minute, and the gray shadows around them were turning to browns and greens.

"Check it out." Liam veered into a stand of trees to examine a small fire pit.

"Think it's him?"

"Don't know. Looks recent, though."

Liam looked but found nothing useful in the charred debris. They resumed their course. As they moved from oaks and hackberries into loblolly pines and long-leafs, the ground underfoot became a carpet of pine needles. Liam felt the grade increase until they reached the top of a ridge.

Then Liam saw it.

"I'll be damned," he muttered. The weathered old wood blended perfectly with the forest.

Except for the right angles.

"Nature doesn't like straight lines," Jeremy said. Liam looked at him and saw the faintest trace of a smile.

"Good find," Liam said, stepping closer to examine the hunting blind. It was a simple platform made of wide slats, accessed by a narrow wooden ladder.

Liam studied the rungs. Any trace of mud or other evidence had washed away in the rain. He climbed the ladder and looked west over the treetops in the direction of Silver Springs Park.

Jeremy handed up a spotting scope. Liam crouched on the platform and checked the view.

"See anything?"

"Yes."

Through the lens, Liam had a clear view of the sign marking the park entrance.

And of a blond newswoman holding a microphone.

Liam skimmed his gaze over the crowd. Several police units had been stationed at the scene to shoo away onlookers, creating the perfect dramatic backdrop for at least six different camera crews.

The UNSUB had been up here, Liam could feel it. He'd watched from this exact vantage point, enjoying the spectacle he'd created. He'd watched the police come and go, the ME's van, the news crews.

Tara.

The UNSUB hated women. He'd killed at least five already, including a prominent politician. Who was next, a female cop? The head of the task force?

Liam's gut clenched. His brother had warned him that this man was escalating, that he'd developed a taste for killing and was feeding off not just the act itself but also the surrounding attention. His first few kills had gone unnoticed by the media. But now, with Catie and then a waitress who had been serving up pancakes to news crews all week, the killer had definitely captured the media's attention. Every reporter who'd set foot in the diner now felt a personal connection to the story.

"He's one sick son of a bitch," Jeremy said.

"Smart, though." Liam lowered the scope.

"And trained."

Liam took a last look around and climbed down off the platform. They trekked back in silence, still combing the ground for any tracks or clues. He was the worst kind of enemy. Armed and agile and operating in his comfort zone.

"Kind of surprised to find a deer blind so close to the park," Jeremy said.

"It wasn't always a park. Some lumber heiress donated the land about ten years ago. Turns out she's a tree hugger, didn't want to log it."

"How do you know?"

"She's still around. Sold me some of my acreage a few years back."

They trudged in silence for a while, with Jeremy checking the GPS every few minutes and Liam deep in thought.

Tara was at the autopsy now. But it would be over soon and she'd be out again, working the case right there in broad daylight, tromping around the crime scenes in plain view of anyone with a scope.

And she wouldn't transfer off the case.

Or steer clear of the woods.

Or do a single damn thing he'd asked her to, including come to stay at his house.

He'd seen the resistance in her eyes this morning, the distrust, and there wasn't a thing he could do about it because it was a part of her, every bit as much as her cool blue eyes. And right then Liam wanted her again. He wanted her lithe body and her strong legs. He wanted her lush mouth that could just as easily tell him off as set him on fire. He wanted her totally, fiercely, and with a possessiveness that shocked him.

For years he'd prided himself on being disciplined and immune to cravings. But Tara had blown all that out of the water. She'd taken over his thoughts, his dreams. She was in his head, and he couldn't get her out. She'd shattered his focus. No woman had ever done that to him before.

Keeping Tara safe had become his core mission. And she wasn't even his client. She wasn't anything at all, except the woman who'd upended his life.

Liam trekked through the forest trying to figure out when it had happened, when fifteen years' worth of training and mental discipline had ceased to matter. He didn't give a shit about his job right now. He didn't give a shit about his obligations or his clients or even his men. Tara was it.

Problem was, she was wary. Skeptical. And she had a chip on her shoulder for reasons he could only guess. Liam understood having a chip—he'd had one, too, but the Marines had mostly beaten it out of him. So her distrust was an obstacle, but it wasn't insurmountable. Over time she'd see that she could trust him, that he didn't break commitments. Eventually, maybe she'd open the door to him—just a crack, just enough for him to get a foothold.

They were alike. Even without knowing everything about her, Liam could sense it. They both had experiences that had hardened them. But there were moments, like last night, when she'd softened around him. She'd let down her guard, and he was clinging to that because it meant he had a chance.

The terrain leveled out as they neared the road.

"You want a camera set up again?" Jeremy asked.

"He's onto it." Liam wasn't sure why he felt sure of that, but he did. "He won't be back here." He stopped and glanced around at the woods, discouraged. "I feel like we know this guy, like this is his backyard."

Jeremy looked at him. "Ours, too."

They moved soundlessly through the trees as Liam refined his plan.

"I want a tight group," Liam said. "You, me, Lopez."

"You want a manhunt."

"We need three men, four maximum. Total radio silence."

A flash of movement through the trees caught Liam's eye.

"You have a tail out here?" He looked at Jeremy.

"Didn't think so."

"One of us did."

Liam ducked through the barbed-wire fence and stepped over to the road, where a light brown cruiser was parked beside his pickup. Ingram and two of his deputies leaned against the grille of the sheriff's SUV.

"Liam Wolfe." Ingram stepped forward and tipped his hat. "Just the man I wanted to see." He smiled slyly. "You're under arrest."

CHAPTER TWENTY-FIVE

M.J. looked around anxiously as she approached the little brick house. She counted three separate BEWARE OF DOG signs hooked to the chain-link fence, but the only barks she heard were coming from the neighbors'.

She knocked on the door, and it was answered by a woman with greasy blond hair and pink, watery eyes.

"Amy Leahy? I'm Special Agent Martinez. We spoke on the phone."

"Come on in. Sorry about the mess."

Her voice was low and nasal, and she pinched a tissue over her nose as she ushered M.J. inside. She wore a gray sweatshirt over pajamas, and her house smelled like Lipton Cup-a-Soup. She led M.J. to the living room, where a tissue box sat on the coffee table beside a purple yearbook. Still no sign of a dog.

"Feeling any better?" M.J. asked.

"No. I was going to go in anyway, but . . ." Her face crumpled, and she looked down at her bare feet.

"Sorry." She sank onto the end of the sofa beside a bunched-up nap blanket. She picked up the TV remote and muted the sound on a news broadcast.

M.J. took a seat on a worn armchair. "Did you know Crystal Marshall?"

She nodded and blew a *honk* into her tissue. "Sorry," she said. "I'm a wreck today. Crystal and me went to school together. She was a year behind, in my brother's grade."

M.J. gave her a sympathetic look, but she couldn't bring herself to say any canned words of condolence. Not with that yearbook sitting there. Instead, she took a notepad from her purse and let Amy have a moment to compose herself.

"I realize this is a bad time," she said, "so I'll try to keep it quick—"

"I don't mind. Really. I want to help."

"You took the call last Monday morning. Let's see . . . five fifty A.M.?"

"That's right." She squared her shoulders and seemed to settle in for the interview. "He didn't give his name."

"He gave his location, though?"

"Yeah, he was very specific. Said he was at Corrine Timber, northwest quadrant, near the capped gas well. Said he'd been walking through the woods with his dog and came across a skull."

"Did you think it was strange to get a call like that? So early, I mean, from someone walking his dog?"

"Not really. We get all kinda calls all the time, day and night." She shrugged. "Anyway, the sheriff said it was probably a poacher, so in that case it makes sense he'd be out early."

M.J. consulted her notes. That assumption was the reason she was here. What if it wasn't a poacher? The profiler who'd briefed the task force said he believed the UNSUB was interested in the investigation, interested enough to insert himself in some way.

Such as calling in an anonymous tip to investigators. Maybe he felt overlooked and wanted to make sure he got credit for every one of his kills.

"I asked did he live in town, but he wouldn't answer," Amy said. "Just repeated the location of the skull and hung up."

M.J. nodded. She'd listened to the tape.

"We traced the call, though," Amy added. "It bounced off the cell tower right there near the Corrine Timber field office. The address popped up there on my screen. There's nothing much out that way, you know. Nothing at all, really, but a bunch of woods. So either he was standing right near the timber office with his cell phone or he was right there in it."

"That's what we thought, too. We had some of our tech people take a look at the call." M.J. didn't mention that they'd traced not only the call but the number itself. The call had come from a no-contract phone, a throwaway.

And that was another red flag. What was a hunter doing walking around with a burner phone? Sure, it was possible, but M.J. thought it seemed odd.

"Have you thought about asking their landsman there in the timber office?" Amy said. "Maybe he saw something. He might not have been there that early, but you could ask."

"Good idea." M.J. jotted some notes. She already had plans to talk to him.

Amy cast a glance at the TV, where they were running camera footage of Silver Springs Park on an endless loop.

M.J. cleared her throat to pull Amy's attention back. "You probably get hundreds of calls a day, so this may sound like a strange question, but . . . any chance you recognized the voice?"

She brightened. "Actually, I do sometimes. We're not that big a county. And Dunn's Landing is so small, so . . . yeah, sometimes I know people." Her brow furrowed. "You want to know if I recognized him?"

"That's what I was wondering, yeah."

"I didn't. I mean, I would have told the sheriff that." The crease in her brow deepened. "You don't think it's *him*, do you? The killer?" She twisted the tissue in her hands. "Oh, Lord. You do, don't you? You think he was the one who called in those bones?"

"We're just tying up loose ends, really. The sheriff's probably right about it being a poacher, but I just thought I'd ask."

Amy darted a look at the door, as if someone might come bursting in, and M.J. regretted coming. Clearly, she was freaking this girl out.

But if there was even a chance she knew something, it was worth the visit. M.J. couldn't stop thinking about the profiler, about how certain he'd been that their UNSUB would at some point find a way to involve himself because it would give him some sort of thrill.

"Are you sure you don't remember anything else about the call? Maybe a background noise or any kind of detail about his voice?"

Amy shook her head, looking flat-out scared now.

M.J. flipped shut her notebook. "Well, thanks for your time. I'm sorry to bother you."

"It's no bother. I've just been stuck here nursing this cold and watching the news."

M.J. glanced at the TV screen, where the footage had shifted to a live report. She read the headline crawling across the bottom of the screen, and her heart skipped a beat.

TARA COMBED THROUGH Liam's files, getting more and more bleary-eyed with each passing minute. Her head throbbed, and it wasn't just the computer work. It was the anxiety, the steadily mounting pressure.

The autopsy.

She closed her eyes and tried to shake it off. She couldn't think about it right now or it would paralyze her. She took a deep breath and refocused her attention on the information before her, looking for that crucial clue. More than three hundred men had been through Liam's training camps. Tara had culled through almost half of them but still had a long way to go. And she still hadn't found the psych evaluations. Did he keep them on a different system, or had someone deleted them? Tara had put in a call to their tech expert earlier, but he hadn't yet finished with the thumb drives.

She glanced at her phone. It was after four. What was Liam up to all day that he'd been so evasive about? And why hadn't he called? She looked at her phone again and felt a wave of apprehension. Followed by a wave of disgust.

Would this be the new normal if they started up a relationship?

He seemed to think they were already in one. She thought of the amused look on his face this morning and felt a fresh onslaught of nerves. Thoroughly annoyed with herself now, she slid her phone under a file and focused back on the screen.

Brannon walked in and dropped a fast-food bag on the table. "Hungry?"

"No, thanks."

He sank into a chair. "I finished with the ViCAP search," he said, pulling out a sandwich. "You know how I told you I had hundreds of results for strangulation homicides? I've narrowed it down to two. In both cases the bodies were dumped near military bases."

Tara leaned back in her chair. "Sounds interesting."

"One is a ligature strangulation and the body was recovered just outside Camp Pendleton in California."

"That's a Marine base," she said. A lot of Liam's men had been through there. "What's the year?"

"Oh-two."

"Hmm."

"Second case is more recent." He picked up his drink and took a slurp. "Two thousand seven. Manual, no ligature. Victim was a stripper, found in a wooded park not far from Fort Benning."

"That's Army. You used to be stationed there, didn't you?"

"The place is huge. Practically everyone in the Army's been through there at some point. But what really caught my eye is the killer used a knife. She had defensive wounds on one of her hands."

"Any particular details—"

"Not on the weapon. And no DNA recovered, from the looks of it. But I've got a call in to the lead detective in Georgia. This case has been on ice for a while, but I'm hoping he has a list of suspects somewhere."

"That's a good lead."

"I know." He chomped into his sandwich and glanced around. "Where's M.J.?"

"Out on an interview."

"What about Jason?"

"He's supposed to be picking up surveillance tapes."

As for Ingram, Tara didn't know. He'd been conspicuously absent from Crystal Marshall's autopsy. It was possible he hadn't wanted to observe because he knew the victim, but he should have at least sent a deputy.

Tara returned her attention to her computer. She still had a hundred names to go.

"That looks fun," Brannon said around a mouthful of food. "You need a hand?"

"I got it."

"That the spreadsheet from before? You're obsessed with that."

She looked at him. "Lot of potential leads here."

"If you buy into the profile."

"You don't?"

He shrugged. "Maybe. I prefer physical evidence."

"Same with me," she said. "Such as the murder weapon, which happens to be a Full Black knife with a seven-inch blade. Wolfe Security took a shipment of those two years ago. And a shard of glass recovered from Catalina Reyes matches the optical glass from some of the rifle scopes Wolfe Security uses. How's that for physical evidence?"

"Okay, fine. I hear you." He slid his chair closer. "Sure you don't want a hand?"

She started to refuse him but then remembered Mark.

You need all the help you can get from anywhere you can get it, so lose the pride.

Tara had never been good at delegating, but she needed to learn. There was more to leadership than bringing people doughnuts.

"Here." She scooted her chair aside to make room for Brannon's. "This is a database of trainees. They all went through one or more of the boot camps at Liam Wolfe's ranch, and many later applied to work for him. Right now I'm going through the names and anything about their background that jumps out. If something flags my attention I click on the name and it links to the biographical info and a photo. That's where you can get date of birth, physical stats, detailed employment history."

"Lot of info for a bunch of trainees," he said.

"I know. The camps are sort of a proving ground for job applicants. They get a hundred applicants for every spot so they use this as a way to pare things down."

"Separate the men from the boys, I get it," Brannon said. "Is there any way to look up military service, see if anyone was at Fort Benning that year I mentioned?"

"Not a bad idea." She clicked on the cell for military experience. "It lists branch of service. You could at least narrow it down to Army."

"Here, let me try."

Tara's phone chimed, and she grabbed it, letting Brannon take over at the computer.

"Are you watching this?" M.J. asked, and Tara caught the urgency in her voice.

"Watching what?"

"Turn on a TV."

"I don't have one. I'm in the basement." Tara glanced around. "Why?"

"Pull up a local news Web site. Anything. Everyone's running it."

Tara's pulse picked up as she moved to her laptop and entered one of the Houston TV stations. Beneath the station's logo was a shot of Sheriff Ingram standing behind a podium.

"God damn it." Tara clicked the video. "Where is he?"

"Silver Springs, I think. He called a joint news conference with the police chief."

". . . investigation is ongoing," Ingram was telling reporters.

"Sheriff, has he been charged with a crime?" came a voice from the audience.

"Has *who* been charged?" Tara asked, dismayed.

"He's being held for questioning," Ingram said.

"Sheriff, has Mr. Wolfe confessed to the murders?"

Tara's blood ran cold as she stared at the screen.

"No comment," Ingram stated. "Like I said, this is an ongoing investigation."

"He arrested *Liam*? When the hell did this happen?"

"I'm trying to find out," M.J. said. "I think the arrest was this morning."

"On what charges?" She glanced at Brannon, but he seemed as confused as she was.

"Criminal trespass," M.J. said. "At least, that's what Jason told me. I haven't confirmed it yet."

"That's a misdemeanor! He's making it sound like they're charging him with murder."

"I know," M.J. said.

"This is a disaster." Tara stood up and looked around helplessly. Her gaze settled on the grisly crime-scene photos taped to the case board. She pressed her hand to her forehead. "Does Ingram even realize what he's doing? He's trashing a man's reputation just to have an excuse to stand in front of a camera."

"I know, it's bad," M.J. said.

Bad didn't even begin to describe it. Tara felt like her head was going to explode. "Where are you?" she asked M.J.

"In my car. I'm following up on that anonymous phone call. The dispatcher tells me it came from Corrine Timber's field office, so I'm headed over there to interview the property manager, Oscar Valero."

Tara looked at Brannon, who was now on his phone. He glanced at her and took the call into the hallway.

"Need me to come in?" M.J. asked. "I could help with damage control."

"No, I'll handle it."

"Okay, I'll call you if I get anything."

Tara clicked off and stared at the phone in her hand. She felt sick to her stomach. She had to get control of this. She couldn't have a rogue sheriff out there calling press conferences. And she couldn't have the time and resources of his entire department being wasted on publicity stunts.

And what about Liam? The professional reputation he'd spent years building was being dragged through the mud. Even if they released him without charges, the damage was done.

Tara's gaze landed on the computer where Brannon had been scrolling through files.

The picture on the screen made her breath catch.

The man in the photo stood beside a tree, holding a rifle. He wore an Army-green T-shirt that stretched over bulging muscles, and his face was covered in green greasepaint right up to his hairline. He looked like the Incredible Hulk, and Tara remembered Corey Bower in his pajamas playing with his action figures.

I saw the Hulk down by the creek once . . .

An unfiltered observation from a little boy. And Tara had dismissed it.

She sank into the chair, her heart pounding as she studied the man's face, his build, his military haircut.

"Holy shit," she breathed.

Even with the greasepaint, she recognized his eyes.

M.J. PULLED UP the driveway searching for the white Toyota pickup registered to Oscar Valero, fifty-six, of Dunn's Landing. As she rolled through the gate, she spotted the vehicle parked beside the double-wide trailer that Corrine Timber used as a field office.

She parked and got out, glancing around. The woods were quiet, no whine of a chain saw or grumble of a truck engine or even the faint tap of a wood-pecker to break the silence. She picked her way across the muddy parking area and mounted the wooden steps to knock on the door.

No answer.

She looked through the window. A fluorescent light glowed over a work station in back. She tried the door, but it was locked. Again she knocked.

"Mr. Valero?"

Nothing.

M.J. checked her watch and blew out a sigh as she scanned the area. The sound of distant voices made her turn around. Across the firebreak she spotted a shed.

"Mr. Valero?"

She went down the steps and crossed the muddy road. The shed was prefab aluminum, like the trailer, but forest green instead of white. A sign beside the door warned away trespassers: CYPRESS COUNTY FIRE DEPT AUTHORIZED PERSONNEL ONLY.

The noise came again, definitely voices. M.J. knocked on the door, then looked through a grimy windowpane. It was a two-room storage building crammed with equipment—chain saws, axes, a four-wheel ATV with a missing back tire. A loud squawk drew her attention to a table in the corner where someone had left a handheld radio.

She knocked again. "Señor Valero?"

She tried the door, but it was locked. She cupped her hand against the dirty glass again and peered inside. In the back room were coiled fire hoses, a chair, a cot stacked with boxes. She glanced at the chattering radio again. Beside it was something blue and rectangular. She shifted against the glass for a better angle. It was a phone case.

A queasy feeling settled in her stomach. It was Tara's lost phone case, right there on the table. It had been missing since the night someone shot at her.

M.J.'s pulse started to thrum. She scanned the room again, picking up details she hadn't noticed at first glance—the fast-food wrappers, the muddy footprints, the chunky plastic ashtray filled with cigarette butts. Someone had been here recently, and for an extended period of time.

The sound of an engine had her whirling around. As the noise grew louder, she glanced across the road, suddenly panicked for reasons she couldn't pinpoint.

Yes, she could.

She'd stumbled across someone's hideout, and she was about to get caught.

She darted a look at her car, but it was by the trailer on the other side of the firebreak, at least thirty yards away. The engine noise was close now as she ducked around the side of the building and pulled out her Glock. She clutched it in her hand.

It could be nothing, maybe Oscar Valero back from an errand down the logging road.

She listened, heart pounding, thinking of the phone case and the radio and the muddy footprints. Valero didn't fit the profile. He wasn't their UNSUB.

A black pickup rolled to a halt just beside the shed. Flat black paint, no hubcaps. M.J. couldn't see the cab.

She held her breath. The door squeaked open, slammed shut. Heavy footsteps across the grass. She gripped her gun. Sweat beaded at her temples as she tried to decide what to do. Fight or flight, a simple decision. But it wasn't simple at all. She didn't know whether he was armed or even whether he was alone.

The lock rattled. M.J. stood there, pulse racing, as he rummaged around the shed. A low curse. Something clattered to the ground.

Then silence.

She waited, holding her breath. Had he spotted her car? But it was tucked behind the trailer. Had she left footprints by the door or a smudge on the window?

More rummaging. The door opened again, closed. A metallic *click* as he secured the padlock. Then a high-pitched *squeak* as the truck door opened and shut.

M.J. flattened herself back against the building, gun ready. The engine grumbled to life again. She watched the truck bed as the vehicle pulled away. She stood still until the engine noise faded into the woods and all that remained was an eerie silence.

She let out a breath. Slowly, cautiously, she eased to the edge of the building and looked around the corner.

Gone.

M.J. dashed across the firebreak and back to her car. She slipped on a patch of mud and caught herself on the bumper just before she could take a header into the muck. She jerked the door open and reached for her phone charging in the cup holder. With a trembling hand, she dialed Tara's number.

A blinding burst of pain as something smashed into her temple. She dropped to her knees and screamed, but the sound was cut off as a giant arm yanked back against her windpipe and hauled her to her feet. Another stifled scream as her arm was twisted violently behind her and her gun was ripped from her grasp.

"Fucking bitch." The voice in her ear was a low growl. "You think you're fucking smarter than me?"

Pain bolted up her arm, her shoulder, her neck. She gasped for air. Something hard dug into her back as she tried to breathe, to yell, to see past the spots dancing before her eyes.

"Fucking whore—"

She kicked back, a frantic jab at his kneecap. A sharp howl. His grip loosened. M.J. dropped to her knees and lunged away from him, landing on her face in the mud. She scrambled to her feet and ran.

CHAPTER TWENTY-SIX

Jeremy rolled to a stop in the alley behind the court-house just long enough for Liam to get in.

"Your phone's in the console," Jeremy said. "And there's a mob of reporters out front, so you might want to duck."

"They can fuck off," Liam said, retrieving his phone. He'd missed half a dozen calls.

Jeremy turned onto Main Street and handed him a printed list. "Second one from the bottom," he said.

Liam skimmed the list to the second-to-last name. "Shit." He looked up. "Did you call Tara?"

"No answer."

Liam's thumb was on her number when his phone buzzed with a call.

"It's the fire chief, Alex Sears," Tara said. "I can't prove it, but everything fits."

Her voice sounded excited and choppy, like she was on the move.

"He spent five years in the Army," she rushed on.

"Three tours in Afghanistan. Took a discharge six years ago and became a firefighter. He went through one of your training camps and applied for a job with Wolfe Security. You rejected him a year ago."

Liam's brain was spinning as the elements fell into place. Alex Sears, Army veteran turned firefighter. He'd come through training three cycles ago. Liam recalled a talented shooter with mediocre PT scores and an attitude problem.

"Liam? Are you there?"

"He knew Catalina," he said, thinking aloud. "He met her when the homemade bomb was thrown at her house. Have you told the task force yet?"

"No way. I don't know who his friends are. I'm keeping the locals out of it while I nail this down. But listen, that's not why I called. I need Jeremy's phone number. I can't reach M.J."

Liam looked at Jeremy. "You heard from M.J.?"

He frowned. "No, why?"

"Jeremy hasn't talked to her."

"She's not answering her phone, which is totally out of character. I've been calling and texting. I—"

"You need to have emergency services ping her cell. They'll be able to locate it with GPS unless the battery's been removed or destroyed for some reason."

"I did all that! Nothing. It's totally dead. Liam, I'm getting worried."

He could tell by her voice that she was beyond worried. "Where's her last known location?"

"She was on her way to Corrine Timber."

"What's at Corrine Timber?" He looked at Jeremy, who took the information aboard and stepped on the gas.

"She was interviewing the property manager. Oscar Somebody."

"Listen to me, Tara. You're dead on about Alex Sears. I just got a customer list from my contact at Full Black. They shipped a custom-made tactical knife, camo green, to Sears's Silver Springs address two years ago."

"Why didn't you tell me?" Her voice was shrill.

"I've been in the damn jail all day! I just got this. Tara, Sears knows this area inside out. He can slip through our fingers in a heartbeat. We need to find out where he is without tipping him off that we're looking for him."

"That's not easy! He's got contacts everywhere. And he's probably monitoring the police frequency."

"Call backup from your office."

"I will, but they're thirty minutes away, minimum, and she's missing *now*. I—"

"Jeremy and I are en route to Corrine Timber. Meet us at the turnoff."

"I'm already on my way."

"Wait for me."

"Not happening."

"Tara—"

"I'm almost there and you're where? Cypress?"

"I'm on the highway."

"What if he has her *now*? I can't wait, Liam."

"God damn it! I can't protect you if you won't god-damn listen to me!"

"It's not your job to protect me."

Yes. Yes, it was. At this moment, it was the one job that mattered more than anything in his whole life. He gripped the phone and tried to get a grip on his emotions. "Tara. Think this through. You need to wait for backup. You can't go after her alone." But as he said the words, he knew she'd see the double standard—she had a radar for it. He was asking her to refrain from doing something he'd do without hesitation if one of his men needed him.

"Tara?"

"Liam, I have to."

M.J.'S THROAT WAS on fire.

She blinked into the darkness and felt the flames sweeping up and down her esophagus. She tried to swallow and would have cried out at the pain, but her tongue was thick and swollen, and her lips wouldn't move.

She couldn't see. The blackness around her seemed to hum, and she was on a hard floor. Her head throbbed. Her brain felt fuzzy. Had she been drugged or just deprived of oxygen? Her body pitched sideways. White-hot pain zinged up her arm, and a realization flashed through her mind.

She was in a trunk. Using her uninjured arm, she groped in the darkness. The walls around her were hard metal. She moved her legs and gradually realized it wasn't a trunk but a truck bed, something with a lid.

Blurry snippets came into focus. Black truck bed. Flat black paint. Murdered out.

You're with him, an inner voice told her. *He's taking you . . . somewhere.*

The floor pitched again. She rolled sideways, and the fiery bolt of pain brought tears to her eyes.

She was on a bumpy road. He was taking her somewhere deep in the woods.

The horror of that fact seeped in as she explored the metal box. She groped for a latch, a weapon, a tool—anything to help her—but her fingers touched only hard, vibrating metal.

Fear churned in her stomach as she thought about what the groping meant, what it really told her. Bits of memory came back of how he'd choked her and choked her until she felt like she was drowning. She'd blacked out. And now the fear inside her turned to panic as she realized why he'd left her hands free.

He thinks you're dead, the inner voice told her. *And now he's going to cut you.*

TARA SPED DOWN the bumpy road and whipped into the parking lot of Corrine Timber. The sight of M.J.'s car beside the double-wide trailer sent her pulse into overdrive.

She parked and jumped out. "M.J.?" She was nowhere in sight. Tara slid her gun from her holster as she circled the car. A phone charger was plugged into the dash but no phone.

"M.J.?" she called again, scanning the surrounding woods. She hurried up the steps to the office, hoping the white pickup parked out front meant someone was there.

No one answered.

"Shit!"

She tried the door. Locked. Not a sound from the office or the forest or anywhere.

Tara rushed down the stairs and noticed the grooves in the mud near M.J.'s car, as if someone had slipped.

Blood on the ground. Tara's heart skittered.

She crouched down to confirm. Only a few small droplets, but it was definitely blood right there beside the door.

She spied more droplets several feet away. And a few more. Icy dread filled her stomach as she followed the blood trail until it disappeared in the grass beside the firebreak where fresh tracks had been made in the mud.

She whipped out her phone and texted Liam. Then she texted Brannon. She knew both would get here as quickly as they could. And she knew both would tell her to wait.

She eyed the heavy-duty gate blocking the dirt road. Her SUV could probably plow through it, but there was a log blocking the road. She would bet it wasn't there by accident.

Tara gripped her weapon and scanned the woods around her. Dark, quiet. Full of shadows and secrets.

Her phone buzzed with a text from Brannon: ETA 15 MIN.

Fifteen minutes.

No time at all.

But to M.J. maybe an eternity.

Tara ducked through the gate.

PANIC SET IN as M.J. felt around in the darkness. She couldn't fight it. She bumped along in the hard metal box and searched for the slightest object that would give her hope, but her hands came up empty.

She had no weapon.

Her right arm was useless.

She probably couldn't even scream effectively—her throat felt like she'd swallowed a bottle of Drano.

The tears started to come, making her shake and gasp and hyperventilate. She tried to calm herself, tried saying a prayer over and over. But then the words jumbled together and all she could think of was the knife.

And what could she do? She didn't even have her gun.

It's your service weapon, and it could save your life.

She thought of Jeremy and wished desperately for her pistol.

But wishing wouldn't help her.

Another bump and she rolled to the side, jostling her arm and sending a spear of pain through her body. By the sticky puddle beneath her, she knew she was bleeding, probably from the cut on her mouth. She ran her tongue over it. Her arm was on fire, maybe broken. She had to think.

What did she have?

No gun. No tool. No weapon.

She had her hands free.

And her legs.

He thinks you're dead. And now he's going to cut you.

The panic was back again, but this time she fought it. She ignored the last part and focused on the first: *He thinks you're dead.*

She had the element of surprise. It was the only weapon she had.

When he dragged her from the truck, she had to play dead. She couldn't be crying or shaking or sniveling with fear. She had to surprise him and disable him somehow and get away.

Right.

It was impossible. He was armed and probably crazy, and he outweighed her by at least a hundred pounds. It would never work. She needed a better plan.

The humming changed pitch, and the truck rolled to a stop.

CHAPTER TWENTY-SEVEN

Liam cursed and smacked his fist against the door as he read Tara's message.

"What?" Jeremy asked.

"A blood trail."

"Where?"

"Near M.J.'s car. And tire tracks leading into the woods."

Liam pulled up a satellite map on his phone. He scanned the area, analyzing roads and firebreaks and exfil routes. They were five minutes away thanks to Jeremy's driving, but still Tara had rushed ahead.

Jeremy swerved onto the shoulder and skidded to a halt. "I'm going in."

"You're going to drop down on him?"

"Yes." He hopped out of the truck and grabbed his rifle from the back of the cab, then a box of ammo. "He won't leave the way he came, which means he'll exit west or south."

Liam slid over the console and into the driver's seat. "Or east if he's on foot."

"He won't be." Jeremy was right. He'd need transportation if he planned to escape. Jeremy slung the rifle over his shoulder. "You find anything, text me the coordinates."

Liam shoved the truck into gear. "Careful what you shoot."

M.J. LAY STILL. Her throat burned and her arm throbbed and her heart was pounding so hard she thought it might burst right out of her chest. But she didn't move. She held her breath and waited as he shifted around in the front of the truck.

A soft *thunk* of the glove box. M.J.'s blood ran cold. Was he getting a knife? A gun? She wanted to kick or scream at the top of her lungs, but instead she lay completely still.

A loud *screech*. Then the door slammed, rocking the truck and jarring her arm. She bit her tongue to keep from yelping.

Footsteps.

M.J. held her breath. She visualized her attacker, pictured his hands, his weapons. She pictured her strike. It would have to be fast and accurate. She'd only get one chance. One.

God, help me.

Another sound, loud and metallic, at the back of the truck. The lid lifted. Cold air wafted over her and she struggled not to flinch or even move her eyelids.

Her heart hammered. She held her breath. *Wait, wait, wait.*

He clamped a hand around her ankle and dragged her across the metal, sending pain shooting up her arm.

With every ounce of power she had, she kicked. Her boot connected with something soft, she hoped his groin.

He made a low noise and doubled over. She slid off the tailgate, landing hard on her butt, then kicking and punching as she scrambled away. He was on his side, clutching himself and spewing curses as he rolled to his knees.

She staggered to her feet and sprinted for the trees.

DARKNESS WAS FALLING fast as Tara ran along the road. She stayed as close as possible to the tree cover, trying to penetrate the gloom of the forest as she moved between the stands of pines. She was exposed out here. She knew it. She tried to keep low, moving swiftly as she followed the curving road.

Her mind raced. She'd come up with three scenarios, all bad.

There had been a struggle at the car. Had M.J. made a run for it? Had she been subdued and abducted? Had she been strangled and hauled into the woods?

Tara's stomach knotted as she thought through each possibility. Alex Sears had a cop now, whether by accident or design. Tara took it as a sign of desperation. She'd seen many desperate people through her SWAT work, and they were the most dangerous kind because they had nothing to lose.

He had to know the net was closing. He had to know killing a cop would send every law-enforcement officer in the state after him like the hounds of hell.

Did he care? Would butchering a woman with a badge be his grand finale before he offed himself? Or did he plan to slip away? He was elusive—and seemed to take pride in that. Maybe he believed he could escape to bask in the glow of what he'd done or to do it again.

Tara looked up at the slate-gray sky, which seemed to be darkening with every minute. She looked at the forest, still and ominous all around her.

All at once she understood. He was about control. He was playing God with these women, taking their lives and their bodies, too. And then disappearing into the woods like mist. He was the ultimate controller. A force of nature.

He was God, or at least he thought he was. A wrathful, hateful God who meted out punishment.

What sort of twisted past must he have? What sort of childhood wounds?

Tara's chest tightened with anger. She didn't give a shit. She had wounds, too, but she hadn't let them make her into a monster.

She heard a noise and stopped. She glanced around, listening, but the forest was dead quiet.

She started moving again, picking up the pace now as she scanned for any sign of movement, but there was nothing but trees and bushes and ever-darkening shadows.

She halted again.

A noise. Something metal?

She darted to the cover of a pine and looked around. No person, no vehicle. But she'd definitely heard something. She moved in the direction of the sound.

A white light flickered, deep in the thicket.

She ducked low and looked around, then darted for another tree. She could make out a beam of light now . . . two beams.

Headlights.

She took a quick look around, assessing and analyzing. She crouched low and pulled out her phone, then checked her GPS coordinates and sent them to Liam.

Another visual sweep. Staying as low as she could, she moved closer to the truck. It was hard to make out in the shadows, and the glare of the headlights messed with her perception, but it was definitely a pickup. Black, from the looks of it. As she crept closer, she took in the details: engine off, headlights on. A muffled *ding-ding-ding* told her the key had been left inside.

She picked her steps carefully, hyperalert for any movement around her as she eased to the next tree. And the next. And the next, until she was within pistol range. She slipped around the back . . .

The truck bed was empty.

She moved closer, clutching her weapon in both hands. Her gaze swept over the darkening forest, and she knew he might be watching her at this very moment, lining her up in his sights.

She pressed her back against a tree trunk and eased

around until she had a view of the driver's-side door. It was open, but she saw no one inside.

M.J., where the hell are you?

Tara wanted to scream her name. But stealth might be her only advantage here.

She went absolutely still and listened.

In the woods to her right . . . rustling? She couldn't tell. She strained to hear. All was quiet except for that faint *ding-ding-ding*.

She crept up to the truck, gripping her Glock. She paused to detect any sign of life. Then she moved slowly toward the truck bed.

The lid was propped up with a plastic arm. The tailgate hung open. Tara's stomach clenched as she saw the smears of blood.

A noise close by.

She lunged for a tree. Bark exploded beside her, sending splinters into her cheek as she dropped to the ground. She dived behind the trunk, clutching her gun.

Her ears rang. Her heart thundered. That had been close, forty feet max. She was within range. She had to answer the shot before he took aim at her again or fled into the forest.

Or would he make a run for the truck?

She gripped her weapon and tried to think over the ringing in her ears.

The truck. He needed it. His keys were inside.

She knelt low and waited.

LIAM RAN TOWARD the gunshot, Sig in hand. Four hundred yards out, maybe five. Fear pounded through him as he dodged through trees and ducked under branches, no longer following the road.

It had been a pistol shot but not a Glock, which meant it hadn't come from M.J. or Tara. Liam raced through the forest, hurdling logs and fallen limbs.

In the far, far distance he saw a flicker of light.

M.J. CROUCHED BESIDE the rotten log with her arm cradled against her stomach. She'd heard the shot. It had been far away but not far enough, and now she tried to make herself small, invisible. Her best chance was to hide. She knew it instinctively. She'd managed to evade him for now, but it was getting dark, and blindly crashing through the woods would give away her location in no time.

She hunkered down and looked at her arm. It was bent like a banana. A wave of nausea hit her every time she looked at it, so instead she focused on her surroundings.

She was in the shadows, hidden. Her only weapon was a sharp rock in her left hand.

She stayed silent, as silent as she could with her heart frantically thumping and every one of her limbs shaking. She leaned back against the log and tried to calm herself, tried to talk herself into the idea that she was going to be okay.

Even though she knew he was out there right now, hunting her down like a wounded animal. He was searching, combing, probably more determined than ever to finish her off.

Snick.

She froze. She went totally still, not even blinking an eye.

Something was behind her. She could hear it. Soft, slow footsteps creeping nearer.

She sucked in air, held it in. She was trembling with every cell of her body.

Slowly, the footsteps moved closer. She gripped the rock in her hand, gripped it so hard the edges cut into her skin. Blood pooled in her palm.

Closer.

Closer.

Her thighs quivered, and she thought she might lose her balance and fall over. Another footstep behind her, even closer now. She sucked in a breath. A hiccup escaped.

Silence.

She clutched the rock. He'd stopped moving. He'd heard her.

Her heart hammered. She held her breath. Without moving her head, she shifted her gaze right as a figure emerged from the trees. A giant man holding a rifle.

Jeremy.

She gave a startled yelp and tipped to the side, falling against the log. The rock slipped from her fingers.

He rushed forward and dropped to his knees beside her.

"Oh, my God," she rasped.

"Are you okay?"

She could hardly see his face in the dimness, but his voice was like a warm blanket wrapping around her. She reached for his arm, and the solid heat of him made her want to cry.

"It's Alex Sears," she croaked.

"I know." He carefully pulled her arm from her side. "It's fractured." He looked at her. "What else? Your lip's bleeding."

"I bit my tongue."

Her throat burned and her voice didn't even sound like hers, but the relief was so intense she didn't care.

Jeremy pulled out his phone and sent a text message.

"Who are you—"

"Liam."

"He's here?"

He wrapped his arm around her waist. "Can you stand?"

"Jeremy, Sears is out here. I heard a gunshot."

"I know. Can you stand?"

She nodded, and he helped her to her feet. Her legs felt wobbly, but he took most of her weight.

From deep in the woods, the pop of gunfire.

TARA TOOK THE shot, but it wasn't like in the movies. He hadn't collapsed to the ground or fallen over dead. He'd grabbed his arm and lurched into the brush.

She crouched beside a tree, paralyzed with indecision and fear. Should she follow or not? Was it a lethal shot? A flesh wound? The thought of him escaping into the woods again made her rise to her feet.

She took off following in the direction he'd gone and soon found herself surrounded by shadows. Branches lashed at her cheeks as she plowed through, looking and listening for any sign of him. Her toe caught a root and she stumbled.

A tremendous weight slammed down on her. Her face hit the dirt and the air rushed from her lungs. She threw an elbow and managed to flip onto her back. She brought up her Glock, but a stunning blow blocked her arm and sent her gun flying.

She reached up, frantically clawing for his eyes as his hand closed around her throat. She scratched at his face, his neck, but his arms were longer, and he had the advantage. She clawed and fought, struggling for air. Amid the pain and panic, she realized he was fighting one-handed. His right arm hung limp at his side, so her shot must have hit something important, maybe an elbow.

She jabbed a fist at his injury and heard a pained grunt. His hand squeezed tighter around her neck, and her head started to swim as she battled for air. She felt like she was sinking, going under. Her vision tunneled, and all the grays and shadows blurred together. She felt her arms weakening, her legs. She tried to buck him off, but he was too damn heavy and she couldn't *breathe*.

She made a swipe at his injured elbow, but the blow had no power behind it, and her vision dimmed. She was suddenly filled with a blinding outrage that she was losing to him, that he controlled her, even injured, and he was going to win. Fury surged through her.

She remembered the knife. He must have it with him. She flailed her hand around, fumbling for his sheath. His weight shifted as her fingers closed around something hard. With all her might, she jerked it from the sheath at his side and jabbed it, but he reared back. She jabbed again, connecting, and he made an animal-like grunt as he rolled off of her.

She scrambled to her feet and charged him, falling on him with the knife, stabbing and stabbing, but he caught her around the waist and tackled her to the ground under him.

I'm dead now. I should have run.

He tried to pry the knife from her fingers, but she gripped it fiercely. It was her only chance. His knees were on her chest now, smashing her lungs and pressing out her air. With a frantic, smothered screech, she jerked her hand free and plunged the blade into his thigh.

A deafening *bang*.

He tipped forward, crashing down on her like a giant tree. She sucked in air and coughed and tried to move beneath him, but he was too heavy and she didn't have the strength. She took a deep breath and heaved him off of her and onto his side.

She scrambled away from him and stumbled to her feet. She choked and wheezed, and her lungs burned from the shock of being filled finally. She glanced around, desperately looking for her gun in the near-darkness. It couldn't have gone far.

She spied it at the base of a tree and snatched it up. Her arms felt like noodles, but she managed to aim her pistol at the lump on the ground.

He lay on his side, eyes open and lifeless. His throat was a gaping exit wound, and Tara stared down at him, shaking and gasping. He was dead. *Dead.* But she kept her gun pointed at him as she backed away.

"Tara!"

She turned toward the voice. She opened her mouth to speak, but all that came out was a strangled rasp.

And then Liam was there, grabbing her arm and hauling her behind a tree. He dropped to a knee beside the body and quickly confirmed his kill shot. Then he touched the hilt of the knife. "You stabbed him?" He looked up at her, and she nodded numbly.

"Where's M.J.?" she rasped.

He stood up and pulled her into his arms. "Jeremy has her. She's safe."

"But—"

"She's injured but safe." His arms wrapped around her, and she rested her head against the wall of his chest. Even through his jacket she could feel his body vibrating with adrenaline as he squeezed her hard. "You scared me."

She slid her arm around him and gripped his jacket with her free hand. In her other hand she clutched her gun in a death grip.

She heard the faint wail of sirens in the distance. She pulled away from Liam and looked around.

How deep in the woods were they? She had no idea. The distant *whump-whump* of a helicopter made them tip their faces to the sky.

"My backup," she said.

Liam shook his head. "Just in time."

CHAPTER TWENTY-EIGHT

Tara stepped out of the FBI building into the cold night air. The temperature had plummeted while she'd been inside, and the wind had picked up. She gazed out over the parking lot in search of a black Silverado.

Brannon walked up beside her. "M.J.'s at County General getting her arm set."

"I know. I talked to her."

The doors behind them opened, and Ingram stepped out. The sheriff looked tired, shell-shocked. His gaze landed on Tara as he nestled his hat on his head.

"What's the update on Sears?" Brannon asked him.

He cast a glance at the visitors' lot, as if longing for his truck, and Tara knew he'd like nothing more than to dodge this conversation. He reluctantly stepped over.

"I tracked down his wife. She's living at her mother's." Ingram rubbed his chin. "Turns out she filed for divorce a year ago. The house was in foreclosure. He was knee-deep in unpaid bills."

A year ago. Maybe his wife leaving him was the trigger Mark had said they'd find. But who knew? He could have started before that. The triggering incident could have happened on some distant battlefield.

"How'd she take it?" Tara asked.

"How you'd expect, I guess. Hard." He looked out at the parking lot. "Not that surprised, though. It was almost like she saw it coming. She said he was never right in the head since he got home. He'd been having insomnia, flashbacks. Knocked her around some. Finally she'd had it." Ingram glanced at Tara. "I didn't know any of that beforehand."

Looking into his eyes, she could tell it was the truth. He'd been blindsided. For the first time since she'd met the sheriff, he looked flummoxed.

He glanced away, shaking his head. "I guess you never really know a man."

For a while they stood silently on the steps of the building. A frigid gust whipped up, breaking the quiet, and Tara zipped her jacket.

Ingram trudged down the steps without a goodbye. Tara watched him climb into his truck and drive away.

She took out her phone and checked it. Nothing from Liam. She looked at the lot again.

"He left," Brannon said. "They kicked him loose about an hour ago."

She didn't say anything.

"Good job today." He turned to face her.

"Thanks."

He reached up to touch the bruise on her face, and

she flinched. He glanced away. "You know, you could have called me," he said.

"I did."

"You could have called me first." He gave her a long look. "I would have had your back."

"I know."

She could see the disappointment in his eyes. Brannon, her teammate. They'd been through so much together. And he *would* have had her back if she'd bothered to wait for him.

She gazed out over the parking lot and confirmed that he was right, the person she'd been hoping to see was long gone. Liam had finished his marathon interrogation and headed home, which was exactly what he should have done. Why had she expected anything else?

Beside her, Brannon scrolled through his phone. Tara thought about what he'd said. Should she have waited? Would things have turned out differently or better? Those were the questions she'd been grappling with during her debriefing as she'd recounted the day's events, documenting every last detail. If she'd waited for backup, Alex Sears might be alive right now to stand trial.

And M.J. might be dead.

She didn't know. She only knew that this case had done something to her, and she was a different person now from when she'd started.

A few hours ago she'd helped kill a man. Her actions had led to his death. And when she'd seen his exit wound and watched his blood seeping into the forest floor, she'd thought how fast it had happened. She'd stood there in those woods on legs that could barely hold her, and all she could think was how undeserving he was and how it should have been worse.

She shuddered at her own thoughts. She didn't know how it might have ended differently if she'd waited, but it didn't matter now. She hadn't. She'd followed her impulse. Some might take it as proof that she wasn't a team player. They might see it as a flaw that could one day prove fatal.

"Well, I'm beat. How about you?" Brannon tucked his phone away.

"Yeah."

"Some of us are meeting up for a beer," he said. "Want to come?"

"I'm good."

"You sure?"

"Yeah."

"All right, then." He shook his head and smiled. "Catch you later."

Tara watched him leave. And then she was alone on the steps of her office building. She looked up at the night sky. Not a star in sight. She tucked her hands into her pockets and wrestled with what to do next.

Her stuff was at the Big Pines Motel fifty minutes away.

Her apartment was just ten minutes away. She pictured her dark window and her empty balcony.

And then there was the third option. Her fingers closed around the object in her pocket. Liam had left it in her motel room this morning like a gift.

Or maybe a dare.

She took out the gate key and looked at it.

For so long she'd thought of herself as brave. Tough. After making it through the police academy and Quantico and SWAT training, she'd felt confident, almost cocky. So sure of herself and her ability to handle anything. But it wasn't real. In so many ways that mattered, she wasn't tough at all, not in the slightest.

Tara rubbed her thumb over the key. She slipped it into her pocket and walked down the steps.

M.J. SIGNED THE last of the paperwork and pretended to listen as the nurse gave stern instructions about taking care of her cast.

"And that should cover it. Everything clear?"

"Yes," M.J. croaked, cringing at the sound of her own voice.

"All right, then. You're all set."

The nurse disappeared through the curtain, leaving her alone in the exam area where she'd spent the past four hours having her cuts sutured and her arm set and then being debriefed by agents.

M.J. stared down at her black ballet flats, the only things left of the outfit she'd worn in here. She'd traded her torn pantsuit and blouse for a set of blue surgical scrubs. Staring at her muddy shoes now, she remembered how she'd slipped beside her car the moment before the ambush.

She closed her eyes. She didn't want to do this now. Her mind was still spinning from all the questions and responses. Not to mention the pain meds. All she wanted now was to get out of here.

The air stirred, and she opened her eyes to see Jeremy stepping through the curtain.

"How'd you get back here?" she asked hoarsely.

"Talked my way past the nurses."

Instead of commando gear, he now wore jeans and a leather jacket, and M.J. glimpsed the gun holstered at his side. Even armed, he'd somehow gotten past the hospital security guard and the federal agents in the hallway. But what was more surprising was that he'd *talked* his way past the nurses.

He stepped closer. "How's the arm?"

"Fine."

"How are *you*?"

She glanced down at her feet and nodded, not trusting her voice. Her uninjured arm rested on her lap, and through the veil of tears she watched him gently pick up her hand. For a moment she just sat there, absorbing the feeling of his big, warm fingers surrounding hers.

She tugged her hand away and slid off the table. "My paperwork's done, so I can leave now."

"I'll take you home."

"No, it's—" *It's what?* Fine? It wasn't fine at all. She'd come here in an ambulance. And her car had been hauled away to be processed for evidence. She glanced up, and Jeremy was watching her, patiently waiting for her to put it together.

And then her mind was spinning for a totally different reason. He wanted to take her home. To her motel room, where her suitcase was? To his place? She felt tired and dirty and hungry and, yes, scared. And the last place she wanted to be right now was that dumpy motel. But the prospect of going home with him . . .

What she wanted more than anything was a hot bath and a mug of tea and her own bed.

"I'll take you home," he repeated, as if she hadn't heard him.

She cleared her throat. "You sure? It's a fifty-minute drive."

"That's fine."

"Both ways," she added pointedly.

He arched his eyebrows. "Sounds like a tough assignment." He stepped over and picked up the brown paper bag on the counter. Her ruined clothes were inside, along with her pain meds. "This your stuff?"

"Yeah."

He grabbed her things and led her past the crowd of people bunched in the hallway, somehow shielding her from having to make eye contact with everyone and field more questions. He pushed through several sets of double doors, and then they were standing outside the hospital beside a circular driveway. M.J. stifled a shiver as she glanced around and spotted his truck along the curb. And she realized she'd never ridden in it before.

"Jeremy, really, this is a hassle. I can get a ride with one of the other agents."

"Don't."

She glanced up, and the look in his eyes put a lump in her still-sore throat.

He took her hand again. "Just let me do this. Please? I need to get you home safe."

CHAPTER TWENTY-NINE

Tara awoke in Liam's bed, but this time she wasn't alone. They were tangled together, arms and legs, and it was hard to tell where her body stopped and his began.

She lay there wrapped in his sheets, watching the slow rise and fall of his chest. The room was gray and quiet. She had no idea what time it was, and she didn't want to.

Her throat felt sore and parched. Slowly, she extricated herself from his arms and slipped from the bed. She crept into the bathroom and gulped down a handful of water, carefully avoiding the mirrors because she didn't want to see her bruises. When she'd first arrived last night, he'd made her spend half an hour lying flat on his sofa with ice packs, but she knew it hadn't done any good.

She crept back into the bedroom, where the light had a strange quality to it. She felt drawn toward the window and gently lifted a slat in the blinds to peer out.

Her breath caught.

She glanced back at Liam, sprawled on his stomach now, still completely out. She took his flannel shirt from the arm of the leather chair, shrugged into it, and buttoned it up as she watched him sleep. Careful not to make a sound, she unlatched the door to the porch and stepped outside. The planks were cold under her feet as she walked to the wooden railing and looked out.

The world was blanketed in snow. Tiny flakes drifted down from the white sky, and she gazed up, awestruck. Everything was so *quiet*, so utterly tranquil. She pulled Liam's cuffs over her hands and crossed her arms against the chill as she gazed out.

Twenty-nine winters she'd lived here, and only a handful of times had it snowed. She envisioned her grandparents' roof covered in white, probably brighter than the aging paint on their house. She gazed across the lawn at the pines and the maples. Beyond them near the creek, she saw the lacy cypress branches that hung low over the water, and they looked like they'd been dusted with sugar.

She shivered and pulled her arms closer. When she'd first come here, the woods had seemed dark and sinister. Now everything looked fresh and pure and otherworldly. As she stood there, the flurry picked up energy. She reached out her hand. Flakes landed on her palm and instantly disappeared.

The door opened behind her, and Liam stepped out, bare-chested. He wore jeans and carried his leather jacket.

"I had no idea it was supposed to snow overnight," she said.

"It wasn't." He settled the jacket on her shoulders, and she slipped her arms into the sleeves. "Want me to make coffee?"

"Maybe later."

He slid his arms around her and tugged her back against the firm wall of his body. "How do you feel?"

"Good."

He lifted the hair off her neck and planted a kiss below her ear. "I don't believe you."

She snuggled closer, not wanting to argue about it. Right now she only wanted to think about his warmth and his smell and the weight of his arms around her waist.

"Through the trees there," she said. "Is that a dock?"

"Yeah. I don't have a boat, though. I sometimes use it for fishing."

"What's in the creek?"

"Catfish, mostly."

"My granddad used to take me to the Neches River. We caught perch."

He kissed the back of her neck again, and warm shivers swept over her skin as she gazed out at the trees. The wind gusted and snow flitted off the branches.

She sighed. "It's beautiful here."

"I know." He paused. "Think you could get used to it?"

She went still. For a moment she didn't move or even breathe.

He eased back and turned her to face him. His green eyes were dark and serious, and her heart was thumping.

"Could I get used to visiting here?"

"Living here."

She turned to look out again. "I don't know, that's . . . I mean, that's a big step." She looked up at him, trying to read his face for clues. "It seems fast. You barely know me. You've never even seen where I live."

"That's not hard to fix."

Panic welled inside her. He was serious. "Liam . . . there's so much you don't know about me. And so much I don't know about *you*, too. And it doesn't make sense," she babbled, "especially right now after everything that's happened."

She gazed up at him, but he was just watching her calmly. How could he be so calm?

"Things feel confused right now," she said. "And to be honest, I'm scared."

"Why?"

She turned to look at the trees again. Her heart was racing, and she felt him watching her. She truly could not believe they were having this conversation. "Because I think . . . I think I love you."

Her stomach dropped the instant she said the words. They were out there, hovering in front of her mouth like frost, and every muscle in her body tensed as she stared out at the woods and Liam stayed silent beside her.

She glanced at him. "Sorry."

"Why?"

"I'm jumping the gun."

He pulled her against him, and her heart was pounding like crazy now because she'd blurted it out, the thing that had been dawning on her for days now.

"You're not." He gazed down at her. "I think I've loved you since that first day you showed up here." He smiled. "You should see the look on your face."

"I just—the first *day*? That's impossible."

"You were ready to slap the cuffs on first and ask questions later. I was hooked."

Tara felt numb.

"If it makes you feel any better, I'm scared, too." He pulled her into a hug. "I never asked a woman to live with me before. Maybe you'll hate it after a day."

"People will think we're crazy. I know I do. This is all so fast."

For a few moments they just stood there. Tara rested her head against his chest and heard his heart thudding. And she realized he *was* scared. It wasn't just her. She could get burned here, but so could he.

"You know when you have a raid coming?" he said. "You get your intel together, you plan everything, you gear up. But even after all that, when the time comes, you're worried anyway because no matter what you do, you never really know what's waiting behind that door." He went quiet for a moment. "It's an unknown, Tara. Everything is."

Unknown.

She understood that. She knew all about fear. It had a texture, a taste. And in those critical moments all she could do was take a deep breath and summon her courage—even if it was fake—and go in anyway. He'd been in those situations, too, and he knew. He knew *her*. It didn't seem possible, but somehow he did.

And now he was offering her a chance at something. She knew that chance was rare, as fleeting as a snowflake.

He tipped her chin up gently and kissed her. She wrapped her arms around him and kissed him back, absorbing his heat and his strength and his passion, all the good things she loved about him and hadn't even known she was missing. She didn't want to go back to not knowing. She wanted warmth and love and intimacy. She wanted *him*. He felt right. He fit.

She pulled back. "Okay."

He smiled down at her. "Okay what?"

"Okay, I'm in."

Turn the page for a sneak peek of Laura Griffin's next
heart-pounding Tracers novel,

DEEP DARK

Coming spring 2016 from Pocket Books

Laney Knox blinked into the darkness and listened. Something . . . no.

She closed her eyes and slid deeper into the warm sheets, dismissing the sound. Probably her neighbor's cat on the patio again.

Her eyes flew open. It wasn't the sound but the light that had her attention now. Or *lack* of light. She gazed at the bedroom window, but didn't see a band of white seeping through the gap between the shade and the wall.

She stared into the void, trying to shake off her grogginess. The outdoor lightbulb was new—her landlord had changed it yesterday. Had he botched the job? She should have done it herself, but her shoestring budget didn't cover LED lights. It barely covered ramen noodles and Red Bull.

Laney looked around the pitch-black room. She wasn't afraid of the dark, never had been. Roaches terrified her. And block parties. But darkness had always been no big deal.

Except this darkness was all wrong.

How many software developers does it take to change a lightbulb? None, it's a hardware problem.

She strained her ears and listened for whatever sound had awakened her, but she heard nothing. She saw nothing. All her senses could discern was a slight chill against her skin and the lingering scent of the kung pao chicken she'd had for dinner. But something seemed off. As the seconds ticked by, a feeling of dread settled over her.

Creak.

She bolted upright. The noise was soft but unmistakable. Someone was *inside* her house.

Her heart skittered. Her thoughts zinged in a thousand directions. She lived in an old bungalow, more dilapidated than charming, and her bedroom was at the back, a virtual dead end. She glanced at her windows. She'd reinforced the original latches with screw locks to deter burglars—which had seemed like a good idea at the time. But now she felt trapped. She reached over and groped around on the nightstand for her phone.

Crap.

Crap crap crap. It was charging in the kitchen.

Her blood turned icy as stark reality sank in. She had no phone, no weapon, no exit route. And someone was *inside*.

Should she hide in the closet? Or try to slip past him somehow, maybe if he stepped into her room? It would never work, but—

Creak.

A burst of panic made the decision for her and she was across the room in a flash. She scurried behind the door and flattened herself against the wall. Her breath came in shallow gasps. Her heart pounded wildly as she *felt* more than heard him creeping closer.

That's what he was doing. *Creeping.* He was easing down the hallway with quiet, deliberate steps while she cowered behind the door, quivering and naked except for her oversized Florence and the Machine

T-shirt. Sweat sprang up on the back of her neck and her chest tightened.

Who the hell was he? What did he want? She had no cash, no jewelry, just a few thousand dollars' worth of hardware sitting on her desk. Maybe she could slip out while he stole it.

Yeah, right. Her ancient hatchback in the driveway was a neon sign announcing that whoever lived here was not only Dead Broke, but Obviously Home. This intruder was no burglar—he was here for her.

Laney's pulse sprinted. Her hands formed useless little fists at her sides, and she was overwhelmed with the absurd notion that she should have followed through on that kickboxing class.

She forced a breath into her lungs and tried to *think*.

She had to think her way out of this because she was five-three, one-hundred-ten pounds, and weaponless. She didn't stand much chance against even an average-size man, and if he was armed, forget it.

The air moved. Laney's throat went dry. She stayed perfectly still and felt a faint shifting of molecules on the other side of the door. Then a soft sound, barely a whisper, as the door drifted open.

She held her breath. Her heart hammered. Everything was black, but gradually there was a hole in the blackness—a tall, man-shaped hole—and she stood paralyzed with disbelief as the shape eased into her bedroom and crept toward her bed. She watched it, rooted in place, waiting . . . waiting . . . waiting.

She bolted.

Her feet slapped against the wood floor as she

raced down the hallway. Air *swooshed* behind her. A scream tore from her throat, then became a shrill yelp as he grabbed her hair and slammed her against the wall.

A stunning blow knocked her to the floor. Stars burst behind her eyes as her cheek hit wood. She scrambled to her feet. She made a frantic dash and tripped over the coffee table, sending glasses and dishes flying as she crashed to her knees.

He flipped her onto her back and then he was on her, pinning her with his massive weight as something sharp cut into her shoulder blade.

She clawed at his face, his eyes. He wore a ski mask, and all she could see were three round holes and a sinister flash of teeth amid the blackness. She shrieked, but an elbow against her throat cut off all sound, all breath, as she fought and bucked beneath him.

He was strong, immovable. And terrifyingly calm as he pinned her arms one by one under his knees and reached for something in the pocket of his jacket. She expected a weapon—a knife or a gun—and she tried to heave him off. Panic seized her as his shadow shifted in the dimness. Above her frantic grunts she heard the tear of duct tape. And suddenly the idea of being silenced that way was more horrifying than even a blade.

With a fresh burst of adrenaline she wriggled her arm out from under his knee and flailed for any kind of weapon. She groped around the floor until her fingers closed around something smooth and slender— a pen, a chopstick, she didn't know. She gripped it in her hand and jabbed at his face with all her might. He reared back with a howl.

Laney bucked hard and rolled out from under him as he clutched his face.

A scream erupted from deep inside her. She tripped to her feet and rocketed for the door.

THIS CASE WAS going to throw him. Reed Novak knew it the second he saw the volleyball court.

Taut net, sugary white sand. Beside the court was a swimming pool that sparkled like a sapphire under the blazing August sun.

"Hell, if I had a pool like that, I'd use it."

Reed looked at his partner in the passenger seat. Jay Wallace had his window rolled down and his hefty arm resting on the door.

"Otherwise, what's the point?"

Reed didn't answer. The point was probably to slap a photo on a Web site to justify the astronomical rent Bellaterra charged for one- and two-bedroom units five minutes from downtown.

Reed pulled in beside the white ME's van and climbed out, glancing around. Even with a few emergency vehicles, the parking lot was quiet. Bellaterra's young and athletically inclined tenants were either at jobs or classes, or maybe home with their parents for the summer, letting their luxury apartments sit empty.

Reed stood for a moment, getting a feel. Heat radiated up from the blacktop, and the drone of cicadas drowned out the traffic noise on Lake Austin Boulevard. He glanced across the parking lot to the ground-floor unit, where a female patrol officer stood guard.

"First responder, Lena Guitierrez."

Reed looked at Jay. "You know her?"

"Think she's new."

They crossed the lot and exchanged introductions. Guitierrez looked nervous in her wilted uniform. Her gaze darted to the detective shield clipped to Reed's belt.

"I secured the perimeter, sir."

"Good. Tell us what you got."

She cleared her throat. "Apartment's rented to April Abrams, twenty-five. Didn't show up for work today, didn't answer her phone. One of her coworkers dropped by. The door was reportedly unlocked, so she went inside to check . . ."

Her voice trailed off as though they should fill in the blank.

Reed stepped around her and examined the door, which stood ajar. No visible scratches on the locking mechanism. No gouges on the door frame.

Jay was already covering his shiny black wingtips with paper booties. Reed did the same. Austin was casual, but they always wore business attire—suit pants and button-down shirts—because of days like today. Reed never wanted to do a death knock dressed like he was on his way to a keg party.

He stepped into the cool foyer and let his eyes adjust. To his right was a living area. White sectional sofa, bleached wood coffee table, white shag rug over beige carpet. The pristine room was a contrast to the hallway, where yellow evidence markers littered the tile floor. A picture on the wall had been knocked askew, and a pair of ME's assistants bent over a body.

A bare foot jutted out from the huddle. Pale skin, red toenail polish.

Reed walked into the hall, sidestepping numbered pieces of plastic that flagged evidence he couldn't see. A slender guy with premature gray hair glanced up. Reed knew the man, and his expression was even grimmer than usual.

April Abrams was young.

Reed knelt down for a closer look. She lay on her side, her head resting in a pool of coagulated blood. Long auburn hair partially obscured her face, and her arm was bent behind her at an impossible angle. A strip of silver duct tape covered her mouth.

"Jesus," Jay muttered behind him.

Her bare legs scissored out to the side. A pink T-shirt was bunched up under her armpits, and Reed noted extensive scratches on both breasts.

"What do you have?" Reed asked.

"Twelve to eighteen hours, ballpark," the ME's assistant said. "The pathologist should be able to pin that down better."

Reed studied her face again. No visible abrasions. No ligature marks on her neck. The right side of her skull was smashed in, and her hair was matted with dried blood.

"Murder weapon?" Reed asked.

"Not that we've seen. You might ask the photog, though. She's in the kitchen."

Reed stood up, looking again at the tape covering

April's mouth. A lock of her hair was stuck under it, which for some reason pissed him off.

He moved into the kitchen and paused beside a sliding glass door that opened onto a fenced patio. Outside on the concrete sat a pair of plastic bowls, both empty.

"I haven't seen a weapon," the crime scene photographer said over her shoulder. "You'll be the first to know."

Reed glanced around her to see what had her attention. On the granite countertop was an ID badge attached to one of those plastic clips with a retractable cord. The badge showed April's mug shot with her name and the words *ChatWare Solutions* printed below. April had light blue eyes, pale skin. Her hair was pulled back in a ponytail, and she smiled tentatively for the camera.

The photographer finished with the badge and shifted to get a shot of the door.

"Come across a phone?" Reed asked, looking around. No dirty dishes on the counters. Empty sink.

"Not so far." She glanced up from her camera as Jay stepped into the kitchen and silently handed Reed a pair of latex gloves. "I haven't done the bedroom yet, though, so don't you guys move anything."

Reed pulled on the gloves and opened the fridge. It took him a moment to identify the unfamiliar contents: spinach, beets, bean sprouts. Something green and frilly that might or might not be kale. The dietary train wreck continued in the pantry, where he found three boxes of Kashi, six bottles of vitamins, and a bag of flaxseed.

Opening the cabinet under the sink Reed found a bag of cat food and a plastic trash can. The can was empty, not even a plastic bag inside it despite the box of them right there in the cabinet. He'd check out Bellaterra's Dumpsters. Reed opened several drawers and found the usual assortment of utensils.

"That's an eight-hundred-dollar juicer." Jay nodded at the silver appliance near the sink.

"That thing?"

"At least. Maybe a thousand. My sister got one last Christmas."

Guitierrez was standing in the foyer now, watching them with interest.

"Did you come across a phone?" Reed asked her. "A purse? A wallet?"

"No on all three, sir. I did a full walk-through, didn't see anything."

Reed exchanged a look with Jay before moving back into the hallway. The ME's people were now taping paper bags over the victim's hands.

Reed stepped into the bedroom. A ceiling fan moved on low speed, stirring the air. The queen-size bed was heaped with plump white pillows like a fancy hotel. The pillows were piled to the side and the bedspread was thrown back, suggesting April had gone to bed and then gotten up.

"Think she heard him?" Jay asked.

"Maybe."

The bedside lamp was off, and the only light in the room came from sunlight streaming through vertical blinds. Reed ducked into the bathroom. Makeup was scattered across the counter. A gold watch with a diamond bezel sat beside the sink. Reed opened the medicine cabinet.

"Sleeping pills, nasal spray, laxatives, OxyContin," he said.

Reed examined the latch on the window above the toilet. Then he moved into the bedroom. Peering under the bed, he found a pair of white sandals and a folded shopping bag. On the nightstand was a stack of magazines: *Entertainment Weekly, People, Wired*. He opened the nightstand drawer and stared down.

"Huh."

Jay glanced over. "Vibrator?"

"Chocolate." Four bars of Godiva, seventy-two percent cocoa. One of the bars had the wrapper partially removed and a hunk bitten off.

Reed was more or less numb to going through people's stuff, but the chocolate bar struck him as both sad and infinitely personal. He closed the drawer.

"We ID'd her vehicle," Guitierrez said, stepping into the room, "case you guys want to have a look."

Reed and Jay followed her back through the apartment, catching annoyed looks from the ME's people as they squeezed past again.

"So, what's our game plan?" Jay asked as they exited the home and stripped off their shoe covers.

Reed watched the gurney being rolled across the lot. Twenty minutes into the case, and already they needed a game plan. That was how it worked now, and Reed didn't waste his energy cursing social media.

He thought of April's mug shot. He thought of her anxious smile as she'd stood before the camera, probably her first day on the job. She'd probably been feeling a heady mix of hope and anticipation as she embarked on something new.

He pictured the slash of duct tape over her mouth now. It would stay there until she reached the autopsy table.

"Reed?"

"No forced entry. No purse, no phone. But he left jewelry, pain meds, and a Bose stereo."

Jay nodded because he knew what Reed was thinking. At this point, everything pointed to someone she knew.

Jay glanced across the lot. "Damn."

Reed turned to see an SUV easing through the gate, tailgated by a white news van. Just in time for the money shot of the body coming out. In a matter of minutes the image would be ping-ponging between satellites.

"Dirtbags," Jay muttered.

Reed shook his head. "Right on time."